CUBS V CARDINALS

A NOVEL BY

J. W. WHEELER

Alan
Keep swinging for the fences.

Dedication

This book is dedicated to my family. To my parents, Herman and Vera Wheeler, thank you for all the nurturing and raising me in an atmosphere that demanded I explore my mind to the fullest. To my sisters, Barbara, Mary Ann, and Brenda, thank you for protecting me, berating me, encouraging me and never letting me forget the little boy I was and still am. To my wife Tia, thank you for the many years of companionship and understanding as I uncorked my creative mind after decades of analytical thinking. To my children Kai and Jasmine, thank you for sharing your childhoods with me, without which I would never have been able to recall my own with such compassion or known why I should.

And last of all to my brother Richard, thank you for the many manly things you have taught me: how to catch and throw a football, the intricacies of the pitcher's wind up, what the hop-skip-and-jump was, and how to do it without falling sometimes, how to drive a stick shift, and so many others (too numerous to write here or for either of us to remember) whether I wanted to learn these things or not. Just know that I will always call you Punch, no matter what you call yourself to other people, whether you want me to or not.

I love you all forever.

Acknowledgments

The author wishes to extend his sincere thanks to the following: Julie Goldman, Jasmine Wheeler, and Jerry and Christie Bustamante for their help and support with editing and vital encouragement to continue with the project, without which this book would not have been completed; Tonja Daniels, her invaluable skill for turning a manuscript into a book was an unexpected blessing; Theo Simon for his webmaster skills and social media savvy; and last but not least to my wife Tia, for allowing the space, time and stillness required to carry all this out.

CHAPTER
One

Each of us is born into our own unique universe. We all expand at the speed of self-awareness as we grow. We are each conceived with a bundle of talents, features, and personality traits crammed inside our tiny bodies and we are cast out into the cosmos in our own individual big bangs of birth to fend for ourselves, and we can only use what our own universe brings to us to mold our bundles into the persons we will become.

At first, we are alone, only vaguely aware there are other, alternate universes containing beings such as us, but as our consciousness develops our universe begins to overlap with other universes, and things get complicated. There are universes so close to us and so much larger and older they seem to entirely envelope ours, and there are others which barely touch us. There are still others that can only be imagined, but they are just as real in our dreams, and when we awake we cling to them more than the reality facing our open eyes.

Jimmy Williams' universe was not very vast when he finished the second grade. A few square blocks were all that was contained inside its slowly expanding boundaries, just enough to encompass his school, his church, his friends, and his family. By eight years old that was more than enough to make things difficult.

"Take back what you said, Jimmy, and I'll let you up."

As Jimmy lay pinned underneath the heavy weight that was his older sister, he wasn't thinking about the universe or its boundaries, but instead about how to get out of his current predicament.

He wasn't thinking about taking anything back either, that was for sure, he was too stubborn for that. The best tactic would be to keep wiggling and swinging his arms, and in general trying to be as uncomfortable to sit on as possible. Plus, why would he take back something he meant? That would be a lie. And while not being above lying, he made the choice to not do so in this instance.

"Take it back!!" screamed JoAnn. She was furious, looking down at his pencil thin arms and legs, and glasses larger than his narrow face. She was sitting on him with a knee on the floor on either side of his body, and she had him trapped in the narrow aisle way of the bedroom the boys in the family shared, the only open space between the bunk beds and dressers.

As he could not roll over and use his considerable wriggling skills to get away, which would have been his first choice, Jimmy cried out, "I'll take it back when your feet shrink, instead of just stink!"

His second choice did not calm his sister one bit. She pressed down on him as hard as she could, too angry to make any noise other than to sputter. As he struggled to catch his breath, Jimmy admired his poetry and its dual purpose of restating what had gotten him pinned in the first place while at the same time rhyming.

"I'm being crushed by an elephant!!" he bellowed as soon as enough air was back in his lungs to allow it.

Universes are blends of time and space, and to function both must be present. One great thing about being eight years old is time is abundant, and even though it seems to pass so, so, slowly in universes so new, it brings about constant change, because change is the only proof a universe exists. Jimmy and JoAnn's were changed irrevocably when another big bang occurred two years before and the baby of the family, Belinda, started her expansion into the cosmos.

By this day she had expanded to the point she could walk, more of an awkward trot with her arms waving above her head as if still celebrating the achievement, and she could express two emotions very clearly; either laughing and giggling with pleasure or wailing and screaming with displeasure. Her universe mainly consisted of observing those around her and deciding which vocalizations their behavior warranted. When she ambled through the doorway of the bedroom and saw JoAnn sitting on Jimmy she let out a howl anyone in the surrounding universes could not help but hear.

JoAnn was a very meek and practical girl. It took a lot to make her angry, which was the main reason Jimmy took such pride in accomplishing it. By ten years old she had learned many things about the universe she inhabited, and among the things she had learned was her mother responded to Belinda's cries within thirty seconds of hearing them, and her mother did not necessarily ask why fights happened before punishing the fighters. Peace came first and justice came later, if it came at all. The only practical thing to do was to stand up and walk away before the half minute time limit and not let her anger get her into trouble. JoAnn stood without a word and stared down for a moment at Jimmy as he lay on the floor before she started her walk out of the bedroom toward her younger sister.

"Don't trip," said Jimmy as he grabbed at her foot and almost sent her tumbling.

Jimmy sat up and was facing the door at the opposite end of the bedroom. He took a few breaths with his knees up and head down, smiling at his recent escape and the words which had led to his need of it. This being the first day of freedom from school meant he had a whole summer to torment his sisters ahead of him. As he reveled in the many ways he would aggravate them, the feeling of another presence invading his time space forced him out of his mental merriment. He looked up to see his brother in the doorway.

The universe of Slugger was much older than Jimmy's, more than twice as old. It was quite a strange universe, from the observations of it Jimmy had made. First off, Slugger was not his real name, it was Theodore. No one, not even his mother, called him Theodore so maybe that led to some of the confusion. What was most confusing about him to Jimmy was his unpredictability. Sometimes he was playful and full of fun, and other times angry and violent, but mostly he was both at the same time. Dealing with his brother was one of the most complicated aspects of Jimmy's universe. The look on Slugger's face suggested he had witnessed the whole sorry scene of his brother being taken down by his sister, but Jimmy could not be sure he had been there watching. He had a smile on his face, which in Jimmy's memory could mean several different things, and no matter what it meant now it could mean something different later.

The toy wooden blocks were a prime example. Slugger had smiled when he had given them to Jimmy after he outgrew them a couple of years before, and spent a few happy hours showing him how to stack them into forts or castles or towers. Then one day Jimmy forgot to put them away under the bed as he was supposed to, again, and Slugger's gift became an excuse for Slugger's torture. He threw Jimmy under the bunk beds, shouting, "If you can't remember to put the blocks back under the bed when you're done playing with 'em, I'm gonna keep YOU under it!" After Jimmy begged and pleaded to be let out and Slugger realized how it terrified him to be confined in such a dark small space, it became a daily game, whether the blocks were in their proper place or not. He told Jimmy it was good for him, because if the Viet Cong ever buried him alive he'd already know what it felt like.

His universe, as always, brought things back into balance when it revealed to Jimmy the blocks could serve other purposes than building, they could be effective weapons as well. When Slugger threw him under the bed the next time he did not beg or whine or cry, he lay silently, except for his open-mouthed inhalations to calm his terror of confinement, and waited for what he knew Slugger would do eventually, to get on his hands and knees and look under the bed. As soon as that happened he threw the block in his hand with all his might and by some divine guidance it hit Slugger's upper lip and it exploded in blood. Slugger ran screaming into the bathroom bleeding on the floor, the walls, and the sink, which of course got the attention of the girls across the hall, and Jacky, the oldest sister, went running to her mother. Mom used her legendary interrogation skills to force out the details, and that resulted in the banning of the Under the Bunk Bed Prison system.

This was followed by the Dart Practice Torture, made possible by their mother, who decided one day the bunk beds should be unstacked and placed on opposite sides of the room. Jimmy was on the inside wall, Slugger on the outside. Everything went well until someone had the bright idea to give the boys a dart board for Christmas. It was not a happy Christmas for Jimmy, as it turned out.

As happened often, Slugger taught Jimmy how to play darts, even though Jimmy did not want to learn how to play darts. Experience had taught him the odds favored it ending badly. Precedent had been set in this area already. His siblings were constantly teaching him how to do something, sometimes because he asked them to and sometimes whether he asked them to or not, and it usually didn't take long for him to master it. The problem came when he learned to do it better than they could, which he often did, and when he did he did not hesitate to let them know it.

What happened was after two weeks of Slugger beating Jimmy in darts every single game, Jimmy won a game fifteen to twelve, and Jimmy was not a gracious winner. In fact, even though the record might still have been 212 games for Slugger to 1 for Jimmy, he infuriated Slugger by telling his friends about it, and writing '15–12' in Slugger's notebook so he wouldn't see until the next day at school, and then when they were at the dinner table he asked Slugger, "Could you please pass me the 15 to 12 salt?", which was the topper because Slugger could not react in any way other than to pass the salt. The second quickest, easiest, way to get a whipping from their father was to have bad manners at the dinner table. The only easier way was to misbehave in church.

After this, Slugger came up with a plan. He took the darts from their place in the dart board that night, and kept them next to him in the bed. Once their mother had come and tucked the boys in and turned out the light, Slugger said to Jimmy, "You know Jimmy, I need more practice at darts, since you think you're better than me now. I'm gonna practice by throwing darts across the room in the dark. You better lie completely flat, or you're gonna get stuck." Then he started tossing the darts across the room, and Jimmy had to lie as flat as a pancake or the missiles would land in his leg, or stomach, or arm. He wisely kept his pillow in front of his face, to eliminate the possibility of being stuck with a dart in the head.

This went on for the couple of weeks. Slugger would only stick Jimmy with a dart occasionally. It wasn't like he was trying to hit him, he would assure Jimmy, he just wanted to see how low he could put marks on the wall without hitting Jimmy. If sometimes he threw it too low and stuck Jimmy, that just meant he need-ed more practice. Jimmy should understand, seeing how much better at darts he was than Slugger. The end of this torture came the next time their mother changed the bed sheets and saw the wall marked by scores of tiny holes. Not only was Dart Practice in the Dark banned, the dartboard was removed from the bedroom, never to be seen again, and the beds were once again stacked.

Those memories flooded in when Jimmy saw Slugger in the doorway, as the smile on his face meant Slugger was plotting something with him in mind. He had no idea what Slugger was planning would change his life. He could only assume it would hurt in some way, and there was little chance of avoiding it.

CHAPTER
Two

T he universe Slugger had been thrust into was filled with the violence and mayhem which accompany the birth of new galaxies, which swirled about him, spinning away before he could reach them. His nickname, Slugger, was well earned, and in his mind, it was earned by necessity. Being the only black kid in a white neighborhood in the 1950's meant having to fight for everything. Grade school for him was a succession of battles, initial defeats and subsequent victories, until the other boys learned he would not tolerate being called a Nigger, even if four boys surrounded him. If they beat him up that day, he would wait until he could catch each one alone and beat them twice as badly on another day. By the time he reached high school his skill level at combat had reached the point if he had to face two of them together they were more likely to end the encounter leaking blood than he was.

Slugger loved no one in his universe more than his little brother Jimmy, despite him being the favorite son. The friction between Slugger and his parents caused by this reality did not change that. In his mind, there was no one who knew better what was best for Jimmy and was willing to make sure he obtained it than he was, and he had been waiting for this day since his little brother had blown out eight candles during the winter just past.

It had been at just about this age when the war had started in his life, and he assumed it would be the same for his brother. There could be no survival for the timid or the weak. Reading the encyclopedia and being the smartest kid on the block may earn

13

him praise from the adults, but it was pointless if he didn't survive high school. Jimmy had to learn to fight, to be tough, to fill his chest with the heart of a warrior to be able to overcome what was coming, and time was running out for Slugger to help him do that. The Viet Cong were still hiding in the jungle and he was in a hurry to go track them down.

That was what was on his mind as he stood in the doorway looking at his brother getting roughed up by his sister again, licking his lip along the contour of the bump which never quite healed from the wooden block. That and the plan he was so happy to be putting into motion this very day.

"Get up, Jimmy, and put your sneakers on and a sweater," he said with a voice full of both resolution and resignation, shifting his weight to lean against the doorframe.

"Why?" asked Jimmy, without moving. After being trapped in this very spot for much longer than he would have liked, he now felt it was the most comfortable place in the universe and he wanted to stay there and lounge.

"Just do what I say and shut up!" commanded Slugger, stiffening his body to full height, and mimicking the tone he imagined his future drill sergeant would use.

Jimmy stared at his brother silently, knowing more questions would be fruitless, and his brother stared back for a moment before shouting out his next order, "Follow me!" and with that he turned on his heels, quasi-military style, and marched through his parents' bedroom, through their tiny master half bathroom - large enough only for a single sink, cramped shower, a small metal hamper for the collection of dirty clothes, and a toilet – and out the back door. He glanced over his shoulder before he turned the corner into the bathroom, to see Jimmy still immobile on the scratchy carpet of the bedroom, his mind spinning with the decision of what to do next.

Jimmy recognized after a few turns of the wheel the choice boiled down to the same one he had to make over-and-over again over the duration of the short expansion of his universe, the risk of doing something which may turn out to be painful, if not downright fatal, versus the absolute certainty of unpleasantness if he did not take that risk. So with an air of inevitability he rose from his position of comfort and did as he was instructed, that is, he put on his light blue PF Flyers with the laces barely long enough to tie after so many breakages, and his brown sweater with the thick patches on the elbows, and walked much more solemnly than his brother past his parents' bed, past the medicine cabinet which held his father's shaving cream and his mother's secret potions, past the hamper he had peed in in his sleep a few years earlier, and out the back door into the chilly swirling air of the larger world. It was early June, and in Illinois, that meant it was still winter some days and summer on others.

As the metal screen of the door closed behind him, Jimmy stood facing his brother, who was standing on the walkway that led from the house to the garage which stood separately behind it, the walkway made up of square cement blocks spread like stepping stones down the slight slope between the buildings.

"Took you long enough," observed his brother, and not waiting for a response to his critique, said, "Come on."

With that he turned and walked through the screen door of the patio which their father had converted half of the garage into, and left Jimmy to decide whether to take a step off the small back porch he was standing on, or to run back into the house and hide. An expanding universe cannot hide, so the choice had been made for him already. Jimmy skipped down the steps gingerly, as if there was water filled with crocodiles between the footholds, not the crab grass and dandelions his lying eyes were exposing, and followed his brother on to his destiny of the day.

The patio half of the garage had wire mesh screens instead of outer walls their father enclosed with thick plastic sheets every fall and had recently taken off for the warmer half of the year. A solid wall separated it from the other side, in which the car was parked and their father's sturdy work bench imposingly stood, along with his storage bins and tools. Slugger reached into the toy box which was strategically located in the patio and motioned for his little brother to follow him into the other side. It was empty, as their dad had left for work before Jimmy opened his eyes that morning, and even with the garage door down it was cold enough for the boys to see their breath as it escaped from their lips. Opposite the door was a small window from which a view of the back of the house was obtained, and on the floor near that window was a grease spot which marked the limit to which the car could be pulled in.

As Jimmy stared at the kaleidoscope of colors shifting in the oil as he walked into the space, he failed to notice what his brother had taken from the box, his old baseball glove and a smaller, newer version. He was startled by the sight of both when he heard his brother's gruff command, "Put this on," as he held out the small glove to his young sibling. His shock was such he did not question, he followed the command and tried to put the glove on his left hand, quite unsuccessfully.

Slugger, using the tone he had developed specially for Jimmy, to let him know how stupid whatever he had just said or done was, said with an air of impatience and amusement, "The other hand, genius. You're left handed, aren't you? You throw with your left, and catch with your right."

Jimmy tried the other hand and it still wouldn't go on. Instead of laughing or yelling, or the combination of both Jimmy expected, Slugger silently snatched the glove from his brother's hand, separated his fingers correctly, and shoved it on. Again, Jimmy was startled, except this time it was not from a sound or sight, it was from a smell, the scent of the oiled leather of the glove, and Jimmy held it close to his face to breathe it in fully, and it was then he became aware of the feel of it, so strange and comfortable at the same time. Dazed as he was by the new sensations, Jimmy did not say a word as Slugger produced a ball, smaller than the ones Jimmy had seen Slugger play with before, and held it out for him to take.

In Slugger's universe, sports were mastered easily, the rough and tumble actions required to be proficient were the very stuff his being was composed for. He succeeded whether the ball was round or oblong, if the victorious needed to be stronger, or quicker, or faster, or some delicate combination of the three, or if stamina and denial of the urge to crumple in pain were required. If the game rewarded aggression and meekness was vanquished, he was adequately equipped for the task.

But above all he was a fighter, and his rebellious nature would not allow him to be coached easily in team sports. After lettering in baseball, basketball, and football as an underclassman he quit each and ran track in his senior year instead, which allowed him his freedom and brought records and medals. Despite having the talent to make a living on a baseball diamond his destiny lay elsewhere, on the many battlefields of his heart and soul, and his universe was not to be deterred from the multitude of armed conflicts in his future.

"I got this ball for you to practice with," said Slugger. "It's a regulation Minor League ball."

"Where'd you get it?" asked Jimmy, trying to change the subject. The word "practice" always made him cringe. He had been subjected to it many times and could not remember it not turning out to be boring or painful or painfully boring, and he had little trouble imagining which would occur with the word emanating from his brother's violent universe.

Slugger stared down at his younger sibling and said in a tone that let Jimmy know to drop this line of questioning, "Don't worry about that," which of course was the trigger for the rush of worry flooding into the little boy, but before his imagination could take full flight his brother continued, quite jauntily, by saying, "I'm gonna to teach you how to pitch!!" with a triumphant flourish which was not reciprocated.

"What?" cried out Jimmy, with amazement overcoming his shock, "Who says I want to learn how to pitch?" Jimmy had never even considered being anything more than an imaginary athlete until this exact moment in his expansion. Why would he, when up to this point his life had been filled with the kinds of health problems which would not have allowed him to survive in an earlier era? He was born so weak with dehydration he had to stay behind at the hospital after his mother was released, as he struggled to nurse and maintain his body temperature. The doctor told his mother he would make it, barely, but he should be her last child, because the next would probably not survive at all. It became clear once he started to walk something was wrong with his gait, which resulted in surgery when he was four for a hernia. He was hospitalized for pneumonia a year later, fever racking his body for days, but once again he pulled through. Then his nose started erupting with blood when he was sitting at the dinner table, or laughing at the television, or asleep in his bed, and this led to a diagnosis of anemia and the need for him to have an appointment every three months at the local clinic to allow a nurse to puncture his tiny middle finger, exactly where the nerve endings all congregate, far enough in to make blood spill out to match his tears. The result was his mother would have to go to the pharmacy and buy big brown pills half as large as his mouth for him to take, with the choice of chewing them and tasting the foulest taste he could imagine, even worse than peas, or risk choking by swallowing them whole. The year before he had pains searing through his chest so severe his mother rushed him to the doctor, praying for his young life as she sped through stop signs on her way to the hospital, but they could not find anything wrong with his heart. He had excruciating headaches, which had lessened since he started wearing the thick glasses he had been prescribed in kindergarten, the result of astigmatism, but they still came and went unexplained even after. He may have not been the shortest boy in the second grade, but he was by far the frailest.

Slugger stepped up to Jimmy as close as he could so when he stared down at him his evil smile would have the greatest affect, and said, "Who says I was asking you?" Then Slugger, almost tenderly, put his hand on Jimmy's shoulder. "Here is what I want you to do. Hold this," he said, handing the ball to Jimmy.

He turned and walked away and left Jimmy staring down at his destiny, round and hard and smooth, white with red seams sown around it in a wobbly figure eight. With the ball in his hand his mind went quiet, not crowded with competing thoughts and fears as it normally was, a calm energy flooding into it he hadn't felt before.

Slugger was standing at the end of the garage closest to the house, where the window was. He squatted down with his butt touching his heels, in the classic catcher's relaxed position. Just when he was about to tell Jimmy to throw him the ball, he stopped himself, walked back to Jimmy, and said, "Before I show you how to throw, you need to learn how to wind up."

Without giving Jimmy a chance to respond, he stood behind Jimmy, towering above him, and told him to stand straight with his arms at his sides. Then he leaned over him and grabbed his arms, and brought them together in front of his chest, bent at the elbow, with the ball in his left hand tucked into the glove on his right hand.

"The first thing you do is step back with your right foot," said Slugger, and before he could continue Jimmy did, stepping on Slugger's foot. Instead of the slap to the back of the head Jimmy expected in response, Slugger didn't react negatively. He moved back and said, "Don't step back too far, 'cause you don't want to lose balance. You just step back far enough for your left heel to come off the ground, but keep the front of your left foot on the ground. Then you turn it to the side and step back forward with your right foot."

Step back forward? This seemed like a contradiction to Jimmy, and was too much information for him to process as he was still trying to get over the fact he hadn't gotten slapped, and his only response was to look up at his brother like he was crazy. Instead of yelling at him, which was his first instinct, Slugger realized if he was going to do what he needed to do he had to stay calm and not let Jimmy upset him or get frustrated and scared, so he reached down and did it for him, he turned Jimmy's left foot so it was pointed to the left, and raised Jimmy's right leg and brought it forward, past where it started.

"OK, Jimmy, do it," he commanded, after moving back again so he didn't get stepped on.

Jimmy tried it, but it felt like an awkward dance, the kind his sisters were always trying to teach him. He wondered when Slugger would start laughing at him like they did, and blurt out a punch line.

"Try it again, Jimmy," said Slugger patiently, another surprise for Jimmy. After about ten tries it didn't feel so awkward and he looked at Slugger for some sign of acceptance, but Slugger said nothing. After a few more times Jimmy was the impatient one.

"Now what?" he asked.

"You think you've got it now?" Slugger countered. "OK, now don't just step forward with your right foot, lift your right leg as high as you can and twist your whole body when you turn your left foot, then step forward."

Jimmy looked at him like he was crazy again. Slugger stepped up, bent over and turned Jimmy's foot as he had before, but this time lifted Jimmy's leg so his knee was as high as his waist, and turned Jimmy's torso so his whole body was facing left, along with his foot. Jimmy realized he was dangling in the air and would have fallen if Slugger wasn't holding him up. Maybe that was the trick. Slugger was about to let go and send him crashing into their father's immaculately maintained work bench, and then run into the house to tell their mother what Jimmy had just done and get him in trouble again. But Slugger didn't let go, and brought Jimmy's leg back down as he had tried to instruct him, then stood and looked down at his brother sternly.

"Think you can do it?" he asked.

As he stared up at his brother, the look on his face said no, but he had a heart full of the type of stubborn maleness that would not allow him to voice it. Instead he focused on the task at hand by squeezing down on his tongue firmly with his left side molars and churning his jaws, just hard enough to grip but not so hard as to bite, and lifted his leg a bit too quickly, lost his balance, and without a quick lunge from Slugger he would have crashed into their father's bench.

As he stood his brother upright, Slugger said softly, "Keep trying. Your right foot should be pointing straight forward when you bring it down, then you step forward with your left to bring it even."

Jimmy tried again, and this time maintained his balance awkwardly, even though he did not have his feet in the right place when he finished. Then he did it again, and again, gaining balance with each repetition, for what seemed like an hour in the time scale of an eight-year-old, with Slugger urging and correcting and finally standing with arms crossed and brows furrowed to admire his teaching skills, as if he were watching ballet practice.

"Now you need to bring your arms into this," he continued. "When you take that first step back, swing your arms up and over

21

your head and touch the back of your neck. Keep your left hand in the glove. And when you step back forward, bring your arms back down and touch your thighs with the glove, then let your hand fall out and dangle by your side."

Jimmy looked at Slugger like he was speaking French. Slugger grabbed him, turned his leg, put his arms in the right positions, and tweaked his body until he was in balance, then let go. "See?" asked Slugger, "Not as hard as it sounds, huh?"

The look on Jimmy's face told Slugger he did not agree. "And what am I doing all that for?" asked Jimmy as a stalling tactic. Whether he thought he could do it or not, and he had serious doubts about being able to, he needed to know what the end game was.

"To get yourself in the right position to throw the ball, dummy," said Slugger. "This way you can not only throw it hard, you can control it. If you get to the point where you can repeat your windup exactly the same way every pitch, you can throw the ball where you want to throw it every time."

Jimmy did not look convinced, and did not understand what his brother was trying to accomplish. There had to be a sinister motive buried in there somewhere. Slugger saw the look on his brother's face, and knew he needed to change it, so he did what he knew would be irresistible to him, he issued a challenge.

"What, you don't think you can do it?" he asked.

Jimmy looked back at his brother with a flash of anger, just like Slugger knew he would. Jimmy hated to be told he couldn't do something. That was the surest way to get him past fear, or lethargy, or whatever other emotional roadblocks were keeping him from acting. Without thinking about whether he could or could not do it he started at it with a vengeance, but as he repeated the motions, and focused on not falling over, his anger turned to a calm resolve. He couldn't quite understand why, but somehow what Slugger was saying seemed right, and even though the whole episode felt strange, it also felt fun, and the more Jimmy tried it, the more it began to make sense. When he stepped forward with his arm down by his leg, it was obvious to him the next thing to do would be to whip his arm around his shoulder and release the ball. But Slugger never said anything about that. He just told Jimmy to keep practicing the windup. When Jimmy reached the point where he could bend down with his leg above his head and still step forward without losing his balance at any point, and still Slugger would not go to the end of the garage and let Jimmy throw it to him, Jimmy reverted to the trait so many fast learners do when they get bored and their short attention span ends, he starting goofing off, doing his windups with silly hitches and exaggerated twists.

"Quit clowning around, Jimmy," Slugger finally commanded.

"Well, why don't you let me throw you the ball?" Jimmy fired back, now full of confidence at what he had achieved so far.

"Two reasons," hissed Slugger. "First, we haven't gotten that far yet. Second, I don't like you clownin' around when I am tryin' to show you how to do something. If you keep practicin' your wind up the way I just taught you, next time I'll let you throw it."

And with that he spun on his heels and strode out of the garage and into the patio on his way back into the house before giving his brother the chance to argue, which he knew he would, and left Jimmy standing there with no one to complain to. With nothing better to do to quell the frustration rising in his chest he repeated the windup in the most perfect way he knew about twenty times, waiting for Slugger to come back but knowing that was a fading hope with each passing second, until he finally gave up and went back in the house, his heart beating wildly and his imagination stirred.

CHAPTER
Three

Normally on wet or cold days, or on lazy days, or after dark, or when he came home from school before dinner, or whenever else the mood struck, Jimmy would have his face buried in a book. It seemed to him there was never enough to read in the house. But that had all changed when Jimmy started exploring the family's encyclopedia, with its twenty big thick books displaying the smallest print Jimmy had ever seen and filled with pictures, some even in color. He had been led to this journal of discovery because his great grandmother always told him when she could not answer one of the multitudes of questions he was constantly asking to look it up in the dictionary, and when some of those questions were not answered in it, the thickest book he had ever seen, even thicker than the Bible, he had been instructed by his mother to look it up in the encyclopedia.

The Williams family had kept the firmly bound set of books in the master bedroom on the bottom shelf of a long bookcase. The many volumes stretched across the entire shelf, each having a number and a letter, such that they could be kept in proper order either by arithmetic or by alphabetization. Before being given the de facto permission by his mother, he had thought those books were for his parents use only, but after being given it he stopped asking his elders questions first and instead went to this treasure trove of knowledge to find out if it held the secret before troubling those who might not give him the correct answer anyway. And in Jimmy's universe there was nothing better than knowing things his older siblings did not, so after becoming used to going to it for unanswered questions he began reading it for pleasure, or at least to avoid watching soap operas with his mother and sisters on those days the weather or his health dictated he stay inside. After opening it randomly for a while, he decided to read it from start to finish, from volume 1-A, using it to fill in the unexpected and infrequent gaps of solitude in his days and vowing he wouldn't stop until he finished the Z's or high school, whichever came first, and learn as much as he possibly could to successfully negotiate the life he would lead beyond the current boundaries of his existence.

When he returned to the house he made a beeline to the living room where the encyclopedia was now kept. His father had grown tired of stepping over Jimmy in the bedroom as he read on the floor in front of the bookcase, and had moved it to the living room to allow Jimmy to read whenever he wanted without being a tripping hazard. Jimmy first pulled out the P volume to look up pitching but found nothing, then he put that volume back and remembered, as he was up to the D volume by this time in his life, there was an article on baseball in the B's. He flipped through the pages until he found it, and there on the fourth of the twelve-page article was a description of a pitcher's windup. Amazingly, Slugger was teaching him exactly what the book showed. This had a profound effect on Jimmy, as this may have been the first time anything Slugger had taught him was confirmed in this kind of detail from such a reliable source. Maybe Slugger knew what he was talking about!

He read on. The article had another, even more engrossing section. It concerned statistics, and since Jimmy loved to do math problems, he spent the next hour calculating batting averages, earned run averages, and how many home runs per year Babe Ruth averaged over his career.

But there was never enough time to read everything. Not with so many girls around. Whenever Jimmy was deep into something, one of them would always break the spell. This time it was Jacqueline, his oldest sister. She was the second child after Slugger, four years behind him, and despite the difference in size and age, she would never back down to her older brother. Slugger had long ago learned fighting with her was more often than not a losing proposition. And one of the main things they fought about, since he was born anyway, was Jimmy. She thought she was his second mother, but despite being his protector at times, to Jimmy she was still overwhelmingly a girl, and therefore more trouble than helpful.

"So, what are you reading about this time, Jimmy?" she asked.

"Baseball," he replied, so engrossed he forgot to pause to think of a funny answer.

"What for?" she continued.

"Because Slugger says he's gonna show me how to pitch, and I wanna make sure he knows what he's talkin' about."

"And does he?" she asked.

"Seems like it," he responded.

And with that off she went, looking for Slugger. As always, she wanted to know what Slugger's real motive was, so she could protect Jimmy. In her mind the chances of Slugger's motives being pure were slim. Slugger was always doing something Jimmy needed her protection from, like the time they were playing Sorry at the dinner table.

The Williams family played board games or card games sitting around the dinner table, usually when it was raining or snowing or winter's darkness had fallen and no good television shows were on. On this occasion the game was Sorry, which was a game with cards and a board, and each of the 4 players had 4 pieces of the same color; 4 red, 4 blue, 4 green or 4 yellow; and the object of the game was to get your pieces from the Start Line to your color's Home. Since this game and so many others required 4 players, and Jimmy was the fourth child in age, Jimmy had to learn to play or the others couldn't play, and therefore was forced to learn this game by his older siblings, like it or not, but this one he liked.

He liked it because as the game was played each player picked a card from the stack and moved one of their pieces around the board the number of spaces the card dictated, selecting which of the 4 to move based on the best strategy to get all 4 Home, the first player to do so being the winner. If one player's piece landed on the space another player's piece already occupied, the player who landed on the space called out SORRY!, and the player's piece already on the space had to go back to its Start Line. The most fun part of the game, for Jimmy anyway, was not winning, but yelling SORRY! as often as he could at the top of his lungs. His strategy, therefore, was to always move the piece that caused someone else's to go back, without considering if a different move would be more advantageous to winning the game, and if he had to choose which other player's piece to send back he prioritized Slugger's first, then Jaqueline's, then JoAnn's, because that was the way things worked in his universe.

Jimmy's mom, as was her personality, often started dinner and forgot one of the ingredients and had to rush to the store to pick it up after peeling the potatoes, putting them in a pot filled with water and turning on the burner. It was on one such occasion the kids had decided to pass the time before their now delayed dinner playing Sorry. As they had been trained since they were old enough to sit at the dinner table instead of a high chair, Slugger sat next to Jimmy on one side of the table, and the Jaqueline and JoAnn sat on the opposite side. Because of the clockwise rotation of turns in the game, Jimmy's turn followed Slugger's and he could see where Slugger's pieces were and move his pieces to thwart Slugger's strategy.

This game Slugger had the unfortunate luck to have a piece five spots ahead of Jimmy's and of course Jimmy drew a five card.

Jimmy had a choice to move another piece to Home, which would be the proper strategy in the minds of most players, especially Slugger's, but he knew as well as everyone else sitting at the table that was not what made the most sense to Jimmy. Despite what Slugger knew would be his brother's next move, he tried to influence him in the best way his universe had taught him to exert it, which was to threaten him.

"Don't do it, Jimmy," he said menacingly, before Jimmy had a chance to move.

Jimmy thought about it, weighing the possible pain of retribution against the sure pleasure of hearing his still unbroken contralto voice, and in the end, he made the only choice his universe would accept, regardless of consequences. He moved the piece which would land his piece on the space occupied by Slugger's, and called out in a loud sing-song tone, "SORRY!"

Slugger was not pleased. In his universe, the orders of superiors were followed without question, and if not, punishment must be meted out. Something had to be done or chaos would triumph! Jimmy could have moved a different piece and should have moved a different piece. The anger suddenly boiling up within him was tripled when he looked at the board and saw a third move Jimmy could have made which would have bumped one of JoAnn's pieces. That's when the form of punishment became clear. He stood from his chair, grabbed the pot off the stove, and said "I better drain some of this water off before it boils over," and he swung the pot over Jimmy, tilting it purposely to splash an unpleasant amount of it on Jimmy's head. "SORRY!" he called out derisively. Then he poured a bit of the water in the sink and sat back down, smiling at his obviously necessary adjustment to an improper attitude. Jimmy, hot water screaming down his face and neck, was both humiliated and injured, and burst out crying from the injustice and the pain; by the fact his brother wanted to hurt him more than its actual feel.

Jaqueline, as she looked on, was enraged. She stood from her chair behind the table, went to the cabinet, picked out the biggest glass she could reach, filled it with water, raised it to her lips as if to take a drink, but then instead dumped it, the whole glass, on Slugger's head.

"SORRY!!" she said to Slugger, and then went back to her chair. Jimmy, still crying, started to laugh at the same time, in the way only a child can do. The game continued.

She smiled at this memory as she walked around the circle of rooms that was their house, but could not find Slugger. After she realized he was nowhere to be found, she did what she thought was the next best thing, she took the risk of telling their mother what she had just learned.

The reason why this was a risk was her mother had been raised by her grandmother, and her grandmother had drilled into her the morals of the prior century. There was a wise old saying for every situation, and one of her favorites was if you were bored, there was always something useful you should be doing, The Idle Mind being the Devil's Workshop, and if Jacqueline wasn't careful, she would be put to work doing something that wasn't on her long list of regimented chores already. But for Jimmy's safety she would take the risk.

"Mom, guess what Slugger's doing to Jimmy now!" she said.

Her mother just looked at Jacqueline without responding. In her house her children could talk at the dinner table, which was a shock to the older generation that had raised her, but she had an old-school attitude when it came to raising daughters versus sons.

"He is teaching him how to pitch….." Jacqueline paused trying to determine if her mother would know what she meant without further clarification, and for dramatic reasons, "a baseball." Little did she know her mother knew all about baseball. She had met their father at a baseball game, where she was trying to learn how to keep score. He was the guy who volunteered to teach her, then gave her a ride home from the baseball field, then asked her to a movie.

"OK, I'll talk to your dad about it," she answered, and Jacqueline could only hope she had done enough to protect Jimmy. She wondered how bad Slugger would get in trouble this time. Before the term was known to her, she thought this was probably going to be a win-win situation: Jimmy saved; Slugger whipped. She disappeared as quickly as possible, before her mother could find something unpleasant for her to do.

CHAPTER
Four

W hen their father came home the atmosphere changed in the house. As with most men, he had a routine he felt driven to follow, and it usually meant woe to the child who forced him to alter it. On a typical day, he would announce his arrival, sometime between 4:15 and 4:30 in the afternoon, either by the sound of the creaking garage door as he lifted it or the rumble of the car over the gravel as he drove up the alley toward it. After pulling in and closing the door behind him, he would trudge with shoulders drooped through the patio and up the steps between it and the house swinging his metal lunch pail, empty except for the Thermos bottle he placed inside after completing his noon time meal, and open the back screen-door, turning immediately into the small bathroom and closing the door behind him. From there he would continue into the master bedroom, sitting his pail on his dresser and himself on the bed, and wait for his wife to join him if she wasn't already there, to discuss the events which occurred while he was away.

Most days it was a calm discussion, filled with the kind of hurried pleasantries lovers turned into parents can only find time for in precious snippets such as these. He was the quiet one, always focused on the burdens ahead and subdued by those just completed, and she was the boisterous blessing that was given to him at the end of each day because of his diligence. The universe he was born into required the work he did to be well beneath his intellect and she more than anyone knew this, how it drained and pained him not only physically, so she tried to let him know how much he was loved and appreciated in the short space of time they had to themselves before they had dinner with their brood, her goal being to bring him some cheer and lighten his heart, even if only for a minute or two. This was also the time for her to let him in on whatever the children had done that day; who deserved punishment or praise or both, who was suspected of being or becoming sick, who needed something and how it could be paid for along with all the bills staring up at him from the dresser top whenever he walked by, and most importantly, what should be on the grocery list. If the result of this conference was one or more of the children were summoned into the room before dinner, it was a good bet it was going to be a negative experience for that person, and it did not necessarily bode well if laughter was heard before the summons came, as they were the type of parents who believed it was their utmost duty to punish whatever they saw as bad behavior, even if the antics had made them chuckle.

Once Slugger was summoned, and he for sure was summoned more often than the other children, he came to the bedroom door and stood in the doorway. Dread would be an accurate emotion to describe his state of mind, but he could not recall anything he had done to deserve a whipping, but it wouldn't be the tenth time it happened and he hadn't done anything deserving, at least in his mind.

His dad started by saying, "Come in and close the door."

This was not good for Slugger. "What had he done this time?" he thought. He did as he was told. His mother was sitting on the bed, and he noticed she didn't look angry, but his father was standing by his tall dresser with a stern look on his face.

"I hear you are teaching Jimmy how to pitch," he said.

Slugger mind raced. Had Jimmy gone crying to his mother again? That would ruin his plan completely. But Slugger wasn't going to back down. He straightened his back, and set his jaw and responded, "Yes, I am."

When that got no reaction from his father; no back hand, no yank on his arm, just silence, in his mind it was a signal to become bolder. He continued.

"And I'm gonna sign him up for Minor League, too. Practice starts in a week."

His dad's eyes widened, and then narrowed, his mind racing through a possibility that had not occurred to it before. Unlike Slugger, he had not even considered his younger son would play any sports, as just keeping him alive had been enough of a challenge until now. His male ego started to swarm over his skepticism, but he wasn't about to drown in it.

"You know Jimmy isn't very strong, or healthy like you," he retorted, his mind resisting the urge to lift its feet and start floating.

"Well, he won't get strong reading those encyclopedias," Slugger challenged. Lack of boldness was never an issue in Slugger's universe, and during its expansion he had experienced many times how his rashness could unravel his plans, but he couldn't back down now. "I'll make sure he doesn't get hurt," he spat out before thinking of how he could possibly ensure that, but the tone of confidence in his voice somehow remarkably worked.

"OK, Slugger, make sure he doesn't," responded his dad with a stare, letting Slugger know he was giving him a responsibility for which he would ultimately be held accountable in the clearest way he could. Then he turned away, to study the economic challenges on his dresser top, which under normal circumstances would result in the immediate vacating of the room by whomever had been summoned, but Slugger did not move.

"I haven't told him yet about signing him up," he said firmly.

His father stared back at him, but remained silent. He realized Slugger had thought this out and it wasn't just today's whim, that he had assumed Jimmy would revolt against the idea if he told him too soon, before he had built some confidence in him. Slugger had a plan.

The silence went on too long for Slugger. Instead of engaging his father again, he turned to his mother and said, "Could you let me tell him when I know he's ready?" thinking she would be more likely to support him.

She smiled, but did not answer. His father finally broke away from his revelry and stated with an air that was undisputedly the last word on the subject, "OK, Slugger, I'll let you tell him. But if he says no, I'm not going to force him to play."

And with that, Slugger left the room as quickly as possible, before he could give his parents a chance to change their minds. When he opened the door, Jacqueline had to jump back quickly or she'd have been hit by it, as she was standing outside, too close to not be attempting to listen to what was happening on the other side.

"So," Slugger said with the half smile he could patent, "You're the one who tattled."

She said nothing in response, but straightened her back, put her hand on her hip, and tilted her head back in her typical confrontational stance. Then she said, "So what if I did? Are you in trouble?"

Obviously, she hadn't been able to hear clearly through the door.

"No," he said, "but you might be." And with that he walked past his sister and gave her the slight push out of his way siblings often do, even if there was plenty of room to walk past.

Jaqueline stared at her brother in disbelief, having not expected this outcome, but it did not take her long to recover, as in her universe her mother never sided with her.

34

CHAPTER
Five

The next Saturday morning, after their dad left to run his weekend errands, Slugger led Jimmy into the garage again. It was cold and damp, typical of spring days in the Midwest when every breath could be seen in the cool mist of the mornings followed by afternoons dripping with sweat. Once again Slugger went to the end of the garage where the window was, and told Jimmy to stand by the opposite end.

As he stood there shivering, Jimmy blurted out before his brother could say a word; "OK, I've been practicing the windup."

This was better news than Slugger could have hoped for, but he managed to mask his pleasure with his inscrutable trademark half smile and said, "Let me see," in the dull tone of the unconvinced.

"Give me the ball," retorted Jimmy, not pleased by his brother's lack of conviction. How dare he not believe him?

"Just show me the windup, Jimmy." ordered Slugger. It was not a request.

Jimmy was old enough to understand he did not have to take orders from his older siblings, that is unless it was mandated by his parents, and even then, he wouldn't do it unless it made total sense to him, having been tricked by them so many times before, but this time a higher form of energy was in control of his actions which overcame his universe's natural inertia of rebellion. He had something to prove, and the gravity of the anger he felt toward his brother for his lack of faith overcame the forces which were otherwise constantly pushing him away from authority's grip, even the weak grip his older brother had on him, and so Jimmy felt compelled to go through the motions he had been practicing and threw an imaginary ball right at Slugger's head. In his mind, Slugger missed it and it hit him square in the mouth, just like the block had years before.

"That looks pretty good!" said Slugger, with a tone of surprise he could not hide in his voice.

"I told you I've been practicing," said Jimmy, with the air of someone who already knew what he had just been told. What did his brother think he meant when he said it to him in the first place? "So can you give me the ball now?"

Pleased at his brother's defiance, Slugger replied, "OK, Jimmy. But first you need to learn how to throw it. Let me show you." Then he walked over to his brother, stood behind him and lifted his left arm so it was above his shoulder, angled outward. "When you step forward, bring your arm up like this. Not too low or too high. Bring it around as you bring your foot down. Try it," was the command.

Jimmy knew this already, there was a picture of it in the encyclopedia. He had, in fact been practicing it. He went through the motions again, adding the proper arm motion as he took the last step forward in his windup.

"Good," said Slugger.

Then he put the ball in Jimmy's little hand, and to Jimmy, the ball fit perfectly as he held it in his palm.

"That's not how you hold it," said Slugger, and with that he grabbed each of Jimmy fingers and placed them on the ball, the little and ring fingers curled together on the left side of the ball, the thumb on the right side of the ball, and the middle and pointer fingers straight out, split slightly, so the fingertips touched the seams of the ball at right angles. Jimmy had also seen this in the encyclopedia. It was called a "cross seamed grip".

Slugger walked back across the garage, squatted in his catcher's position, and held the glove in front of his chest.

"I want you to look at my glove at all times during the windup. You should step toward my glove, with your foot pointed straight at the glove, and when you release the ball your pointer finger should be pointed right at the glove. If you do it right I shouldn't have to move the glove to catch it." Slugger paused for emphasis. "And if you do it wrong you'll throw it too high and I might not catch it and you'll break the window. And Dad will kill you if that happens. So you better keep it down. And in order to keep it down, you have to follow through."

Jimmy knew instantly Slugger was bluffing. If the window was broken, it would be Slugger getting into trouble, not him. But his experience had also taught him Slugger getting punished by their dad often led to Jimmy getting punished in some way by Slugger, so it was in his best interest to keep it down in any case. After reaching that conclusion Jimmy realized he might have trouble doing it, since he had no clue what Slugger was talking about when he made his warning.

"Follow through?" asked Jimmy.

"Yeah, follow through. That means after you let go of the ball, keep swinging your arm down and step forward with your left foot until it is even with your right. Make sure you are bent at the waist, but don't bend too far. You want to be in a position to catch the ball if it gets hit back at you."

Those words startled Jimmy, as he hadn't considered the idea of a batter entering his universe, or the possibility this new entrant could hit the ball back at him. Up to this point it had all been theoretical, and Jimmy had assumed Slugger would get bored with teaching him after a few days, and that was where this would all end. Now, with not only the possibility of breaking the window on his mind, but also the idea of being hit with a batted ball, he started his windup. His first attempt with the added weight of the ball in his hand upset his balance and he stumbled once he kicked up his leg and he couldn't throw it at all, instead extending his arms and using the ball and his glove to keep from crashing face first to the ground. Slugger laughed as anyone would have who saw his tumble, but in Jimmy's world getting laughed at was worse than getting beaten, and Slugger needed to be shown he would not tolerate it. He wanted to hit Slugger with the ball so earnestly the second time he went into his windup he lifted his leg a little lower to keep his balance, and brought his arm around, stepped forward, and let the ball go without thinking about anything other than Slugger's lip splitting on the impact and thereby stopping the laughter. The ball flew straight into Slugger's glove, as he held it in front of his face.

"Good pitch!" said Slugger, somewhat surprised by the fact Jimmy had hit the glove without his having to move it. Not only that, but the ball hadn't come directly into his mitt in a straight line, it seemed to curve its way into it. Lefthanders, he pondered, can never throw a ball straight for some reason. He threw it back to Jimmy. "OK, now try to throw it a little harder."

Harder? Jimmy thought he had thrown it with all his might the first time, but he also instinctively knew the only way to throw it any harder was for him to raise his leg higher than the last time. But he also knew that made the odds of controlling it decrease, so he made an extra effort to bend his knee more, and bring it down farther when he stepped forward. The result was the ball seemed to go faster, but it remained low off the ground, and went straight into Slugger's glove.

"That was better," said Slugger, and he threw the ball back to Jimmy. "Now do it again."

And Jimmy did, again and again. Slugger was amazed at the accuracy, but then, not quite so amazed. Jimmy always learned everything so fast, if he wanted to learn it, anyway. The trick was making him want to learn it. After about 25 throws, he ordered Jimmy to stop. The last few were getting more and more wild, and Slugger had to reach for the last one before it hit the window.

Jimmy was getting tired, but having so much fun he didn't want to stop. "One more!" he cried.

"OK, Jimmy, but just one more. I don't want you getting a rag arm," responded his brother.

Jimmy paused to consider what that meant, probably something Slugger made up because he was bored and wanted to stop, but then focused completely on getting the last pitch into the glove with as much velocity as he could muster and threw it straight into the mitt. The sound it made as Slugger caught it was wonderful to Jimmy. It was part pop, part snap, part drumbeat, and it filled him with the same kind of joy he felt when he took the first lick from an ice cream cone.

CHAPTER
Six

After that last pitch Slugger left Jimmy standing in the garage, still working on his windup and throwing imaginary pitches, by opening the garage door and walking out into the driveway, leaving Jimmy exposed to whoever was walking or driving down the alley behind it. The alley was not paved, just dirt covered by loose gravel, so every time a car would pass it made a grinding sound coupled with the pings of the rocks hitting the underside of the car, and on days when it hadn't rained, dust would rise leaving a cloudy trail in the air after the car passed. It was not the pinging or the grinding which woke Jimmy from his day dreaming as he was still twirling his body in the pre-described sequence he was trying to perfect, it was the sound of an even more familiar voice, the voice of his best friend, Joe Gurnsey.

"Hey, Jimmy, whatcha doin'?" called out the voice. He was riding in the open back of his father's ancient, dirty pickup truck.

"Nothing!" Jimmy shouted back as he watched the truck roll past. However, it was obvious to Joe what Jimmy was doing, standing there with a glove and ball in his hands.

"Wanna play catch?" asked Joe, now standing with his hands clasped to the side of the pickup for balance as his father continued past, allowing him to see Jimmy for a few more seconds.

By the time Jimmy could respond with a shrug, the truck had almost reached the Gurnseys' shack of a garage, three doors down the alley on the same side as the Williams'. Jimmy and Joe's universes overlapped quite a bit, seeing as how they originated so close together in space and time, Joe having started his expansion only a couple of months earlier. They were in the same class at school and Joe had older brothers, one the same age as Slugger, and another even older one who was already living on his own, in the house next door, two doors away. Jimmy never felt poor because he had neighbors like Joe, who were plainly more desperate economically than even Jimmy's modest family. Joe proudly proclaimed to be of Native American decent, even though he looked white to Jimmy. Joe's dad however, had the look and bearing of an Indian. Whether he was asked or not, Joe would stick out his chest and declare himself as a mix of the Choctaw, Chickasaw, and Cherokee tribes whenever he felt the need to proclaim it. He never had new clothes or shoes, and everything he wore seemed to be passed down from his older brother, slightly too big as he had not quite grown into it before he had to start wearing it. The Gurnseys were good, simple, and plain folk, still capable of living happily with bare floors while sharing their living space with cockroaches relaxed enough to stroll across the sparsely decorated rooms in broad daylight. Jimmy's mother was most emphatically not of the same mindset, and entering the Gurnsey house had been forbidden ever since Slugger had contracted a skin disease she was convinced he picked up there years before.

As soon as Joe jumped out of the back of the truck, he came running down the alley before Jimmy could think to run into his house. Joe knew Jimmy sometimes did that to avoid him, and this time he didn't want to give him the chance. As he came into Jimmy's view in the driveway he had an old glove in his hands, another well-worn hand-me-down from an older brother.

"Where'd you get the glove and ball?" asked Joe without so much as a "hello". Joe's universe, like that of so many other little boys, was too full of wonder and energy to have the patience for pleasantries like hellos.

"Slugger," said Jimmy.

Nothing else needed to be said, because both knew their older brothers were resourceful types, and very close mouthed about where the things they brought home came from. It was best to just use what was made available, and not ask questions.

"Throw it to me!" said Joe, his universe also having no time for introspection.

Jimmy had not had that luxury in his life, to do things without thinking and get positive results, so he thought about it for a few seconds, and said, "You've got to throw it back."

Jimmy did not think Joe wouldn't, but that didn't stop him from making the statement. Joe had "borrowed" things from Jimmy in the past, and even though he always got them back, sometimes Slugger had to get them back for him.

"We won't be playin' catch if I don't throw it back," said Joe, quite sensibly.

"OK, let's go out into the alley, so we don't hit anything," responded Jimmy, because he doubted if Joe could throw with any accuracy, and if the window was broken when Slugger wasn't around he would be unable to blame him.

And as games of catch go between boys their age, their egos far outstripped their arm strength and they stood too far apart to get the ball through the air between them on most throws, and on the rare occasions they did, neither could catch it cleanly unless luck intervened. Three out of every four throws resulted in one of the boys having to run up or down the alley, into the backyards on either side of the alley, or at best stooping down to pick up the ball after they dropped it.

Unless Joe threw the ball at his face, Jimmy had no fear of trying to catch it, which surprised him. He was usually afraid of everything. He amazed himself and Joe too, by catching one which had bounced in front of him and tried to squirt away. This was the highlight of their game, which by their internal clocks went on for what seemed like hours, but was probably closer to fifteen minutes, when Joe, who was facing the direction toward the street at the end of the alley, looked over Jimmy's shoulder and said "Oh no, here comes Donny Gomes."

Donny was the bully of their grade school class, even though he was no bigger than either of them, or no bigger than Joe, anyway. His pale white skin was sunken into his face, like the skeleton drawn on a Halloween costume, and that scared the other kids more than anything. No one wanted to fight him, because anyone who looked like that had to be tough. When Donny figured out the other kids feared the way he looked, he enjoyed the power it gave him, but deep down, he just wanted to have friends like everyone else. Donny saw them in the alley, but did not walk toward them.

"What are you sissies doin'?" yelled Donny. He knew what they were doing, but didn't want to waste the opportunity to call them sissies.

Before Jimmy could supply an answer, Joe blurted out, "Nothing!" with an air of defiance Jimmy thought was uncalled for.

"Looks like you're doin' sumpthin' to me," said Donny, responding in kind.

Joe called back, "Don't worry about what we're doin'," as if not telling Donny something he could easily figure out for himself was very important.

Donny took a couple of steps toward them, but stopped as soon as he saw the other boys start to fidget, which was the reaction he wanted. "I don't have time to pound you right now, Injun, but I'll make the time some other day," he promised, and then he turned away and continued walking down the street toward his house, which was at the first corner, a half a block away.

Joe couldn't hide the look of concern on his face, but the risk was worth it to him. He couldn't look scared in front of Jimmy. Jimmy was his best friend, and to be Jimmy's friend meant, to him anyway, to be Jimmy's protector. Jimmy was so smart and funny he did not want anything bad to happen to him, and Jimmy obviously couldn't protect himself. But they both decided they didn't feel like playing catch anymore. Suddenly the wind was too strong, the air was too cold, and it was time for a snack. Joe trotted up the alley toward his house with the ball in his hand. After going a few steps further away than he knew he could throw it, he turned and yelled at Jimmy "Catch!" and heaved it with all his might. The balled sailed far into Jimmy's backyard, thankfully missing the patio next to the garage his father had recently removed the plastic from. Joe thought he would scare Jimmy into thinking he would keep the ball, but Jimmy hadn't had a chance to get scared thinking about that. He was far too concerned about getting pounded by Donny Gomes.

CHAPTER
Seven

The only television in the Williams' home was in the family
room. It sat in the corner of the room, in the corner of
the house, with a cord running up and through the wall
near the ceiling to the outside, where Jimmy's dad had mounted
an antenna on the roof. Despite this extra effort, the reception was
still not very clear, and could be made worse or better depending
on where people sat in the room. That was why on this afternoon
Jimmy watched the aptly titled baseball Game of the Week with
his father, sprawled on the floor instead of on the couch, because
on the couch the reception had been worse. His dad had his chair,
left of center, which was his and his alone to sit on. The couch was
angled from right of center, so the left end of the couch was the
second-best seat in the house. Jimmy preferred, despite his mother's concerns about his posture, lying on the floor in front of the
couch to sitting on it, and because his father agreed the reception
was better when he was there she was trumped. He had watched
with his father sporadically before, usually getting bored after the
first couple of innings and running off to do something more en-
tertaining, but on this day, he felt compelled to sit and watch, as he
was already tired from his earlier travails in the alley.

His dad almost never missed the Game of the Week because
it was truthful advertising, as it was the one and only game to be
shown on television, once a week, and missing it meant waiting another whole week to watch a game. Jimmy would have easily missed
it, but his universe placed Donny Gomes exactly where and when

he needed to be to force Jimmy to be where he needed to be to meet his first major league heroes. The game was in progress when Jimmy bounded into the family room to join his father.

"Who's playing?" asked Jimmy, after coming out of his bedroom where he had been since the episode in the alley.

"Close the door behind you," commanded his father before answering the question. "The Dodgers against the San Francisco Giants. It's gonna be a real barn burner."

Jimmy didn't ask what that meant, because as he came closer he saw the Giants' pitcher warming up through the static on the screen and felt compelled to flop down to the floor in his favorite spot to watch. As soon as he stopped moving the fuzziness on the screen he had caused by entering the room disappeared, like clouds parting to reveal a brilliant sunrise, and he could clearly see the pitcher going through his windup, and he was dumbfounded. His leg kick was impossibly high and yet so graceful and powerful as it swept down, stormed down, and with a splendidly asymmetric twist he whipped his arm around and down and released the ball as if it exploded out of his hand. And he did it again, and again, his foot reaching the same point, his leg making the same arc, his arm delivering the same explosion. The term "poetry in motion" never had any meaning to Jimmy until he saw this man's windup, its beauty and power too consistent to be real.

"Who is that pitching?" asked Jimmy, after the sequence ended and the trance was broken as a Dodger walked to the batter's box.

"Juan Marichal," said his slightly annoyed father. He, like most black men, rooted for the Dodgers whenever possible, because they had signed Jackie Robinson.

"Is that the team with Willie Mays?" blurted out Jimmy. Jimmy had heard Slugger talking about Willie Mays. Willie Mays was Slugger's idol. Willie Mays was why Slugger never wanted to pitch himself, only play centerfield.

"Yes, Jimmy," his father responded, now in a tone to let Jimmy know he was annoyed. He didn't want Jimmy going on a tear of question after question while he was trying to focus on the game.

But Jimmy didn't. Something else happened to take away his attention. The Dodger hitter managed to miraculously hit one of Mr. Marichal's exquisite deliveries, and it squirted out toward the shortstop of the Giants. He in turn somehow managed to scoop the ball up and throw it, off balanced, toward first base. The screen changed, and now it was on a very large man with the longest, thickest sideburns Jimmy had ever seen, who was stretching his legs to the point of doing a split and reaching his arm out like he was swatting a fly to snag the ball as it bounced far out in front of him.

Jimmy leaped from his pose on the floor when he saw it. "Wow!! What a catch! Who was that, Dad?"

His dad was now resigned to the fact that his son was not rooting for the Dodgers.

"Willie McCovey," he replied.

"He's left handed," said Jimmy, noticing the glove was on his right hand.

"First base is the best position for a left hander," said his dad. "The only others are pitcher and outfielder and maybe catcher."

"Can you play more than one position?" asked Jimmy, not having thought of that possibility before, as he had not thought about playing even one until a few days before.

"Some players do," said his father, who now realized the questions were flowing now, and he had been sucked in without being able to stop it.

But Jimmy fell silent again, watching the magic of Juan Marichal. When the Dodgers had their outs, Jimmy watched the

Dodgers pitcher warm up, a left hander even, but was not impressed by the windup, some guy named Sandy. To survive as a lefty Jimmy had learned long ago to watch the things right handers did, and everyone in his house was right handed except him, and then store them in his brain as the mirror image to be able to repeat it left handed. This was so well ingrained in him by this point he learned best by watching right handers and was confused by left handed explanations. He could not stop watching until every foot placement, every hand position, every arm angle, and every movement of the masterful windup of the artist that was Marichal imprinted in his mind.

When the game ended, Jimmy couldn't even remember the score. The Giants won, and McCovey hit a home run, but by that time both Mr. Koufax and Mr. Marichal were showered and in their street clothes and weren't involved. But to Jimmy, it was better than any game in any World Series he would ever watch. He had acquired what many boys need when they are playing a sport, someone to mimic. Someone to imagine he was when he tried to do what they did. The next time Slugger asked him to pitch he would imagine he was Juan Marichal.

CHAPTER
Eight

S undays were always the same. It was a ritual engrained in the family like no other. In fact, it started the night before, on Saturday night, with each child taking a bath. Showers were not an option for any of them except Slugger, as the children's bathroom had a bath only, and the master bathroom had a shower only. He had graduated to the shower with the birth of Belinda because his mother had calculated long ago that four was the maximum number of baths she could stretch one bathtub full of water into. Jimmy had been taught to shower as well, a frightening experience of being pelted by the hard water drops and his naked father's rough hands washing his back while his mother watched, laughing, but it was agreed by all involved he should continue bathing until he was older. Even their mother preferred taking a bath to a shower, as that was the most soothing and relaxing part of her day, when she could sit for what seemed like hours in the warm water, reading. But there was no such time on Saturday nights, as each child had to take a bath one after the other, starting with the youngest and working their way up. Their mother would lay their Sunday clothes on a chair in their bedrooms and their pajamas on the toilet seat while each child soaked, so they wouldn't get confused about what they were to wear and what sequence they were to wear them in, and then she marched each straight to bed, theoretically to doze off immediately and be fully rested and energized when she roused them in the morning for that most important day of the week, Sunday, when she would lead the choir in the praising of the Lord through music.

Breakfast was best on Sunday, bacon and eggs and toast, hot and ready. The family ate at the dinner table which was placed lengthwise with just enough room for a walkway between the table and the sink, stove, and refrigerator which lined the opposite wall. The house was too small for a separate dining room. When not in use, the table was pushed closer to the wall to make more room for people washing dishes or cooking or looking in the refrigerator, which was of course punished if it lasted more than ten seconds.

After breakfast, they would pile into the station wagon, attired in suits and dresses, with polished shoes, and lotion covering any exposed skin, and take the mile journey to the small white church that was a segregationist's dream. Out of the driveway, down the alley, a right turn out to Eighth Street and over the half block to the corner of Eighth and Anderson. A right turn on Anderson took them past the front of their house to the next street, which was Seventh, where their father would stop at the house on the corner, Gramma's house. After waiting for her to make her slow walk to the car, they would continue another two blocks to Fifth Avenue, one of the two major thoroughfares in town.

In small towns like Canton, a major thoroughfare meant a street which was only one lane each direction, but the streets intersecting it had stop signs. On non-major street intersections, there were no signs at all. There were maybe ten stop lights in the whole town of fifteen thousand. After stopping and waiting for an occasional car to pass, a left turn on Fifth would lead, after another half block, to a set of railroad tracks. These were the same tracks that ran behind the houses on the other side of the street from their house on Anderson. The railroad tracks and Fifth Avenue formed the northeast corner of the church property. Houses stood on Fifth to the south of the property, and a narrow access road to the International Harvester plant which stood to the west of the church formed the north border. Another access road to the plant ran along the west side, and Fifth the east side. The main entrance to the church was on Fifth, but the Williams family never went into the church through the main entrance. Instead, after crossing the tracks they turned right and went down a narrow road which ran next to the railroad tracks, past the small house that was built there by the hands of the congregation where the preacher lived with his family. Even though they did not call their leader a Parson, his house was called a Parsonage. The road led to a gravel path behind the Parsonage, which they turned left onto, and once past the back of the house opened into a larger gravel parking lot, which was behind the church.

There were two back entrances to the church. One door led down a short flight of steps to the church basement, and the other was up a flight of steps to the backdoor of the preacher's office. The family, after parking and greeting whoever may have arrived concurrently, would go into the door leading to the basement, which first led into a small kitchen on the right, and a storage room to the left, where a Ping-Pong table, Christmas and Easter decorations and other miscellaneous items were kept. Past that was the main room which comprised the remainder of what was the basement. This area was sectioned off by portable partitions, with a pathway down the middle, and each section held hard metal folding chairs, some small enough for children Jimmy's size, and others full sized for teenagers and adults. Inside those sections Sunday School classes were held, with the children split into groups by age.

The routine was for the entire family to go through the basement to the short set of steps at what was the front right corner of the building. At the top of those steps was the front entrance of the church, a set of heavy wooden doors which opened onto the sidewalk in front of Fifth Avenue. Instead of walking back out of the church through those doors, an urge which never quite overwhelmed the children, but was always a tempting thought in their minds, they made a hairpin right turn which led to the wide, main stairway, rising from the front entrance to the sanctuary on the main floor of the church.

At the top of the main stairway was a narrow open area, with a wall of windows separating it from the sanctuary that allowed people to look in and find a place to sit. There were small doors at each end of the wall, and double doors in the middle. This area was just large enough for the choir to line up for their entry into the sanctuary at the start of the service, and for wedding parties to do the same on the rare occasions when someone got married there. Each of these doors led into the main room of the church, filled mostly with twenty rows of polished wooden benches, called pews, arranged between outside aisles, which is where the small, outside doors led, and a wider aisle down the middle, where the double doors led.

The pews faced a raised section of the room, with a wide set of stairs leading up to it in the middle, and narrow stairs leading up to it on either end. The outer steps led into small rooms with doors, one of which had a back entrance to the outside of the church, the other did not. The wider steps led to a table, with flowers and a cross on it, which was called the Alter. The table had enough space around it to allow the choir to walk up the stairs, then around the table to either side to an open area behind it where the choir would sit during church services. A piano sat to the side of the choir area.

On either side of the table was a wooden stand, called a pulpit, made of simple wood, the one on the left smaller and less ornate than the one on the right. To the left of the left pulpit was an unadorned small wooden bench and to the right of the right pulpit was a high-backed chair, upholstered in red velvet. Each small room had a door leading out to the choir area, the one on the left with the outside door was the preacher's office, which was called the Study, and the one to the right was where people about to be baptized or grooms about to get married waited to take the plunge. Under the choir space was the baptismal tub, covered by a trap door.

All the families with children would congregate in the sanctuary, each in the same pew every week, at or before 9:30AM. Canton had about one hundred blacks, or Negroes as they were called in polite society, and since all of them who went to church went there, it wasn't hard to know all the members of Mt. Carmel Baptist church. There had been a shocking baby boom among the Negro population in 1959, and it seems about every woman of child bearing age had one. That made Jimmy's Sunday school class of seven the biggest in decades, and at Easter it could swell to ten. He could see Sonny Mathis was there with his family. His little brother, two years younger but already bigger than Jimmy, was also in Jimmy's class. Of course, the preacher's kids were there. The Mathis's neighbors, the Mitchells, were there, and that meant Susan would be there, even though he could not see her.

After the person in charge of the Sunday School said a few words, usually to figure out who would be acting as teachers, and how many classes would be needed based on the numbers of those attending, etc., the children were released to their separate areas in the basement and turned over to the lucky ones, or unlucky ones (as sometimes unsuspecting adults were drafted for the task whether they liked it or not) designated as Sunday School teachers. There were picture books and songs and reading from the Bible, but Jimmy spent most of his time watching Susan and wondering why girls were the way they were. His sisters, his mother, Susan, the girls in his classes in school, it seemed the more they liked him, the more they tormented him. And if they didn't like him, that tormented him even more.

When they talked about the story of Adam and Eve, he could picture it happening easily, because it happened to him all the time. If a girl bugged him about doing something, trying something, eating something, eventually he'd break down and try it, even if he snuck away somewhere and did it alone, where his tormentor could not see him. That was how he pictured Adam doing it. God had told him not to eat the fruit, but this girl kept bugging him about it, and he finally decided he had to try it, snuck off into the woods where no one could see him, and took a bite. After that there was no way to hide the evidence from God because a bite was missing from the fruit which couldn't be put back, especially after he had chewed it up, and Adam was trapped. And to make things worse, when Eve found out she had the extra satisfaction of not only getting Adam in trouble, but also being able to remind him forever of how gullible he was. It probably didn't even taste good.

After an hour and a half that always seemed like three, Sunday school would end and the children would march back up the stairs to rejoin the adults for the main service. Jimmy's siblings would sit in one of the long pews together, with their Gramma to watch over them, as their mother would be seated at the piano and their father sat in the front row with the other church officers. He would sit so he could look over his shoulder at his children, and he would signal his displeasure at excessive fidgeting, whispering, or head bobbing (from falling asleep) by clearing his throat, loudly. All their heads would snap in his direction when they heard that sound, and whoever he was staring at would have to sweat it out until they found out what kind of trouble they were in later that day after Sunday dinner.

Which of course meant the best way to spend the hour minimum the main service lasted was to try to get someone else to laugh, squirm, or otherwise bring attention to their selves in a way that would get them noticed, in a bad way, by their father. Pinching and tickling were favorite tactics. Writing or drawing funny things were good too, but by the time Jimmy came along, Slugger had found out the hard way pranks which left visible evidence were very dangerous, and the younger ones had watched and learned from the negative experiences he had endured because of it.

Jimmy, who was on the receiving end of the pranks the most, tried to avoid the boredom and keep himself out of trouble by reading the Bible. The difference between a pew and a bench was a pew had holders for books in slots on the back, so someone in the pew behind could put their Bibles there, and a book of songs their Gramma called a hymnal, used by those adults who still hadn't memorized the words to the standard hymns as Jimmy had by age six. Reading the Bible would get him into trouble later in his childhood, but for now it was just like reading a different kind of encyclopedia. The main part that fascinated him was how long some of the people lived. Some lived for hundreds of years, which made them quite older than even his Gramma!!

Jimmy would occupy himself in this way during the start of the service, which never changed. First, the preacher and assistant preacher would come out of the Study, and take their places behind their respective pulpits, the assistant to the left at the smaller pulpit, and the head pastor to the right. He would signal Jimmy's mom to start playing the piano, and the choir, standing in line behind the double doors at the back of the sanctuary, would begin filing into the main chamber. They would march down the aisle two by two, swaying side to side with each step, singing the opening song. The Williams children would know it by heart, since their mother would practice the music in their house all week, sometimes drafting them to serve as singers while she played. In church, they sometimes sang along, sometimes hummed along, and most times stared at the ceiling. Their Gramma would always smile when she heard her granddaughter play, and would clap the hands of her great-grandchildren to the rhythm when they were still small enough to fit in her lap. Baby Belinda was occupying that role these days.

The choir would continue to their seats in the choir section singing, and then stand in front of them swaying, until they finished the song. Then the pastor, and the assistant pastor, standing at their pulpits, would take over. The pastor would give a welcome, and then turn it over to the assistant pastor for a few words.

The assistant pastor, Reverend Spotter, was an old man to Jimmy eyes, very dark skinned, of medium height and weight, thinning hair combed straight back with the help of some mysterious oil, who wore a rumpled dark suit and white shirt. He carried two handkerchiefs in his shirt pocket, which he took out and laid on his pulpit when he started to preach. One of the handkerchiefs was to wipe the sweat from his brow, which was considerable and started flowing from the minute he stood at the pulpit until an hour after the service ended. The other he used to blow his nose, or cough or sneeze into. His job was to warm up the crowd for the main sermon, and to cheer lead during it with loud and drawn out "Amens!"

His opening remarks were always the same.

"I would like to start by thanking God for getting me up this morning and making it possible for me to be standing up here with you today. Some of you are too young to remember, but the way I used to live before I found the Lord...."

He would pause for emphasis, and to let the congregation shout out some encouragement, which sometimes he would get, sometimes not. There might be a group of 25 people in the church, including the choir, unless it was Christmas or Easter.

"I used to smoke. Two or three packs a day. I used to drink, gamble..."

He would follow with another pause. If the room remained silent, the main pastor would speak up. "Watch out now, Reverend!" or "Tell it, Reverend!" would be his retort.

"I wasn't looking for the Lord."

If the pastor was feeling frisky, and it was his job to feel frisky about the Lord, he would start to hum "mm-Hmm, mmm-mmm-mmm-mmm."

"The way I was livin' made me so sick the doctor told me I didn't have long to live. And I was still a young man. My lungs were so full of the filth of my life that every breath I took felt like heavy burden."

The pastor would switch to wailing, "Well, well, well, well" by this point, to a tune he had made up, or was taught to him in Black Preacher's College.

"My burden was so heavy. I couldn't stand under its weight. I had to get down on my knees. I tried and tried, but I could not find the strength to get back up on my own. And I said, Lord, if you take this sickness out of me, I will give up all this vice and sin."

"Tell 'em!" was shouted from one pulpit to the other.

"And I prayed and I prayed until the spirit came down into my body and shook me so hard I fell flat on my face. And I laid there so full of the Spirit I couldn't move, couldn't stand, I was overcome by the Holy Spirit!"

At this point Reverend Spot would use one of the handkerchiefs and wipe his brow, and then use the second to cough up some phlegm or blow some snot into before he continued. The Williams children would come to attention during this part of the sermon. Their mother had told them when she was young Rev. Spot had grabbed the wrong handkerchief, and wiped snot all over his forehead. They had never seen this in all their years of watching this same display, but they didn't want to miss it if it ever did happen again.

"And then I fell into a deep sleep. And when I woke up, my lungs were clear and I felt a great weight had been lifted from me!!" he exclaimed, but the effort of the shout brought up another mass of phlegm, and he barely got the handkerchief to his face before it flew out of his mouth.

The kids leaned forward, not knowing which cloth he had picked up. Maybe the next time he swiped his forehead, it would finally happen.

"He took all the sickness. I felt good for the first time in so long. He had not only saved my life; he had given my life purpose. I knew I had to spread this Good Word for the rest of my life."

At that point he wiped his brow. No slime streaked across his face, so he had unfortunately, from the Williams children's standpoint anyway, picked the sweat rag, not the snot rag.

"And I know what the prophet meant when he said, 'I love the Lord. He heard my cry.'"

The main pastor, who had been sitting throughout the speech so far, stood when he heard this. Jimmy's mother turned to the keyboard and started to tinkle the ivories, hinting at the song to come.

"My life has been so full I have never wavered. If you want that kind of peace in your heart, just let Jesus in!"

"Let him in!" sang the pastor. He knew this was the point at which to cut Reverend Spot off, or he would get too full of the Spirit and he might sweat and shout and cough his way into the hospital. Jimmy's mother also knew, and started to play louder, looking at the choir to make sure they saw her signal to stand.

Reverend Spotter's voice rose to a crescendo, "I Love the Lord!! He Heard My Cry!! When I walk through the Valley of the Shadow of Death, I will fear no Evil!! For Thou Art with Me!!!! Aaaaahhhh....Praise be to the Lord!!!"

The pastor would signal, and the choir would rise, their voices beginning the next song: a slow song about redemption, or a fast one about the joy of being a Christian; and he would start to shout, louder than Spot could with his mucus filled chest, "CAN I GET AN AMEN!!!" again and again until the congregation would shout it back and then Spot would pick up both of his rags from the pulpit and crash down onto his bench spent, furiously wiping sweat and coughing chunks.

The choir would be at full throat by now, and when they finished, the ushers took center stage. There were usually four of them. Two would march up the center aisle, each with a deep plate, and two would march up the outside aisles empty handed. Jimmy's mother would play softly in the background as one of the church officers stood and asked for everyone to give, talked about the money needed to fix the church roof or buy the food for the next church function. The ushers would hand the plate to the first person sitting inside the first row on either side, and they would pass it across to the next person until it reached the outside aisle, where the outside usher would hand it to the person on the outside of the second row and it would start across the row toward the middle. The children were given change to specifically put into the collection plate, and since giving in to the temptation to not put in all the required change had also gotten Slugger a beating in the past, none of them tried that again. After the plates reached the last row, the ushers marched back to the front and gave the plates to the treasurer, who took them away into the office.

Next would be the main sermon. The pastor started by saying which verses from the Bible he would be preaching about. Sometimes Jimmy read what was being discussed, but usually he just found where he had left off the last time, because Jimmy never understood why the pastor didn't start at the beginning and go through the Bible chapter by chapter, week by week, like his teachers in school did. Picking random parts to preach about each week was confusing, and Jimmy wondered if that was why it was so hard for people to follow ten simple rules.

Jimmy read it like he read the encyclopedia, starting with Genesis and working toward Revelations. In the first books were some very good stories, but it was mostly about who knew who, and who begat who, and Jimmy hadn't figured out at his age what the word "knew" meant, in the Biblical sense, or what "begat" meant, in any sense, period. But he had learned not to ask his Gramma about it.

He just read it daydreaming until he heard his mother start to play the piano again, which was the first sign the end was near, at least the end of the church service, not the end of the world the pastor was talking about every week. Jimmy was absolutely convinced the end of the world wouldn't come before he finished high school, so he couldn't relate to it. The way his parents talked about the value of a good education, they must not have thought it was coming as soon as the pastor said it was either.

But by this stage of the daydream she would be playing. The birds never chirped so happily as when Jimmy was sitting in a pew on a spring day, and it was warm enough for the stained-glass windows to be open on the outside walls of the church. It seemed the birds were teasing him, mocking him that they could fly away any time they wanted, and he had to sit there until the music ended. The preacher told everyone to stand, and left one piece of drama before the service was ended.

He would ask, "Does anyone here want to be saved today?"

The choir would sing softly an old spiritual, "There's a still, small, voice..."

"Do you want the peace that I have found?" he would continue.

"Quietly, quietly, quiet moments with Him," on went the choir, low enough to be drowned out by the pastor's rising encouragement.

"Will you let Jesus in your heart today?" he would plead.

Jimmy would look around, hoping no one came forward. When that happened, the proceedings would go on even longer, as the newly repented sinner would walk down the aisle to where the preacher was standing, and fall to his knees. Then the pastor, assistant pastor, and sometimes the mother of the convert would join hands with him to wail, moan, or shout, depending on their personal worship style, until the pastor would stand in front with his hand on the supplicant's head and say a special prayer of thanks to God for not only saving the poor sinner's soul, but doing it on his watch so he could count it toward his total of souls saved, which was a very important statistic on a preacher's resume. Luckily on this day there was no one in the church who hadn't been saved already who was old enough to be saved, so it was straight to the benediction, which was the preacher's parting shot, his promise to be back next week to continue his mission to tally as many souls on the path to heaven as possible.

Then came the procession out, led by the pastor and his assistant. He would march down the front stairs, down the main aisle, then down the main stairs and open the front doors of the church where he would stand by the open doors, letting in the sound of the outside world, mostly the blare of the cars racing past down Fifth Avenue, waiting to shake hands with each person, and smile and laugh and let everyone know how happy he was to be saved, and how happy they should be, or could be, themselves. The choir would follow down the center aisle, still singing and swaying in unison as they had as they marched in. All those in the pews would follow, filing past the preachers to smile back and congratulate them on how well they had delivered His message. The Williams siblings always smiled the most, because at no point during the week did the children feel more joy than when they stepped out of the church building and into the light.

CHAPTER
Nine

After church the family would have the main meal in the early afternoon, and once the dishes were washed, the children were free to play until bedtime, since no work was allowed on the Lord's Day. This meal was usually a roast, or some other cut of meat that was the best they would eat all week. They by no means went hungry in that house, but beans, potatoes, and rice took center stage at most meals and the meat was a side dish, or used for flavoring more than sustenance. Their parents encouraged them to talk at the table, which was something thought of as quite progressive among the old folks at the church. When one of them came over for a meal they were somewhat shocked the children could not only speak, but could speak to each other, not only to their parents. Not to say that wasn't dangerous, as their father did not allow much goofing off at the table. No one would ever let Jimmy forget the time he pulled the salt away from his brother when he reached for it, and received a perfectly timed and placed backhand from his father. Stifled laughter was an art form in this situation.

But on this day Jimmy was not in the mood to antagonize Slugger. He wanted to play catch. In fact, when he was using the salt, he had the courtesy to ask Slugger if he wanted some.

"What's up with that?" asked Slugger in response to the unexpected thoughtfulness from his brother.

"What?" responded Jimmy coyly.

"You must want something," said Slugger, not letting it go.

"I want you to play catch with me after we finish eating," admitted Jimmy.

"OK, for a little while, but I've got things to do," his brother replied as if it was a burden.

While Slugger had been staring at the church floor, begging for the clock to turn as quickly as possible, he was thinking of giving Jimmy another lesson, and was wondering how he could convince Jimmy to do it. He couldn't act too eager, however, when Jimmy suggested it. His plan this time was to step it up a notch. Since Jimmy took twice as long to eat as everybody else in the family, Slugger had the time to go outside, retrieve the gloves and ball, and stroll out to the alley before Jimmy left the table. He picked up a rock and drew a square in the gravel, then walked up the alley, counting his paces. He stopped after he had counted off the number he thought was sufficient and reached down and drew a line. When Jimmy finally came out of the back door he picked up the glove Slugger had left on the porch and trotted out to where he saw his brother, still drawing after pacing it off.

"Whatcha doin?" asked Jimmy, as Slugger stood, his task completed.

"I just measured the distance from home plate to the pitcher's mound in Minor League. I want you to pitch from this line, and I'll go there," pointing to the square he had already drawn, "and that will be home plate."

It looked a lot farther to Jimmy than the distance across the garage.

"Are you sure? That's pretty far," said Jimmy as he looked at the gap between the marks.

Slugger responded with an evil stare and said nothing, so Jimmy went to the line as instructed, looked down at it and then turned to face Slugger. His brother was in the catcher's crouch and didn't give Jimmy a chance to complain by saying, "Ready?" in a tone letting Jimmy know he better be ready whether he liked it or not.

"I guess," said Jimmy, who was not as ready as he was ever going to be, but as ready as he was going to be that day.

Slugger tossed him the ball, which Jimmy dropped as he was still thinking about how ready he wasn't and not the ball coming at him.

"Pay attention, Jimmy," said Slugger. "Next time I'll hit you in the face if you don't, and I'll throw it hard."

Jimmy picked up the ball and pondered it, knowing Slugger was not kidding, and took a deep breath to help himself focus. He leaned over at the waist and stared at Slugger, like he had seen Marichal do, then straightened his back and went into his motion. He raised his leg high, but not too high, and swung it down and stepped forward without stumbling, with his foot pointing directly at Slugger, and whipped his arm around and let the ball go. It bounced about three feet in front of Slugger and sprayed gravel in his face.

Jimmy expected an angry response, but Slugger looked puzzled instead. He did not throw the ball back, but instead walked from the square to the line, counting his steps again. He rubbed out the line he had drawn, and then drew another, about two steps closer.

He handed Jimmy the ball, and walked back. It still looked a lot farther than throwing in the garage. But he tried again, and this time it reached Slugger in the air. And then again. And then again. Jimmy decided to try to see how hard he could throw it, to rear back and fling it as strongly as he could. He was proud of his effort, and it came close to landing directly in Slugger's glove, but Slugger stood quickly, and he was not pleased.

"Jimmy, don't throw it too hard!! Just windup the way you know how, and focus on hittin' my glove with the ball. Gettin' the ball over the plate is more important than how hard you throw it!"

So Jimmy did just that. He focused. He made sure his feet were always pointed in the right direction during the windup. He made sure he kicked his leg high, but not too high. And first and foremost, he kept his eyes trained on the middle of Slugger's glove throughout the process. He wasn't counting, but after what seemed like twenty-five straight times, which if he had been counting was more like ten, Jimmy heard laughter coming from behind his shoulder. When he turned around, standing behind him with a more sinister smile than even Slugger could muster on his face, was Donny Gomes.

"So, you're out here again?" said Donny, totally ignoring Slugger. Jimmy didn't know whether to run or cry. He just stood there, undecided.

"Hey, boy," shouted Slugger to Donny. "Get out of the way!"

Now Donny turned to Slugger. Donny had been walking down the alley as Jimmy was pitching, and Slugger had seen him coming but thought nothing of it.

"Get out of the way of what?" asked Donny. If he was afraid of Slugger, he wasn't acting like it. "You're wasting your time trying to teach this little pansy how to pitch."

Slugger said nothing for a moment. In his mind, Jimmy should have jumped Donny the second he called him a pansy. If Jimmy had been born into Slugger's universe, he would have had Donny chewing gravel by this time, but since he wasn't, he just stood there trembling. After pausing long enough to know what was supposed to have happened wasn't going to happen, Slugger had an idea.

"Well," he said back to Donny, "If that's what you think, you should run home and get a bat, and see if you can get a hit off of him."

Jimmy didn't think that was a good idea, but after thinking about it for a second, Donny did. He looked back at Jimmy, then at Slugger.

"OK, I will," he said to Slugger. Then he turned to the skinny kid shaking next to him and said, "And Jimmy, don't get scared and go runnin' in the house!"

Without another word Donny burst into a sprint down the alley past Slugger and tore around the corner, ecstatic at the prospect of showing off his hitting skills. Slugger, to calm his clearly panicked little brother, said, "Keep throwing. He won't be back."

And after hearing those words Jimmy trusted Slugger enough to not come up with an excuse to go back into the house and he threw another pitch. He had thrown a few more when, as he would find out many more times in his life, his brother was proved to not be a prophet. Donny strutted around the corner carrying not one, but two bats. They were obviously his older brothers' bats, as he was having trouble holding them both at the same time, but in his mind, he would look tougher carrying two bats, so he did it anyway.

Slugger was somewhat surprised by Donny's boldness. His two older brothers were not nearly this bold, especially after he had busted one of their lips and swollen the other's eye, in the same week, no less. Donny was standing just far enough away from Slugger that he did not hit him as he swung the bats. He then dropped one and swung the other by itself, and then repeated the process with the other bat, which was heavier. As he watched, Jimmy got goose bumps, his knees started shaking, and he suddenly had to pee, really, really, bad.

Slugger looked at Donny with disdain. He kind of wished he was younger, or Donny was older, so he could hurt him. "I would pick that one," he said, pointing to the shorter and lighter of the two bats. Of course, as Slugger expected, Donny's universe forced him to pick the heavier one. Then Donny stood in what he thought was an aggressive batting stance and looked out at Jimmy with a smirk, but he wasn't standing in the right spot, as Donny hadn't figured out the square Slugger had drawn in the gravel was supposed to represent home plate. Slugger stood from his crouch, picked Donny up and arranged his feet so he was standing in what would have been the batter's box if Slugger had done enough drawing.

"Hey, are you queer or sumpthin?" asked Donny as he looked up at Slugger, waving the bat as if he was contemplating hitting Slugger with it.

Slugger just rolled his eyes and said, "Are you gonna bat or what?"

Jimmy looked around. He was standing in an alley behind his house, with houses and cars in all directions. If Donny hit the ball, even a foul ball, something was getting broken. The only safe place to hit it was right back at Jimmy, and in Jimmy's imagination that would be far worse. He could not run into the house either, because that would only save him from Donny, not from the far more dangerous Slugger. There was no way out. He had to pitch to Donny, and he had to throw it hard enough so Donny wouldn't hit it. And he had to throw it straight enough that he didn't hit Donny. He couldn't think of any other solution. The urge to pee had suddenly left him. His whole body seemed dry, his mouth parched.

Slugger said nothing, but Jimmy could tell he was losing patience. Donny could smell the fear. "Are you gonna throw it, or are you too scared?" he taunted.

With that Jimmy started his motion. All the energy and strength he had in his little body went into that throw. He threw it much harder than he had before, when Slugger was not pleased, but he didn't care. He closed his eyes when the ball left his hand but quickly opened them again, obsessed with knowing where it had flown.

Donny's eyes swelled when he saw the ball coming. He had also been masking his fear this whole episode. His main fear, as always, was not having friends. He had to prove how tough he was to make friends, he thought. They had to be afraid of him. But when he saw the ball coming, a different kind of fear shot through him. The ball was coming fast. He hesitated and then swung the bat with all his might, closing his eyes and gritting his teeth. The bat was so heavy he barely had it off his shoulder when the ball hit Slugger's glove. The fury of the swing shocked Jimmy more than the fact Donny hadn't hit the ball.

Because Jimmy had thrown it so hard, Slugger had to reach up to catch it. No way was it a good pitch. Jimmy was disappointed until he realized since Donny had swung it was a strike regardless of how badly thrown it was. He would have smiled, but when he saw the look on Slugger's face he knew Slugger was not happy, and if he threw it high again, he had more to fear from Slugger than Donny. The next pitch, he knew, had better be on target.

And so, it was. Jimmy did everything perfectly on this pitch. Slugger did not move; Donny did not move. There was no sound other than the crisp "Pop!" as the ball smacked the glove.

Slugger smirked at Donny. "That would be strike 2," said Slugger. "One more and you'll have been struck out by a pansy."

Donny was furious. "You called that a strike?" he yelled.

Slugger responded, "It was right down the middle. You've got one more strike, so if I was you, I'd be swinging."

Now Jimmy was more afraid of Donny. He had never seen a boy so angry in his life. When Donny hit the ball, he would be sure to hit it right back at Jimmy, and the pain and loss of blood would be terrible. But he had to throw it, although this time he wouldn't throw it as hard. He wanted Donny to hit it more than he was afraid of getting hit by the ball even, or of a window getting broken. But Donny didn't. He almost did, as he had more time to swing the bat this time, more awareness of the velocity of the ball as it was coming, but it did not matter. The ball popped into the glove again, Donny spun himself around with the bat in his hands again, and that was that. Still clutching the bat in fury, he took an enraged step toward Jimmy, but he found a firm hand on the back of his neck before he could take a second. Slugger squeezed it.

"OK, boy, run along home now," said Slugger.

Donny strained to turn his head, but Slugger wouldn't let go until Donny relaxed.

"You cheated!" he yelled, once he was let loose. "I'm gonna tell my brothers about this!"

Now Slugger relaxed. "Tell 'em," he said, without much enthusiasm.

Donny hadn't expected that reaction. Something told him his brothers may not be of any help, or at least Slugger didn't think they would be. He decided he would get his revenge on Jimmy some other time. But as he walked home he thought to himself he had to give the little kid some credit for being able to pitch, because his ego wouldn't let him accept being struck out by a pansy.

CHAPTER
Ten

While the marvel of the last moments transfixed Jimmy, Slugger stood, gazing beyond him. "Hey, Jim!!" he called out.

Jimmy spun around, knowing his brother was not addressing him, but someone behind him. As he looked up the alley he could see it was Joe's older brother Jim. He had a long skinny stick in his hand with a string attached and as he strolled down the alley he flipped it from hand to hand. Jim was a taller, lankier version of his younger brother Joe, less than a year younger than Slugger. He was dressed in his family's standard uniform, dirty jeans and a slightly cleaner tee shirt with a couple of holes in out of the way places.

"Is that a fishing pole?" asked Jimmy, and then without waiting for an answer, "What're you gonna do with it?" he continued in his typical questioning mode.

"Is that a baseball glove?" answered Jim. "Whatcha gonna do with that?"

Jimmy stopped before asking another obviously stupid question.

"Hey Slugger, wanna go fishin' in one of those spots I was tellin' you about?" asked Jim, having finished his discussion with Jimmy.

"You mean one of those special spots?" answered Slugger.

"What makes 'em special?" interjected Jimmy.

"Never you mind, Jimmy," Jim shot back. "You wanna come or not, Slug?"

Slugger stood with his gloved hand on his hip and thought about it. He was having a good time with his little brother, but fishing sounded like fun too. Why not combine the two?

"OK, Jim, but I wanna take Jimmy with us," Slugger said, and to sweeten the pot he continued. "I'll drive my car."

Jimmy was listening with even more fascination. He had ridden in Slugger's beat up old Oldsmobile before, but never without a mandate from his parents. And fishing? He had seen Slugger come back to the house with fish before, but never had he considered going fishing himself, and Slugger had certainly not asked him. He wasn't sure why he was being included in such a spontaneous adventure, but he had a hunch the recent strikeout of Donny Gomes had something to do with it.

"Are you sure you want this little snot to come along? Can he keep up, or will he start cryin' and wanna go home when he sees a snake or sumpthin'?" questioned Jim. He did not want Jimmy tagging along, and he wanted to make sure Slugger knew it. "We'll need to hike in close to a mile."

Slugger looked at Jim, and then looked down at Jimmy. He had been walking toward Jim and at this point was standing beside his little brother. He reached down and put his hand on Jimmy's neck, the same way he had Donny's. "No, he'll be OK," he responded, in a way that was a threat and a promise.

Before today Jimmy would now be thinking of a way out of this situation, of how he could tell his mother he didn't want to go so she would forbid it, but at that moment Jimmy was thinking the opposite. How could he get his mother to agree to let him go if she balked? Maybe Jim would not agree and the point would be moot.

But to his surprise Jim softened his stance and said "Sure, if you're drivin'. I'm not bringin' Joe, though, so don't even think about it."

Jimmy thought about it anyway, at first disappointed that Joe wouldn't be coming along, but then he realized it would be better if Joe didn't go. If Joe went it would set him up for a fishing contest, Joe against Jimmy with the older brothers' bragging rights on the line, and he assumed Joe had fished before and knew what to do while he didn't. Instead of a contest, this could be an adventure, a learning experience. He could do something he hadn't before, and observe how the older boys did it and figure out ways to do it better. That is, if he survived the expedition at all. And to his surprise his mother approved of the plan, with the stipulation they came back before dark.

So, before Jimmy could even believe it was happening, he was in the back seat of his brother's car with his head sticking out of the window, letting the breeze wash over his face with the coolness not found in static air. It was an unreasonably warm spring day. Their town was so small reaching the country only took a mile, and within five miles was the wilderness. They rolled past farms with corn low to the ground and wheat fields waving with their soon to be harvested spring crop. They went through an even smaller town, named Banner, which was just an intersection between the smaller county road which led out of Canton and the larger state road that led to Peoria. After turning left at the stop sign as Jimmy remembered his father always doing when they went to his grandparents' house in Peoria, they turned right off the main road to a smaller side road and went through the three blocks that was Banner and into the countryside beyond.

After less than a mile the blacktop gave way to dirt, and the farmers' fields turned into trees on either side. Dirt roads were a wonder to Jimmy. He turned his head and watched the dust cloud which trailed the car. As he was imagining figures in the swirl behind him, and sailing through it with the rest of the Argonauts, he heard Jim say, "Slow down, we're gettin' close."

That got Jimmy's attention. When he turned around to see where they were stopping, he saw nothing on either side of the road but thick trees, without a house or other building in sight. There wasn't a lake either.

"Here it is," said Jim. "You can pull over on the side of the road, on the left." Jimmy couldn't figure out what "it" was. "Grab the stuff out of the trunk and let's go."

While Jimmy had been in the house asking his mother for permission to go on this journey with his brother, the older boys had packed the trunk of Slugger's old Olds with fishing gear. Jimmy was handed 3 fishing poles to carry, and Jim and Slugger grabbed each end of a large chest. Inside that chest was a smaller one, filled with fishing supplies. Among other things there were spools of fishing line, plastic balls, fish hooks, oblong pieces of lead weights, and a jar filled with dirt and wriggling worms. Jim led the way into the trees, and a path appeared out of nowhere which the older boys marched down as if it was a sidewalk in the middle of town. Jimmy trailed behind, and to him they were in the darkest jungle of the Amazon. Bugs buzzed, birds screamed, and animals could be heard scurrying through the bushes.

"Keep up, Jimmy. If you get lost I'm leavin' you out here," reassured Slugger.

After what seemed to Jimmy like an epic journey, they came out of the trees to what looked at Jimmy's height to be a farmer's field, surrounded by a tall berm made of earth, which was too tall for Jimmy to see over. They climbed the berm, just wide enough for a tractor or pickup truck to drive on, and the grass covering the berm was broken by two dirt tracks, evidence of the berm's use as a road. The boys hoisted their gear over the berm and on the other side, instead of the field Jimmy had expected to see was a body of water. A sign was posted next to the water which read "No Fishing Allowed by Order of the Game Warden".

"Is this where we're gonna go fishing?" asked Jimmy, not daring to point to the sign, as he was certain the older boys knew about it already. That was what made this a special spot.

"Yup," said Jim, as Jimmy knew he would.

"It's Banner Lake," explained Slugger, trying to distract Jimmy from the sign he knew he read already.

"Not really the lake, it's an overflow pond created by the Fish and Game people," countered Jim, destroying Slugger's scheme. "See that?" asked Jim, pointing to a horizontal pipe sticking out of the berm a few yards away, to their right. A lazy stream of water poured out of it into the pond. "There's usually fish right there at that outlet."

Slugger walked over and looked down into the water. "There's a bunch of them, right there!!" he shouted. Jimmy walked over and looked in. The water draining from the pipe had caused a depression on the soft bottom of the pond, where a small pool had formed. As the water coming out of the pipe was warmer than the rest of the pond, it was a favorite place for fish to congregate. As Jimmy stared, Jim pulled off his shoes and socks and Slugger did the same. Jim jumped into the water next to the pipe and stood thigh deep in the pond, then reached down and pulled a large fish out with his bare hands. When Slugger saw this, he eased into the water on the other side of the pipe and joined in.

Jim threw his fish on the bank, but Slugger had a better idea. "Hey Jimmy, make yourself useful and take the smaller cooler out of the big one, and drag the big one over here so we can toss the fish in it!"

Jimmy did as he was ordered and slid the cooler as close as he could without falling in the water himself.

"Get out of the way!!" yelled Slugger, and he threw his fish toward the cooler. And then the race was on. Both Slugger and Jim were reaching in and grabbing fish and tossing them in or near the cooler. Those that didn't make it in were flapping about on the ground, trying to wiggle themselves back to safety.

Jimmy was counting 5, 6, 7, then Jim called out, "Grab that one before it gets back in the water!" and pointed to the fish he had thrown out first which was flipping and flopping its way down the slope. Jimmy hesitated, wondering if the fish would bite, and then lunged for the fish after he knew it was too late, as it made its last twist on the dry before reaching the wet. He managed to touch the slimy scales just before the fish made its escape, but more importantly, managed to not fall in himself.

Jim and Slugger, still standing in the water, laughed at Jimmy and their marvelous luck. As there were no more fish in the depression near the pipe, they hauled themselves out of the muck and collected the remaining fish in the grass and dirt. Jimmy's count was confirmed and there were seven good sized fish in the cooler when they were done.

"What kind of fish are they?" asked Jimmy.

"Carp," said Jim. "Not the best eatin', but they'll do."

Jimmy sat next to the cooler to watch the fish struggle for air. In the smaller cooler, Jim had brought a tin cup, which he used to partially fill the cooler with water from the pond. After the fish were covered, he closed the lid.

While he did this, Slugger went to the smaller cooler and opened the jar of worms.

"Here, Jimmy," he said handing him the jar. Jimmy looked inside at the worms squirming in the slimy dirt, and the jar smelled as bad as it looked. Slugger picked up one of the fishing poles Jimmy had dropped on the bank and took a plastic ball, which he called a bobber, and lead weight, which he called a sinker, and a barbed hook from small boxes in the smaller chest they were brought in and tied them spaced apart near the end of the fishing line with fancy knots Jimmy knew he could never duplicate. The bobber was tied furthest from the end, next came the hook, and the sinker at the very end. Slugger had been a Boy Scout for a couple of years before he was kicked out for fighting, so Jimmy figured he had learned it there. Since the jar lid had been off for a while now, a worm was attempting an escape over the top of the rim.

"Don't let it get away!" said Slugger when he saw this, but Jimmy made no effort to touch the worm, and didn't want to close the lid because that would cut the squirming little lifeform in half. After watching what Slugger did next, he realized he shouldn't have been so concerned. Slugger snatched the worm before it managed to drop to the ground and grabbed one end and stuck it on the pointed end of the hook, then pushed it, lengthwise, up the hook. Jimmy had never seen such an act of cruelty in his life. This was far worse than getting stuck with a dart. The worm was wriggling with the sharp hook through its body, still alive!

"Now that is how you bait a hook!" said Slugger proudly. "Take it," he commanded, handing Jimmy the pole. Jimmy obeyed, but held the pole so that the worm was as far away from him as he could get it.

"See this?" he asked, grabbing the fishing reel attached to the pole, with most of the fishing line wound up around it. "When you cast the line, push down on this button," he said. And then you let go of the button once you finish the cast."

"When I do what?" asked Jimmy.

Slugger took the pole and lifted it up and over his head, then held it straight back from his right shoulder. He flipped the pole around, sort of like swinging a badminton racket with just the wrist and arm, and the line unreeled, carried by the weight of the sinker, with the hook, worm and bobber trailing behind it. The lead ball fell into the water far from shore and sank, and the bobber floated on the water. The hook was in the water, suspended between the sinker and the bobber.

"Here," said Slugger, handing Jimmy back the pole. "When you see the bobber drop below the water, yank back on the pole, then turn this," he said, turning the handle of the reel a quarter turn to show him how. Then he turned his head to look for the jar of worms as Jimmy stood dumfounded with the pole in his hands. A second later as he looked at the bobber it dove into the water, and Jimmy yanked the pole as his brother had instructed and it smacked Slugger in the back of the head.

"What did you do that for?" yelled Slugger, spinning around in anger.

Jimmy did not answer, as he was turning the reel handle as furiously as he could. Something was on the other end of the string, and it was tugging on the pole trying to pull it out of Jimmy's hands. When Slugger saw how the bobber had disappeared, his anger instantly turned to excitement and he shouted, "You got one!! You got one already!!!" and he snatched the pole out of Jimmy's hands and started reeling in the line himself. After a few seconds the string was almost reeled all the way in, and the ugliest fish Jimmy had ever seen came out of the water, a black fish with a long funny moustache, wriggling on the hook, impossibly trapped.

"That's a nice catfish YOU caught, Jimmy," said Jim, letting Slugger know he wasn't going to give him the credit for the first catch. "You should let him reel it in the next time," he said to Slugger.

"OK, Jim," said Slugger, realizing Jim was not going to give him any credit anyway, so he might as well use it to encourage his brother. "Looks like you caught the first fish of the day, Jimmy!"

"You mean with a pole!" corrected Jimmy, happily, thinking about the carp gasping in the cooler already.

Slugger leaned the pole over, so the fishing line was close enough for him to disengage the fish from the hook. Jimmy noticed how careful Slugger was in handling this fish, compared to the ones he had reached in and grabbed by hand.

"You have to be careful with catfish," Slugger explained. "They can sting you with their whiskers."

This sounded to Jimmy like another of Slugger's tall tales, but Jimmy was by nature cautious and decided to take Slugger's word for it. Slugger managed to get the fish off the hook and into the smaller cooler.

"You wanna try to bait your own hook this time, Jimmy?" asked Slugger.

Jimmy looked at Slugger with horror. Instead of the reaction he expected, Slugger just smiled and said, "I'll bait your hooks this time, Jimmy, but if you ever wanna go fishin' with me again, you'll have to bait your own hooks next time."

He baited the hook for Jimmy again, and patiently let Jimmy cast and recast the line, and on the third try, he was successful in getting the bobber, hook, and sinker into the pond. And as soon as he took a deep celebratory breath the bobber sunk into the water again. Slugger had turned away to bait his own pole and again did not see it.

"I've got another one!!" screamed Jimmy, again yanking the pole back and cranking the reel wheel.

Slugger looked back, but did not grab the pole this time. No way could there be another fish on the line that quick. But there was. Jimmy reeled it out of the water, and when it was hanging in the air, Jimmy stopped reeling. They all stared at the fish in wonder, another nice catfish. Instead of trying to teach Jimmy how to get the fish off the hook and into the cooler, Slugger grabbed the line and took the fish off himself. Another round of bait and Jimmy was casting again.

This next cast was easier, and the result the same. Another fish on the line before Slugger could finish baiting his. This time Jim took the fish off the line for Jimmy and baited the hook again.

"Wow, Slugger," Jim said to his friend. "Your little brother is either the luckiest fisherman I've ever saw, or he's a natural."

Slugger laughed, and both the older boys set about the task of baiting their own hooks and getting their lines into the water. As they needed enough room to cast, they both walked several paces away once they had done so.

Jimmy, now completely overconfident, decided he was a natural. This time he would cast the line as far as he could. He did everything right except he forgot to push the button. The string was just long enough to whip around and stick Jimmy in the leg with the hook. The pain was worse than the finger pricks he had to take for his quarterly blood tests. He wanted to cry out but he stifled it, because there were more fish in the pond for him to catch, and he knew crying would end that. He carefully pulled the hook from his leg without saying a word and flung the pole again, this time remembering to push the button to let the line out. Slugger saw it all and kept silent as well.

Jim and Slugger were not naturals, Jimmy realized. When they cast their lines, nothing happened. Maybe it was because Jimmy had the best spot, or because they had to stop every five minutes to either bait Jimmy's hook or take another fish off his line. Jimmy lost track after the eighth fish. Eventually Jim caught the prettiest fish, a small white fish which reflected light like a prism as it wriggled back and forth in the air. Jim wasn't happy about it, however. He called it a bluegill, and after detaching it from the hook he threw it back into the water.

"With all this good catfish, why waste time eatin' a bluegill?" he remarked.

Jimmy's best day of fishing did not end because of a drip of blood down his leg, but because of the arrival of a man in a pickup truck, driving down the berm behind them. Jimmy had tired after catching so many fish and was sitting on the bank, looking at the big cooler with the carp and counting the catfish in the smaller cooler, eleven in total, all caught by him. Slugger hadn't caught a single fish, and Jim had thrown the one he caught back. Jimmy couldn't decide which would be the worst outcome when he saw the man in the truck, getting taken to jail or having to give him the fish back. Unless he could show the fish to Joe and his sisters, they would never believe he caught them. But on some days, things were not meant to go wrong, and this, to Jimmy's surprise, might turn out to be one of them.

"Hey, whatcha boys doin' here?" asked the man as he exited his truck and stood next to it on the berm. He had a light brown shirt and pants on, and to Jimmy it looked like a uniform, so he looked official. Plus, the truck had the words "Department of Fish and Game" written on the side.

"Fishin'," replied Jim in a way that seemed much too relaxed for Jimmy.

"Well, you better clear out of here quick, Jim, 'cause my boss will be coming through here in about 15 minutes, and he takes his job a lot more serious than I do," replied the man in brown.

Jim looked back at the man, who he obviously knew, like he was not sure whether he was going to take the advice or not. Slugger looked at Jim, waiting for a cue. No way would he be the first to back down and leave. The man looked over at the coolers, half filled with fish.

"Don't you think you already got enough for today?" asked the man, grinning.

Jim shrugged, and looked over to Slugger. Without saying a word, the boys started to pack up their gear. Slugger put the little boxes with the weights and hooks in Jimmy's pockets, and the older boys put the small cooler on top of the big one, so they could carry everything in one trip.

"This stuff is heavy!" complained Jimmy, as he also had to carry the fishing poles and the jar of worms.

The older boys looked at him incredulously.

"Well, you shouldn't have caught so many fish!" said Jim.

The trip back to the car was laborious, and they had to stop a couple of times along the way to catch their breath, but Jimmy was smiling the entire way. By the time the boys reached the car, Jimmy was smiling so hard his teeth hurt. What a day it had been. He had struck out Donny Gomes on 3 pitches, and he had caught 11 catfish, and he had gotten stuck in the leg with a fish hook and hadn't cried. As they drove away and Jimmy stuck his head out of the window, he was thinking this might be the greatest day of his life. Then he heard these fateful words come out of Jim's mouth: "You wanna go to the other place I know about so we can do some more fishin'?"

CHAPTER
Eleven

"OK, why not?" answered Slugger. Since he had not caught any fish, and his little brother had caught so many, it was not thus far a contender for the greatest day of his life. There was still enough daylight to turn things around.

Even Jimmy thought it was a good idea. Maybe he could catch eleven more fish. He looked up at the sky and saw the white clouds which had been floating by lazily earlier that day were now being pushed along by the wind. The air was moist with the humidity that usually chose to accompany hot days in the Midwest. When they returned to the main road and the trees weren't blocking their view, darker clouds could be seen far, far, in the distance, but the sun still shined brightly.

Jim directed Slugger to return the way they had come, and at a point about midway back to Canton he pointed to a narrow dirt lane leading off from the highway and said, "Turn here."

Slugger looked at him dubiously. It was what was called a farm road. This was a road the farmers owning the land made themselves to access their fields with their tractors, made from graded dirt with a crown in the middle such that it sloped down to the edges of the road, with a ditch on either side which served to drain the fields.

"Yeah, right here," encouraged Jim.

Slugger turned, and the road went straight for about a half mile before turning and dropping down into a valley, more like a ravine, and then rising again. The fields on either side were planted with soybeans and corn, with trees planted along the edges to block the wind. As the car climbed out of the ravine and reached a point with a clear view through the trees, a large hill came into view.

"There's another turn coming up," said Jim. "Slow down."

As Slugger was going slowly already, he wondered what kind of road this was going to be. He found out quickly enough. Jim pointed at two parallel ruts leading off toward the hill. Between the ruts weeds grew as high as the bottom of the undercarriage of a farmer's truck. He'd already gone this far, so Slugger made the fateful decision to turn instead of going back. He managed about fifteen miles an hour pummeling the weeds with his front bumper as the soybeans gave way to a field of grass. The ruts curved such that the hill they could see from a distance was now on the right, and going forward a barbed wire fence came into view separating the road from the field.

"Just a bit further and we can park," said Jim. "Can you see it?" he asked Slugger.

Slugger leaned forward and replied, "Oh, you mean down there?"

"That's it!" proclaimed Jim. "We can park a little ways further down the road, and we can walk across the field. There's a place on the side of the hill we can fish from."

Jimmy couldn't see what they were looking at, but they seemed to be sure there was a lake out there somewhere. With all the twists and turns and rises and falls of the road, Jimmy had no clue where he was. If his brother decided to leave him out there alone, he would never find his way back home. Jimmy wasn't sure why such an ominous thought had come into his mind, but his mood changed dramatically from his elation of a half hour before.

Slugger pulled the car into the grass to the side of the right rut, and the two older boys began unpacking the trunk. Jimmy sat in the car. They took everything out except the cooler with the 11 catfish and were picking up the gear when Slugger saw Jimmy still sitting in the back seat.

"Are you gonna stay here and guard your fish, or are you comin' with us?" he sneered.

Jimmy hesitated, thinking maybe he could stay in the car, but quickly concluded Slugger was not in reality giving him that option. He opened the door and exited the car, and Slugger handed him the fishing poles to carry again. The older boys lifted the cooler and gear over the top strand of the three which made up the barbed wire fence. They had found a break in the trees that lined the inside of the fence, about ten feet wide, where they could sit the boxes and rods and cooler down before they jumped over. Jim hopped over using a fence post and Slugger high jumped over scissors style, befitting his training on the track team. Jimmy tried to calculate his odds at crawling under the bottom strand, or between the bottom and middle strand, but neither seemed a good idea. Slugger looked at Jimmy and laughed. He pulled up on the middle strand and down on the bottom to allow Jimmy to carefully step through, and they were on their way.

As they walked across the field, which was more of a meadow, Jimmy could finally see on the near side of the hill a rather large pond. West Central Illinois had once been coal mining country, the coal beneath a few feet of the some of the most fertile soil in the world. Because the coal was so near the surface, the technique used was called strip mining. This was accomplished by using earth moving equipment to strip off the top soil and then dig out the coal. The dirt would be piled up to one side and when the bottom of the coal seam was reached, what was left was a deep hole, and beside it a hill of stripped dirt and rock. There was no law against it at the time, so the mining companies left it like that and moved on to the next seam. After a few years of rain the hole would fill with water, and the surrounding land not dug up was returned to farmland or meadow, as it was before the coal was found.

It was just such a farm which held the pond and the hill the boys were walking toward. The field which was enclosed by the fence was not planted with crops and wild grasses were growing there. The pond was maybe one hundred yards long and half as wide, with grass surrounding it on three sides, and the steep hill made up the fourth side. The boys walked across the grass until they reached the pond, and walked around it to the hill. A path led up the hill to a shelf-like indentation in the hillside, cut ten feet into the hill at its widest, which ran along its entire length. The trio walked to the widest part, which had obviously been made such that fishermen could stand or sit there and cast into the water a few feet below their dangling toes. When they stopped at what in the minds of the older boys was the perfect spot, Jimmy looked out beyond the water, and off to his right, off into the distance at the far end of the field, was a small herd of cows, maybe eight or ten, grazing on the grass. As Jimmy watched them enjoy their peaceful meal, the largest of the group, a big bull with long impressive horns, turned and stared at Jimmy for a long second, and then turned back to his task at hand.

"OK, Jimmy," said Slugger, handing him his pole with a worm wiggling on the hook. "Here you go."

Jimmy gazed out to a place in the water he thought looked lucky and cast his line. This casting was getting easier and easier, he thought. A fish will bite any second, he was sure. But it didn't. Slugger and Jim both cast their lines, and soon all three were bored, waiting for something to happen. Taking advantage of the situation as only a little boy could do, Jimmy laid down on his back with his hands locked behind his head and looked at the sky. He saw the sun pass behind a cloud, dark and gray, and tried to imagine what it looked like. He couldn't think of anything. There were many more clouds passing by, just like it, for Jimmy to study, but he couldn't make out any shapes that looked like anything other than clouds in them either.

But what he could see was they were getting darker and darker, thicker and thicker. And the wind was becoming more stinging. It had been thick with humidity earlier, and now a dry chill was entering. Late spring days were often like this, beautiful turned horrible, downpours followed by rainbows. There was no hint of such violence in the sky earlier that day, no flashes of light or rumbles of thunder, but in Jimmy's universe such things were possible on very short notice. It brought him out of his daydreaming, and he became aware Jim and Slugger were oblivious to the changing weather. They were too deeply involved in a debate about the pros and cons of the girls they had gone to high school with. Jimmy could follow a conversation with the best of them, but when the topic was girls, he did his best to go in the opposite direction. To avoid listening, he looked across the field to watch the cows. They were not where he expected them to be. They had moved closer to the hill, in fact were nearing the water off to the right of the hill, and were still eating and mooing without a care in the world.

Jimmy looked back at Jim, and he was reeling in his line. "Got something?"

"Nope," said Jim. "I'm gonna to try some diff'rent bait." He opened his dilapidated tackle box and took a brightly colored orange plastic lure out. He pushed it onto his hook, displacing the worm that hadn't attracted anything. He walked a bit down the path and cast it in.

"Got any more of those?" asked Slugger.

"There's a couple more. If you wanna try 'em, go ahead," responded Jim over his shoulder.

Slugger started reeling his in, and Jimmy followed suite. Slugger looked at him and said, "I'm not baitin' your hook this time, you have to do it."

Jimmy didn't mind, since it was just a piece of plastic. Slugger handed him a bright green lure which looked like a little frog in the middle of a leap. To make things even better, Jimmy saw the worm that had been on his hook before had worked its way off while it had been in the water. He didn't even have to touch it. He carefully, but not skillfully, stuck the frog onto the hook and cast it into the water. He did not choose a different spot like Jim, but stayed where he was.

He couldn't understand why a fish would choose a piece of plastic over a living, wiggling worm, but he couldn't understand why a fish would eat a worm either, so he was willing to give it a try. As he contemplated this he sat and watched as his bobber bobbed on the ripples in the pond, but it never even hinted of dropping into the water. Jim reeled in his line and cast again and again, each time getting farther from Jimmy. Slugger repeated the same thing in the opposite direction. Jimmy could see that if this continued, they would both be out of sight in a couple of more casts. To make sure he wasn't being left alone he put his pole on the ground and walked in the direction Jim had taken. As he did so he gazed across the pond and saw the cows again. They had come closer, and the bull was staring straight at Jim. There was no doubt he was staring at Jim, but Jim did not notice, as he was staring at his bobber in the water. Jimmy ran back, picked up his pole, and began furiously reeling in his line. He was not sure why, it might have been a premonition, or just good old survival instinct, but he knew the time had come to stop fishing.

His line was just coming out of the water when the first rain drop fell. He had seen four or five more by the time he had the hook in his hand. Slugger came around the corner, his reel in his hand and said "I was just comin' to tell you to reel it in. It's startin' to rain."

"Let's go, Jim," said Slugger. Jim was not the type to let a little rain stop him from fishing, so he hadn't reeled his line in yet.

Jim looked over, shrugged, and began reeling in his line unhurriedly. He was hoping he could entice a bite by slowly moving the lure through the water. This seemed like torture to Jimmy, as he saw the first flash of lightening in the distance. He forgot to start counting, and therefore did not know how far away it was by the number of seconds it took to hear the thunder as his father had taught him, but it hadn't taken very long. His thoughts shifted to how the cows would react, for some reason, and so he looked out where they had been before and noticed the cows were slowly walking around the water toward the part of the field the boys needed to cross to get back to the car. They were walking at a leisurely pace, munching as they went, and the boys would have plenty of time to get past before the cows blocked the path, but only if Jim would start moving.

"I think we should hurry up," said Jimmy. The rain drops were coming down in heavy globs, infrequently enough to still be a classified as a sprinkle, but the trend was obvious. Jim and Slugger packed the boxes and other gear, and the boys retraced their steps down the hill to the edge of the grass. They were in such a hurry they did not give Jimmy anything to carry this time except the boxes of sinkers and hooks and his own pole. Jimmy watched as the cows meandered with more urgency, but still without much concern, led by the bull. When the boys reached the bottom of the hill and began their walk across the grass, the bull broke into a trot, staring directly at them. All three boys noticed now and Slugger looked at Jim and they both increased their pace to a fast walk. When the bull noticed their reaction, he broke into a run, straight at the trio. The stomping of the bull seemed to break open the clouds and it started pouring, not sprinkling, hard drops of rain which splattered on Jimmy's too big blue jeans, weighing them down and causing them to slide over his shoes. The sinkers in his pocket didn't help much either.

At this point the older boys broke into a sprint, sloshing water out of the cooler they carried between them, and Jimmy, hampered by his too long pants and his too short legs and the fishing pole almost twice as long as his body, quickly fell behind. The bull, enraged by the trespass, the rain, and the fact he was a bull, charged at full speed. Jimmy had one thought in his mind: DON'T FALL. That was the mistake most of the innocent people who died in every scary movie he had ever seen made, they fell when they were running away from the monster. He pulled up his pants, running with a wide legged motion to keep them from tripping him. He could hear the bull gaining on him, hear the strained breaths he was taking to maximize his speed, hear the hoofs striking the ground with their powerful thuds.

Jimmy looked ahead, trying to see the fence line through his terror. He found the older boys ahead of him, already on the other side of the fence. They were trying to suppress a laugh, Jim less successfully than Slugger. As he neared the fence, Jimmy was afraid to look back, another mistake he saw people make in monster movies, but knew he wasn't going to make it by the look he saw on Slugger's face. Slugger dropped the gear he was still holding and jumped up on the middle strand of the fence, balancing himself with one hand and reaching over for Jimmy with the other. "Keep running, Jimmy!" said Slugger, trying to be cool, but not able to mask the panic in his voice.

As Jimmy took the last few steps of what he thought was going to be his short life, he thought, "One last lunge, just one last lunge." When he planted his foot to make that lunge he stepped in what was now mud and slipped, his feet flying out and up over his head, and he was flat on his back and sliding toward his brother. The bull, now only two steps behind, screeched to a halt, startled by Jimmy's fall and the fact that he didn't want to go crashing into the barbs that had cut him many times in the past. In one swift motion, Slugger reached down and grabbed Jimmy by one of his too long pant legs and lifted him over the fence. A barb sliced both Slugger's arm and Jimmy's oversized jeans. Once he was safely over Jimmy looked back at the bull, standing proudly just a few feet away, and he could swear the bull was smiling with satisfaction. He had saved the herd once again and could go proudly back to his harem and brag about his bravery.

Jim was bent over double laughing. He was being pelted by the rain and lapsed into a coughing fit. When he was finally able to stop coughing and catch his breath, he asked Jimmy, "So why dincha drop the pole?"

Wow, Jimmy thought, still clutching the pole with all his might. He had never even thought about dropping the pole during his mad dash. He hesitated, thought it over for a moment, and replied, "Because I caught eleven catfish with that pole!"

CHAPTER
Twelve

J im shook his head and started chuckling again. Slugger stood silently watching the blood trickle down his arm, thinking if Jimmy had gotten gored or stomped by that bull, their dad would have killed him too. The rain came down steadily. "You'll live," said Jim, looking over at his friend. "We better get outta here before the road gets too slick."

Without further debate the trio hustled to the car and stashed the gear. Slugger's first and seemingly most significant problem was how to reverse directions and guide the car onto the two ruts which led to the main dirt road. The car was in the grass and Slugger needed to turn it around without sliding off into the field on either side. This was tricky enough when the ground was dry, but the rain made it even more difficult. Carefully feathering the gas pedal, Slugger rolled forward and back a couple of times and managed to make the turn and they were headed out. The boys breathed a sigh of relief and relaxed a bit as they followed the ruts toward the dirt farm road. When Slugger made the right turn which would take them to the paved county road, they thought they were home free.

Unfortunately, that was not the case. The rain flowing off the crown of the dirt road formed channels where the dirt was softer, leading down and into the ditches on either side, and if a car's driver relaxed for more than a second he could find himself slipping off the crown and into the ditch, following the course of the runoff. About halfway along the road that was exactly what happened to Slugger. He turned to share a laugh with Jim, of course about some girl they knew, and off they went. As soon as the slide started, Slugger tried to correct it, but with the tread on his tires being in the worn condition most tires were on cars owned by teenagers, he didn't get enough traction to pull out of it and continued into the ditch at the side of the road, on the edge of a corn field. The ditch was only a foot or so below the road, but the ground was turning into deeper mud with every second that passed.

Slugger made a few valiant attempts to accelerate the car out of the ditch and it seemed it was only a slight fraction away from the traction needed. "There's too much weight in the car," Slugger said matter-of-factly.

Jim took that as a sign and opened the passenger side door and stepped out gingerly. He expected to sink, but the mud didn't seem that deep. He called out to Slugger, "Give it some gas; you should be able to pull out now."

"Should I get out too?" asked Jimmy.

Slugger sneered at him. "What do you weigh, 50 pounds? Stay in the car."

He gingerly pushed down the gas, and the car slipped and slid and rose slightly toward the road. For one tantalizing moment the car seemed like it would build the necessary momentum, but then the car began to slide back down, and Slugger punching the gas pedal only made the slide worse. The back tires spun and swung in the direction Jim was unfortunately standing, and just when he had made a successful effort to avoid the mud flying off the tires by leaping to the side, his foot betrayed him and he slipped face first into the ditch. Slugger's foot came off the gas before he covered Jim's back with mud, even though that would have made it match his front.

The car was now a few yards further down the road, a few feet farther off the road, and a few inches deeper in the mud. Slugger jumped out of the car and ran around to the back where Jim was picking himself up from the quagmire. Slugger didn't give him a glance.

He was looking at his back tires, trying to see how deep in they were. Jimmy was turned around in the back seat, watching as the boys stood in the rain in deep thought.

"Why don't we both push and let Jimmy hit the gas?" suggested Jim.

Slugger ignored Jim, trying to think of a better solution. The rain continued to fall. Finally, he had to admit he couldn't think of a better answer.

"I don't think his feet will touch the pedals," he said in response.

"Only one way to find out," retorted Jim matter-of-factly.

Jimmy could see the two talking, but not what they were saying. He could tell by the way they both turned to him at the same time and stared for a fraction before his brother walked to the back window they had something in mind for him that was not going to work. He started to roll down the window, but to his surprise, Slugger opened the door instead.

"Get out, Jimmy, we need to push the car out of here," he said.

Jimmy did not budge and stared at Slugger dubiously. "You want me to help push the car out of this mud?"

Slugger would have laughed, but wasting seconds getting even wetter wasn't worth it. "No, I want you to get in the front and push the gas pedal while me and Jim push from behind."

That sounded even more outlandish to Jimmy than him helping to push. Slugger had to be kidding. But Slugger was in no mood for further explanation. He grabbed Jimmy by the same pant leg he used before and pulled Jimmy out of the car and lifted him under the shoulders and dumped him unceremoniously in the front seat. Before closing the door, he rolled down the window.

"See if you can touch the gas pedal, Jimmy," ordered Slugger.

Jimmy looked down, unsure of what the gas pedal was. He had heard of it, but had never had to personally encounter it. Slugger did not wait to explain but instead reached in and grabbed Jimmy by the right leg, scooting him as far forward as he could go without falling off the seat. When his foot touched the pedal, he was so close to the edge he needed to hold onto the steering wheel to keep his butt attached to the lip made by the seat stitching. He looked ahead and he could see a sliver of the sky, above the dash board but below the top quadrant of the steering wheel. Rain pelted the glass in constant, angry bursts. The engine was running, Jimmy noticed.

"You see this, Jimmy?" asked Slugger, pointing to the gear selector which was to the right of the steering wheel, sticking out with an oval shaped knob at the end. "When I tell you to, I want you to pull down on it like this," motioned Slugger without pulling down on the lever, "to here," pointing to the Drive mark on the steering column. "Then push down on the gas, not too hard." With that he straightened up and walked to the back of the car.

Jim had been watching as Slugger talked to his brother and said when Slugger joined him at the rear bumper, "Does he know what he's doing?", and began to wonder if his suggestion had been a good one, but stopped wasting his time because he already knew the answer and it was too late to suggest something else.

Slugger didn't respond. He stared at Jim, and then bent over to put his shoulder to the driver's side of the rear bumper, and Jim put his to the other side.

"Go ahead, Jimmy!" said Slugger, and he waited for the wheels to start turning so he could start pushing, but nothing happened. He quickly stepped up to the driver's side window, which was still rolled all the way down. Rain was splashing inside and out of the door.

Before Slugger could say a word, Jimmy blurted out, "I couldn't get the stick to move!"

"What?" asked Slugger? The rain was coming down so hard it was filling Slugger's ears, making it hard for him to hear.

"It won't move," said Jimmy desperately.

Slugger gathered his thoughts and realized the selector had to be pulled in, then down, or it would not move. He reached his arm in the car and Jimmy flinched, thinking his brother was going to strike him. Instead he reached across and pulled the selector slightly toward him, and then showed Jimmy how it would then slide down. Jimmy was breathing very quickly and his heart was racing as he watched his brother walk away. He knew the time was as short as his legs when he would be expected to put his foot on the gas and drive the car out of the ditch. His brother reached the back of the car in what seemed to Jimmy to be an hour's worth of fear packed into two seconds.

"OK, Jimmy. Do it!" yelled Slugger.

This time Jimmy pulled, then dropped the selector easily into Drive, and reached out his foot as gingerly as if he was stepping on a cactus instead of the gas pedal. The wheels started to turn slowly and the boys started to push.

"Push down harder, Jimmy!" said Slugger, and Jimmy slightly, ever so slightly, pushed down on the pedal. The wheels turned slightly faster, but not enough to gain any traction.

"Damn it Jimmy, floor it!!!" yelled Slugger as loud as his rained soaked lungs would allow.

With this Jimmy slid off the seat and stomped on the pedal. It went down as far as he could push it. He had never heard an engine roar so loudly. The wheels spun and spit out an enormous jet of mud blasting back and into the chest of both Slugger and Jim. It was strong enough to knock both boys off their feet, which in retrospect was a good thing, because despite all the fury of the wheels spinning, the car moved back and sideways further into the ditch. The blast had knocked them both out the way and kept them from getting run over. Jimmy saw nothing of what was going on behind him, but he did not dare let his foot come off the pedal. The engine was roaring so loudly it drowned out the screams of the mud soaked teenagers in the ditch behind him. It took several seconds for Slugger to regain his footing and scramble up alongside the car, and yank the door open. He did not say a word but instead snatched Jimmy out of the car, removing him from the gas pedal, and slipped the selector into Park.

Mud was everywhere. Slugger's hair was infused with it. Every thread of his clothes, inside and out, was drenched in it. Both Slugger and Jim could have been completely naked and Jimmy couldn't have seen the difference. Jimmy, in what was not an instance of the truth setting anyone free, said, "You told me to floor it."

Slugger was so mad he couldn't speak. He couldn't move. Jimmy looked at him, and in this moment of extreme emotion and possible danger he couldn't help but see this may be one of the funniest moments of his life. There was his invincible brother, standing in the middle of a ditch turned quagmire, head to foot covered in mud, and on top of that bewildered as to what to do next. The car was still in the ditch, and now it was so deep the right rear wheel was half buried. As Slugger debated how he would get out of this predicament and get back his dignity, Jim, still at the back of the car trying to get the mud out of his orifices, started yelling, and jumping around, waving his arms up and down.

Coming down the road was a tractor, the smaller kind, but plenty big enough to pull a car out of a ditch. As the tractor neared, Jim stepped from behind the car to the side of the road.

Sitting in the open tractor seat was another teenaged boy, exposed to the elements, but wise enough to be wearing a yellow rain poncho. He observed the trio standing in the rain next to the half-buried car, and he stopped and said, "How you boys doin?" He was chewing on a piece of hay.

Slugger, usually one to start a fight at the mere mention of being called a boy by another boy his own age, wasn't in the mood. "How does it look like we're doing?" he snarled.

Jim, not wanting the obvious solution to their problem to drive off, decided to carry out the negotiations himself. He stepped in front of Slugger and stated the obvious. "We ran off the road."

"I can see that," said the farm boy. "So, you think you can get out?"

Before Slugger could say or do anything which would end in a long walk home for the three of them, Jim replied tactfully, "Maybe, but we would definitely appreciate it if you hitched us up to your tractor and pulled us out."

The farm boy looked at them and laughed. He put the tractor in gear, and just when Jimmy thought he was driving off, he swung the tractor around and aligned the back of it with the back of the car. After a quick hookup to the frame, and a few short grunts of the tractor engine, the farm boy pulled both the tractor and the car out of the ditch in short order.

After both the car and the tractor were sitting safely in the road, the farm boy said, "You guys out here to fish in Farmer Johnson's pond?" When neither of the older boys responded, he knew the answer was yes. "He didn't stock it this year," he continued, with a chuckle. "He figured there was no point, since he put his mean old bull in the pasture with the cows this summer. Anybody'd be crazy to go out in that field with that bull in there."

And with that, and a loud wail of laughter, and a wave of his hand, he turned the tractor around and went bouncing down the road and disappeared into the falling curtains of rain.

Slugger was seething, but even as angry as he was, saw there was no point in standing in the rain any longer just to seethe. Jimmy had already scampered into his seat in the back. Jim followed, without seeming to notice he was mud soaked. Slugger got in last, as he hesitated trying to think of a way to clean himself up before entering, but quickly realized that was impossible, and with Jim sitting inside already, miserably muddy, it didn't matter anyway. He put the car in gear and drove back to the highway without further incident.

When the car was safely on pavement, Jimmy had a feeling he had felt often in his young life. His chest felt warm, and a big smile wouldn't leave his face. He had survived again. To Jimmy peril and terror were never far away. It seemed there was danger lurking around every corner when it wasn't staring him directly in the face. Whether it was his health, the weather, his siblings, and now, as he got older, the outside world, something was always there to remind Jimmy of his mortality, his limitations, and his smallness in the cosmos.

At times like this, when the car was back on the pavement or whatever other signal assured him the adventure he had been through that day was coming to a non-fatal end, he had this feeling. When his parents had picked him up from the hospital and drove him back home after one of his surgeries, he had felt it. When lightening had struck the tree in front of their house and it fell away from the house and not into the house, he had felt it. When he finally escaped from under the bed on the many times Slugger trapped him there, he felt it. Even though the smile he could never get off his face when he felt this way could sometimes get him into trouble.

Slugger, feeling quite ridiculous as he scrapped mud off his person with a folded-up piece of paper he had found in his glove compartment, was even further upset by the fact the rain stopped as soon as the car was on the main road. And then he looked in the rearview mirror and saw Jimmy with a big grin on his face.

"What's so funny, Jimmy?" Slugger growled.

Jimmy was startled from his daydream by the tone of his brother's voice. He felt the menace, but the warmth in his chest could not dissipate fast enough to stop smiling in time to change Slugger's mood. Plus, with what Jimmy had just survived, he didn't want it to. Not only that, he had seen something today of massive importance: a chink in Slugger's armor. Slugger had sworn to him he would beat any white male from 16 to 50 if they called him a boy, and if they were out of that age range he would find an older or younger male relative and beat them, even if that relative happened to be a priest. But Jimmy had now seen that Slugger could be helpless, just like Jimmy was always helpless, and seen Slugger have put up with what he had to, when he had to, to survive in this world. The smile stayed.

"I'm just happy I caught the most fish!" declared Jimmy. Then he had to rub it in. "When can we go fishing again?"

Slugger said nothing and the remainder of the drive went by without incident. When they arrived home, it was hard to tell who smelled worse, the boys or the fish. Their mother made them leave the fish on the back porch, strip to their underwear on the rug by the back door, and stand there until she had drawn Jimmy a bath, and sent Slugger straight to the shower.

Once he was washed and dressed again, Jimmy ended his night under the light of the back porch, using a plastic bat to dispatch the fish, one by one, by smacking them on the head against the concrete. His brother had the job of chopping off the head and tail, slitting them open, cleaning out the guts, and scraping off the scales. Jimmy felt sorry for the fish as he watched them gasping their last breaths, and then flopping in pain as they received their death blows, but not that sorry. Jimmy loved catfish, fried with a corn meal coating. He couldn't wait until the next day's dinner, when his mother would cook them. He had read in the encyclopedia when he died worms and bugs would eat him, and the fish ate worms and bugs, so what's fair is fair.

CHAPTER
Thirteen

J immy was thinking he would sleep in the next morning, but to his surprise Slugger was shaking him awake before his eyes opened on their own. Slugger woke him up often, but not purposely, like this.

"Time to get up, Jimmy," said Slugger. "I can't waste my whole day waiting around."

Jimmy always woke slowly, even when he had gotten his full rest, and this morning he had not.

"What does that have to do with me?" asked Jimmy, not unfolding from the comfortable ball he slept in.

Slugger responded by yanking the covers off Jimmy and throwing them to the floor, exposing his pajama clad body. Slugger was always making fun of his pajamas, but to Jimmy, one of the many reasons he knew his brother was a heathen was he didn't wear pajamas. Jimmy's pajamas were his favorite clothes, because Jimmy loved to sleep, he loved to dream. But like most walking contradictions that are human beings, he hated to go to bed just as much. As he contemplated this, his mother's voice called out, "Did you get Jimmy up yet?"

"I'm tryin'," responded Slugger. Making his little brother do anything was very difficult, but getting him out of bed was the hardest thing of all.

But when Jimmy heard his mother was behind his early wake up, he knew there was no fighting it. He did his usual five-minute routine. He rolled out of the ball and into a sitting position, then after a minute fell over to lay on his side for another minute, then dropped his legs over the side of the bed with his face still on the pillow for another minute, then allowed his body to slide down until his feet touched the ground. He tried to keep his eyes closed throughout the whole process. As on most days they were partially closed by dried tears that had cemented his eyes shut during the night, before he wiped them with a wet washcloth. When he came out of the bathroom and went to the kitchen, his mother was standing at the stove, making eggs to go with the bacon he had smelled since his last dream reached its climax.

"Hurry up and eat, Jimmy, we've got to go soon," said his mother. Jimmy was confused. Slugger was at the table eating, but no one else. Where could the three of them be going?

Jimmy's mother looked at him with a quizzical look. Then she looked at Slugger. "You didn't tell him?" she asked, with some agitation.

"Not yet," responded Slugger.

Jimmy lost his appetite. He had learned in his short life other people's plans for him were never what he would have planned for himself. Some of the worst experiences of his life were caused by someone, usually his mother, thinking something he had no interest in or intentions of wanting to do was something he should want to do. Usually the best outcome was something very awkward, and Jimmy knew how to make it more awkward if it wasn't awkward enough already, but his mother never seemed to learn. Jimmy sat still dreading what was coming next.

"You better tell him now," she commanded, staring hard at Slugger.

Slugger looked at his little brother and said sternly, "We're going to the Park District office and sign you up for Minor League."

Jimmy had managed by this time to take a bite of bacon and a mouthful of eggs. "You mean baseball?" Jimmy asked with more than a hint of terror. He hoped his brother hadn't picked up on that, but of course he had.

"Yes, Jimmy," said Slugger, trying to stay calm in what he knew was the moment of truth. His mother had abandoned him. He now knew she would not do what he had hoped she would do: at least encourage, if not mandate, Jimmy play Minor League baseball. Now he had to convince Jimmy, and he couldn't use the threats he would normally, because his mother and father were the kind of parents who would not waste money on anything. If Jimmy did not want to play, they would happily keep the entry fee and equipment costs in their pockets.

Slugger continued, pleading in the most macho voice he could muster, "Why do you think I've been teaching you to pitch? So you can strike out punks in the alley?"

Jimmy had no response for that one. He had struck out Donny Gomes, in three pitches, no less. And he hadn't even tried hard on the third one. But he also knew all the boys in school who talked about playing in the Minor League were bigger and stronger than he was. He knew he would probably be made fun of and called names. A lot of those same boys who were going to play baseball were the main ones who did, and when he got picked on, it was always someone from that group.

His brother saw there was not much chance Jimmy would play Minor League. He sat at the table silently and watched the wheels turn in his little brother's head. He is thinking of an excuse, thought Slugger. I can never get this kid to do anything. My whole plan is falling apart. I guess I tried. The resignation crept over his face.

Jimmy saw it. Once again, for the second time in two days, he saw his brother vulnerable. His disappointment was clear. Jimmy realized he could crush him by saying, "No way am I going to play

Minor League baseball." But, after all these years of torment, of torture, of trying everything in his power to make Jimmy cry at least once every day, Jimmy couldn't do it. In fact, he found himself being driven by something completely different. He felt an overwhelming need to prove something to Slugger, even though he knew the only way for him to live the life he wanted to live was to never worry about disappointing Slugger. It was like the first twitch of manhood for Jimmy when he said softly "OK, I'll play."

The Park District office was in the same building as the School District office, on the corner of Maple and Main Street. The trip lasted five minutes, like any trip inside the city limits of Canton. His mother drove the same course as they took to church, except she went past it and turned right at one of the few stop lights on Fifth Avenue, at Oak Street. On the northeast corner was a junkyard where on summer days, when the older boys were released from Sunday School but had to return in a short time for the main service, they would go to look at the cars that had been in wrecks. After turning on Oak it was five blocks west to Main Street. Jimmy saw the street signs as they went by: Fourth, Third, Second, First, and then Main. He could feel the food in his stomach, but could not remember swallowing it as he sat in the back seat, his brother and mother sitting in the front. Even though it was Main Street, there was no stop light on the corner, only a stop sign. She turned right onto Main, down a block and over the same railroad tracks that ran past Anderson Street, and on the next corner, Maple, was the building where they were headed.

The building held not only the Park District offices and the School District offices, but also the junior high school. Its brick edifice stretched along Main Street, taking up most of the frontage between Maple and the next street, Walnut. Jimmy's mom turned left onto Maple, drove past the building, which was not nearly as long on Maple as it was on Main, and turned into the parking lot behind it. It shared the parking lot with the city gymnasium, which had started its existence as a World War Two aircraft hangar but had since been converted to its present purpose, with a basketball court taking up most of the space but with enough room for collapsible bleachers on one side, and permanent ones on the other. The locker rooms were underneath the permanent bleachers, Jimmy remembered, as he had been allowed in before one of his brother's basketball games.

As the trio exited the car, they did not walk toward the gym as Jimmy expected, but instead into the brick building next to it. The parking lot, dirt and gravel, made it impossible to sneak in, thought Jimmy, which is what he would have preferred. Everyone inside could see them exiting the car and coming to the door as it had so many windows, Jimmy couldn't count them all. He had never been inside it before, but when they entered the building through a double door and climbed up a short flight of steps, Jimmy realized his brother would know his way around, as he had gone to school there for three years, seventh through ninth.

At the top of the stairs was a big room, with thick plastic mats piled up in the corner. The space was sectioned off with the same kind of dividers that were in the church basement, so less than half of the room was available for the people standing in line ahead of them. Jimmy looked up at Slugger with a questioning look on his face for an explanation, but Slugger wasn't looking at Jimmy, he was looking at a piece of paper he saw stapled to a bulletin board mounted on the partition. Jimmy had to tug on his arm to get his attention.

"What is this room, Slugger?" he asked.

"We're in the junior high gym," he responded impatiently. He went back to his reading.

The answer explained the mats in the corner and his brother's annoyance level at the first question stifled the next, so Jimmy had to be satisfied with it. His mother had taken her place at the end of the line, and it was slowly moving forward. Jimmy left his brother and joined her, reaching up to hold her hand, knowing any more questions would be best directed toward her. Most of those ahead of them were adults, men or women, with young boys in tow, some the same age as Jimmy, some older, but all bigger. When they neared the front of the line, Jimmy could see a folding table with two men sitting behind it in folding metal chairs.

As Jimmy walked around his mother so he could see what was going on at the table, he saw a little boy in front of them, with his father. The boy was staring at Jimmy. Jimmy tried not to stare back, but he couldn't. As they shuffled forward, the boy said to Jimmy, without saying hello or anything, "Are you gonna play for the Cubs? That's the team I'm gonna play for."

Jimmy didn't answer. His brother had joined them by this point, and he looked down at the boy with disdain. He wanted his little brother to play on the Giants, his favorite team.

The boy continued, undeterred. In his universe, he knew not to stop just because he received no response to his first utterance. "My name is Brad!" he shouted in his excitement and pride.

Jimmy's mother looked down at him and he stared back up at her, wondering if she would prefer he stayed silent, but the look on her face seemed say she would be mad if he didn't respond. He took a chance and said, "I'm Jimmy."

"You should play on the Cubs!!" Brad repeated, with even more enthusiasm than the first time.

By this point Brad's dad had finished filling out the paperwork and had handed over the money for the fee, and Brad and his dad walked away. Brad tried to say something else to Jimmy, but his dad herded him away before he could get it out. Jimmy's focus turned to the man behind the table.

"How old is he?" the man asked his mother. "Eight and nine is Minor League, 10, 11, and 12 is the Major League, and 13 and 14 are Pony League."

Jimmy looked up at the man like he was an idiot. "I'm eight!" he declared as if that should be obvious.

His mother looked down on him again with the same look as before, except Jimmy knew it meant the opposite thing this time, it meant Shut Up. She smiled at the man, who looked first at Jimmy, then at his brother, and then at his mom. He said to her, "Minor League. Does he have a team preference?"

He showed her a list of every team, each on its own sheet of paper with a clipboard attached, and on them the names of the players who had already signed up. As she began looking through them Jimmy felt sure he had a better chance of picking the right team than his mother, and he didn't want his brother to pick it either. He looked at the first one; it said Cardinals and he didn't recognize any of the names underneath. Next came the Yankees, then the Giants, the Senators, Dodgers, Braves, the Red Sox, and the White Sox. Jimmy wondered why those team names were misspelled, but didn't dwell on it because next to them was the sheet titled Cubs. He looked down that list, and the last name on it was Brad Schmidt. Even though his mother had given him the look of 'Silence or Else', he blurted out, "I want to play for the Cubs!"

"Why not the Giants?" asked Slugger with obvious disappointment in his voice.

Jimmy looked up at his brother, and replied even more forcefully, "The Cubs!"

"OK, then," said the man behind the table. "Sounds like the little man has made his choice! And they need players on that team! Write your name and phone number right here. The fee is seven dollars." He pointed at the next open row on the Cubs sheet.

His mother looked at him in surprise. She hadn't expected such a large amount.

"It used to be five dollars!" she protested.

The man shrugged. "It includes the team shirt and hat."

Instead of walking away without paying, as Jimmy thought she might, she dutifully did as she had been instructed and wrote down Jimmy Williams, 647-3549. Jimmy watched her carefully, to make sure she didn't make a mistake. After she finished and they turned to walk away, the man behind the table said, "The coach should be calling you in the next few days to set up your first practice."

Jimmy's bravery deserted him when he heard this, but he did not have time to ponder it very long. Theory became reality for universes as young as his every other day and the speed of expansion was oftentimes staggeringly fast, but his attention was quickly torn away from his dread by Slugger, who had drifted off to the side while his mother signed the paper. He called her over to where he was standing as soon as she took her first step from the table.

"Mom, come over here," he motioned. He had gone back to the bulletin board he had been looking at before. A sign on the top said 'Upcoming Events.'

When she was close enough to read the paper, Slugger continued, "It says right here that an Army recruiter will be here day after tomorrow. I want to come and talk to him. You and Dad need to be with me."

His mother stood silently, as if she did not hear what Slugger had said to her, slowly reading the paper. Her body felt suddenly cold, and no words would form. She finally tore her eyes away from the bulletin board and managed to blurt out, "You should talk to your father about it."

"I already did," said Slugger.

"And?" his mother asked, with the hope that what he said next would cause the emotion suddenly welling in her to subside, but knowing it wouldn't.

"He said it didn't sound like a bad idea to him, but I should talk to you about it," Slugger responded.

Then the three of them walked out of the building silently, each lost in their thoughts. Slugger was dreaming of crawling through the jungles of Viet Nam, with his rifle slung over his shoulder. His mother was thinking of all the funerals she had attended, of coffins and the sick smell of flowers in the funeral home, but dropped that line of thinking and began focusing on what she would say to his father, next time she saw him. Jimmy was thinking of so many questions he couldn't ask one before the next one crowded it out of his mind.

As they opened the car doors, Jimmy couldn't wait any longer. He started them rapid fire, without waiting for answers before the next. "Where is practice? Is it outside or inside? What if it rains? What if it's cold? Can I wear a coat? Or too hot? Can we wear shorts? How do they stop bees from flying across the field? What do you do in practice? Do I have to bring my own bat? Do I get to pitch? What clothes do I wear? Can I play with my glasses on? Can I get new shoelaces for my shoes? The ones I have now are too short because I've broken them twice on one shoe and three times on the other. I won't have to get up real early, will I?"

His mother and brother tried to answer them as they came out, but fell too far behind and gave up. They both turned around and gave Jimmy a look which let him know to stop. Not that it mattered, they were pulling into the driveway by this time anyway, and Jimmy jumped out of the car without waiting for the missing responses.

CHAPTER
Fourteen

Jimmy's mother was a product of her culture, a remnant of the time when by the very definition of slavery, a master could not rape his property, and any resulting progeny would also become his to own. She was medium height for a woman, with medium brown long straight hair that only kinked slightly when it got wet. It was what other black people called 'good hair'. Her skin was lighter than a lot of white people who worked in the sun, but dark enough for those around her to immediately label her as black. Her body was what was commonly called in her day a "bombshell". Large breasts, well rounded bottom, and curves which fit snugly into the kind of sweater and skirt combo Marilyn Monroe made famous. Her face was attractive, even with the glasses she constantly wore, narrow with high cheek bones, and thin European lips. Behind those glasses were penetrating eyes, green and hazel mixed. That was where her name came from, Hazel. In Louisiana, she would be labeled a quadroon, or maybe even an octoroon. Her gene pool may not have been more than one quarter black. She had many relatives who looked the same, and they claimed they were mixed with Indians, not Whites, a common thing for light skinned Blacks to claim. That was easier to claim than the truth.

This made her a great prize among the black men of her day. Jimmy's father had worshipped her from afar for many years before ever having the nerve to approach her. And he may have never built up that nerve if she hadn't already run off to Chicago and come back pregnant with no husband. So even though he was a very eligible bachelor and had a good factory job, he wouldn't let his older, wiser, and concerned siblings and other relatives steer him away. He was a quiet man and she was gregarious. He was slightly built, she was voluptuous. He was rational and she was emotional. He was frugal and she was a spender. He was capable and she needed him. He needed to be strong and she needed to be weak.

When he asked her to marry him, she had only one demand. He would have to live in Canton, not Peoria where he was born and raised. She had to take care of her grandmother, who had raised her, who had taken her back in when she needed refuge from the cruelty of the world, who had been the only mother she had ever known. Her grandmother's house, which she would not leave, was in Canton. When he promised to do so, she made her vows to honor and obey, and without being asked he had adopted Slugger. Then they started their own family and moved a few times until they had the house built in which they now lived, but they never lived farther away than walking distance from her Grandma.

Hazel had been raised in the church; her grandmother had made sure of that. She had been one of the two black girls in Canton to receive formal training in the piano, with an eye to her one day leading the church choir. As a child, she had dutifully obeyed, and enjoyed the music she was being taught to make, but like most when she expanded into a teenager she had much bigger and better ideas. She went away to the city as fast as her typing skills could take her, and led the life she dreamed about for a year or so before contracting a common, but nearly almost fatal, disease. She fell in love with the finest, slickest, hustler she met in Chicago and it took missing a period for her to realize the folly of falling for him.

But when she had her personal crisis and returned to Canton to watch her belly swell and her dream life disintegrate, she turned to the faith in which she had been nurtured her whole life. By the time Harry Williams had bought her the house on Anderson Street it was the cornerstone of the relationships she made with her children and the people around her. To her, honesty was the only policy. There was no greater sin than not doing what she promised to do.

As was his normal custom when he came home from work, Harry Williams beelined into the bedroom to change clothes, and as was his wife's normal custom, she sat on the bed to discuss her day with him. As usual the only thing he said was he felt fine, even though he did not feel so fine, and he expected her to do the rest of the talking. Instead of her normal chatter, she sat on the bed, strangely silent. As he stood at his dresser, examining the slips of paper he had collected during the day, he could feel the silence tingling the back of his ears. He turned toward the source.

"What is it?" he asked.

"You remember after dinner we have to go to the..." and her voice trailed off.

It had been a couple of days since Jimmy had signed up for baseball and she had told her husband about the visit the recruiter.

"To see the recruiter? Yes, I remember," he said cheerfully.

She walked out of the room without another word. Harry got that feeling a husband gets when he knows there is an emotional storm brewing, and the path of destruction is headed straight for him. His stomach started to turn, he lost his appetite and his head started to ache. No matter how good he had felt about coming home to his family after his hard day of work, it was not going to end the way he had envisioned. He stopped for a moment to think what it could be this time, but then realized it did not make sense trying to guess, he would find out soon enough.

To Jimmy and all the other children sitting around the kitchen table, this was a normal, family dinner. Dad had positioned the television so he could watch the evening news from his place at the head of the table. Jimmy sat next to his father, and Slugger next to Jimmy, Mom on the far end of the table from Dad and the girls on the opposite side from the boys, youngest to oldest, with the baby still in a high chair in the corner, more for the space consideration than being too small to sit elsewhere. The sound would be on and heads would turn when something of interest was heard, but since it was the news, most of dinner was not spent paying attention to the television. Most of it was the girls talking. Sometimes Jimmy joined in, but usually he tuned his sisters out after the first few minutes.

Their mother encouraged the discussions, as she did not like her children watching the news while they ate. It most commonly started with an uplifting recounting of the day's body count from Viet Nam, usually hundreds of enemy dead and a few dozen US soldiers killed, wounded, or missing in action. Jimmy was drawn to numbers, so that always caught his eye. In fact, he had once kept a tally and added the day's total each day, but gave that up after a few weeks. He wondered how so many people could be killed from such a small country, and they still had enough people to keep fighting.

Then they switched to the riots. It seemed to Jimmy there was always one going on. The scenes were of children being attacked by dogs and fire hoses, and burning buildings lighting up the night; of angry people shouting and running, or peacefully marching with signs and flowers.

As was not uncommon, the normal chatter around the table was interrupted by banging on the back screen-door. In past years, it was a little boy asking for Slugger to come out to play, but now it was almost always Joe, looking for Jimmy. Jimmy had seen the top of his head bobbing past the kitchen window, so he knew he was coming. His sisters had seen him as well, and as soon as they heard the first knock they said in unison, "Get up and tell him to go away, Jimmy!"

At this point in the dinner, Jimmy had eaten all the good stuff, the fried pork chops and applesauce, and the only thing left was the green beans. He looked at his mother and she nodded, allowing him to leave the table with food still on his plate, which was an absolute no-no in this family. Even his father was not allowed that transgression.

When he reached the back door, he saw Joe leaning with his face against the screen, so he could see inside clearly.

"I brought my glove, Jimmy," he said. "Come on out."

"I got to finish eatin'," Jimmy replied.

"Don't take all day!" said Joe, and he sat down on the back porch to wait.

Jimmy went back to the table and slowly ate the green beans. The idea that something that tasted this bad could be good for him was as hard to swallow as the beans themselves, and as usual, all his siblings had left the table before he could force down the last bite. He put his plate in the sink, and trotted off to the back door again where Joe was waiting impatiently, but before he could get out the door the phone rang and as usual, one of his sisters ran to pick it up. What was unusual however was for the call to be for Jimmy, so even though JoAnn called out his name he assumed she was joking, and he stepped outside anyway. He was halfway into the patio to retrieve his glove and ball when his mother called him back. The call was indeed for him.

There were two phones in the house, one in the kitchen on the wall shared with the living room for family use, and a second phone in the parent's bedroom. Jimmy returned to the kitchen, where JoAnn was still holding the phone. He took it from her, but she did not leave to give him any privacy. Instead she called out for his other sisters, so they could listen in on Jimmy's phone call too.

"Hello?" said Jimmy.

"Hello. Is this Jimmy Williams?" said a man's voice.

"Yes," Jimmy responded in wonder.

"Jimmy Williams who plays for the Cubs Minor League baseball team?" the man continued.

Jimmy stopped to think about it, but then was filled with even more wonder when he realized the correct answer was, "Yes."

"Well, I'm Coach Schmidt, and I'm calling to tell you our first practice is tomorrow at 9 AM. Can you make it?"

"I'll have to ask my Mom," said Jimmy, still completely baffled by the fact an adult was calling him on the telephone to ask him such a question.

"Mom!!" he called out in his bewilderment.

His sisters were staring wide eyed. Even their imaginations couldn't conceive of what was being said to Jimmy, and he wasn't giving them any hints. His mother came around the corner.

"Can I go to baseball practice tomorrow morning? The coach is calling."

"Yes, I suppose." His mother replied. "Let me speak to him."

His sisters' eyes got wider and their mouths opened too.

"This is Jimmy's mom. Where is it, again?" she asked the coach.

"Wallace Park. The ball field is right beside Walnut Street. Big Creek runs past it. You can park next to the bridge."

"OK. He'll be there. He has his glove, and he'll be wearing jeans and a tee shirt."

Jimmy stood there, soaking it in. What was up until this moment only a theory was quickly becoming a reality.

"Joe is staring in the house. Can you go outside and play, please?" mocked JoAnn. She had to bring him down to Earth as soon as she could.

It worked and he came out of his daze and returned to the back door, where Joe did indeed have his face once again pressed against the screen, looking inside. Jimmy opened the door, smashing Joe's face even more, but Joe didn't mind.

"What was that about?" he blurted out as soon as Jimmy stepped outside.

"I have baseball practice tomorrow. That was the coach calling," said Jimmy, still trembling with shock.

"You're playin' baseball this summer?" asked Joe.

"Yup. You gotta be eight years old to play," said Jimmy.

"I'm three months older than you, Jimmy," said Joe. "What team you playin' for?"

"The Cubs."

"That's my dad's favorite team. I wonder if I can play on that team with you. Can I play?" asked Joe.

"It's not up to me, Joe. You have to sign up. It may be too late already," said Jimmy, discouragingly, for some reason not wanting Joe to join him in this adventure.

With that Jimmy retrieved his glove and ball and the boys began throwing the ball back and forth in the back yard. They did not go into the alley, but stayed on the grass running between the Williams' family's garage/patio and the neighbor's garage. As they tossed it, Jimmy noticed Joe had a much harder time concentrating on catching the ball than he did. Jimmy was afraid of the ball, so he stared at it and made sure he could either catch it or get out of the way, so it wouldn't hit him either way. Joe would lose focus and let his eyes drift sometimes, and miss the ball even though it was thrown straight at him, and Jimmy could forget about it if the ball bounced or was darting away when it was thrown to Joe. He would never catch those.

The same thing happened when throwing. Both boys, when they did not concentrate, would throw the ball with sometimes startling inaccuracy. But Jimmy, when he went through the motions right, could get it where he was trying to get it. Joe could throw it harder, but Jimmy got a lot more practice catching bouncing balls and jumping to his left or right to catch balls with Joe throwing. Whenever he caught one on the bounce he felt like he had accomplished a great feat of magic. In fact, he preferred it when he had to reach out for the ball, because it couldn't hit him, and if he caught it he wouldn't have to run after it.

After one such dramatic catch, Jimmy forgot to focus on the return throw, and bounced it in front and to the right of Joe, and Joe made an impossible attempt to reach it, but it scooted past him and rolled on into the alley. Joe ran after it with his head down, and when he looked up he saw Donny Gomes standing in the alley. The ball rolled to a stop at Donny's feet, and he reached down to pick it up.

"This ball smells like Injun," Donny said with a sneer.

Joe was standing a few feet away from Donny. "Give it back," said Joe.

"Oh, it's not the ball, it's you!" said Donny.

"Give it back!" said Joe.

Donny laughed. "Make me," he challenged.

Joe did not advance, but he did not retreat. Jimmy stood there watching. At that moment, the back screen-door screeched open, and Slugger walked through it, followed by his parents. Slugger, who could smell a fight from miles away, immediately cocked his head to see Joe and Donny standing not quite toe-to-toe. The boys all looked back at him, and Donny dropped the ball and back pedaled down the alley. "I'll come back and deal with you later, Injun," he said as he rounded the corner.

Slugger and his parents continued on to the garage and into the car and down the alley in the same direction as Donny. Jimmy's mom rolled down the window as the car passed where Jimmy and Joe stood near the alley and said, "We should be back in an hour or two." The car continued to the corner and turned left, same as Donny.

Jimmy watched them go, and Joe said, "I wonder if Donny is coming back."

Jimmy thought about it, and realized Donny would see the car pass his house, or maybe he would see it walking. "Maybe I should go in the house," he responded.

Joe said nothing, staring down at the gravel in the alley. He picked up a rock and threw it. It skipped on the rocks in the alley and bounced at a severe angle, surprising both boys as it almost hit the back of a car parked on the other side.

Jimmy had an idea. "Or we could build a fort, just like in the old days. If he comes back, we can go hide in it and throw rocks at him."

"A fort?" said Joe. He was instantly intrigued as only an eight-year-old boy can be over the idea of building a fort. Then he thought of the practicality. "Out of what?"

Jimmy hadn't thought that far ahead. He had thought of where to build it, though. The side of the garage opposite the patio was solid wall, no windows, and a pathway ran along the side. The ground sloped up from the pathway about two or three feet, and the backyard of the house next door was at that higher level. Jimmy had thought of this as the location because he had watched Slugger play Army in the backyard and use this slope as a trench. All they would need is a wall at both ends of the garage, and they were protected on all four sides.

"Well, we could build it here, and when he comes down the alley, we can nail him with rocks," said Jimmy confidently, walking over to the side of the garage.

Joe had heard enough. He started running back and forth from the gravel driveway which ran from the alley to the garage, with rocks piled up in the front of his tee shirt. His idea was the front wall of the fort would be made up of the ammunition itself. As Jimmy watched him he realized it would take too long to build the wall this way and scampered off in search of better building materials. He went into the patio, where there was not only a toy box, but also toys too big for the box. One of the items too big for the box was an old baby buggy his sisters had used in the past to stroll around with their dolls inside. At one time the buggy may have been used for human babies, but by the time Jimmy was a baby it was already too old and dirty to use for that purpose, and by this time it was too dirty for the girls to even put their dolls in.

The buggy was made of wicker, essentially a flat-bottomed wicker basket with scissor type legs on wheels, covered by a partial hood to act as a sunscreen. Jimmy saw it was about the right length to fit between the garage and the slope, and the basket would be a great place to put the rocks. When Jimmy brought it out through the garage and rolled it into position at the end of the garage nearest the alley, Joe's eyes narrowed as he realized what Jimmy was thinking, and he immediately started filling the basket with the pile of rocks he had collected, and then resumed his trips back and forth to the driveway for more.

Jimmy had been ambushed many times inside his house, due to the fact it had a circular floor plan and his tormentors could get to any room by going either direction, so he knew they needed a back wall as well as a front wall. He found it propped up on the side of the garage, partially covered with a tarp. The tarp was not there to protect it; the tarp was stored on top of it. It was Slugger's ancient bicycle, rusted, with a rotten, torn, seat. It could still be ridden, but Jimmy wasn't big enough or desperate enough to ride it at his age. He managed to free it from the spot it had settled into and roll it over to the spot where a back wall should be. That didn't seem strong enough to Jimmy, plus it might fall over, so he added an old folding table and a garbage can. By the time he had this constructed, Joe had filled the basket completely with rocks.

"We could hold out for days with this many rocks!" said Joe proudly.

At this point the boys sat on the slope, inside their fort, and Jimmy had forgotten about the game of catch, the next day's practice, or anything else for that matter as he waited for the ensuing battle. Somehow both boys knew with certainty that Donny was coming back, and they were not disappointed. Joe was sitting near the buggy where he could see the alley, and sure enough within a few minutes Donny walked around the corner.

Without a word of warning, Joe starting throwing rocks. Donny was well out of range and the rocks bounced harmlessly in front of him, but he stopped, looked down quizzically, and then looked up into the sky, baffled by what was happening. As Donny pondered, Joe couldn't contain himself and ran from behind the buggy with a handful of rocks. He threw them all at once, and by some miracle managed to hit Donny on the leg with one of them. Donny's look of wonder turned to rage. He picked up a rock and with marvelous accuracy hit Joe in the chest.

"Oww!!" Joe yelled as he ran back toward the fort.

Donny ran after him, and when he got close enough, Jimmy started pelting him, stopping him dead in his tracks. The two boys both began taking turns hurling rock after rock, and Donny stepped back far enough to allow him to dodge each as it came, and pick up a few and return fire, but he couldn't get any closer, standing in the middle of the alley.

This went on for a while until Jimmy and Joe grew tired of throwing, but they both held up rocks to let Donny see and know what was coming if he took another step forward.

"Come out from there, Injun," taunted Donny.

"Why should I?" answered Joe.

"You'll be sorry if you hit me with another rock," threatened Donny.

Joe answered by throwing another rock. Donny had to duck as it was over his head.

"Whatcha gonna do about it?" taunted the now brave Joe.

Donny threw a rock back, hitting the buggy and the back and forth tosses resumed. The boys could tell the buggy was emptying quickly, and they would soon be out of ammo. Joe looked around at the rocks Donny had thrown at them, on the hillside, under the buggy, in front of the buggy.

"We need more rocks," he said, stating the obvious.

Jimmy had another idea. He had seen in the toy box when he had rummaged through it earlier a couple of old badminton rackets. They would make effective shields!!

"Cover me," Jimmy said, just like he was in a cowboy movie. He crawled on hands and knees along the side the garage, and slipped around the bike barrier and into the patio door. Joe kept Donny at bay by throwing rocks in a steady stream. Jimmy found the rackets, one of which was torn to the point it would be useless, and brought them back into the fort.

Joe took one look at the rackets and instantly knew what to do. He grabbed the untorn racket by the handle and put the strings in front of his face. "Cover me!!" he shouted. As Jimmy threw rocks to cover him, Joe came from behind the buggy and began picking up the rocks Donny had thrown at him. Some he threw back, others he put back into the buggy to restock it.

Donny could see this was not turning out in a good way for him. It wasn't like either Jimmy or Joe could throw that hard, or straight, but over the course of time he was getting pelted. He had to come up with a strategy to attack the fort and not get hit in the face with a rock, so he ran past the fort and stood in the alley behind Jimmy' neighbor's house and as he stood there contemplated running across the neighbor's back yard and down the slope to where Jimmy and Joe were, but just when he was about to charge, the back door of the neighbor's house opened.

Jimmy's neighbors were older, a married couple with children even older than Slugger. Jimmy didn't see them anymore like he did when he was smaller. The father was a man who frightened all the neighborhood children, and not because of anything he had ever done or said to any of them. The reason he was feared was because he was a monster, right out of a fairy tale. He was big and hairy, always grouchy, had a smoker's hack and cleared his throat so roughly and loudly that when it was warm enough to keep the windows open he could be heard any time of the day or night bellowing to clear his throat of the thick brown phlegm he was constantly spitting out.

But that wasn't what made him a monster. What made him a monster was he only had one full arm. The other was cut off at the elbow. To the neighborhood kids, that qualified him as an ogre. No one went to their house on Halloween for that reason. No one crossed their backyard for that reason. Donny was angry and hurt, but he wasn't crazy. He decided against going into ogre country. He didn't need to see who had opened the door. He returned to his spot in the alley behind Jimmy's garage.

He was still there when Jimmy saw the never more welcome sight of his family's car coming up the alley. Donny, so angry he couldn't move, refused to yield to the car as it came toward him. He folded his arms and glared as Jimmy's dad honked.

At this point Jimmy and Joe came out from the side of the garage, and to say the adults were perplexed would be putting it mildly. Jimmy's dad turned to Slugger, who was sitting in the passenger's front seat, and said, "Can you get him out of my way so I can park?"

Slugger jumped out and stood over Donny, cocking his head so he could stare directly into the boy's eyes.

"Are you going to move, or am I going to have to move you?" he asked Donny.

Donny did not respond. Slugger reached down and grabbed Donny around the neck, and lifted him off the ground in this fashion and carried him to the side of the alley. Jimmy's dad pulled the car into the driveway, looked at the buggy, the rocks, and Jimmy and Joe. He shook his head and drove into the garage. After getting out of the car and surveying the scene again, he turned to Slugger and said, "Can you take that boy home?" and then turned to Jimmy and Joe and said "I want every rock back where you got it from, I want the toys back where they belong, and it better be done before dark." Then he closed the garage door and walked into the house with his wife.

Once the back door closed, a sick smile came over Slugger's face. This day was one of the most important in his life. He had gone with his parents to talk to an Army recruiter who would soon get him out of the hole he had grown up in and into the big world he craved. All he needed now was his dad's signature, and a few months to pass until his birthday, and his adult life would begin. No way was the little punk standing a few feet away from him going to change his mood. The sick smile was because he starting thinking of how this day could be even better. Donny had two older brothers, one a year younger than Slugger and another two years older. The older had made the mistake years ago of jumping in when Slugger was whipping the younger one, and the two of them had fought him off. Not only that, but warned him to never mess with his younger brother again, Nigger. Slugger waited a couple of days, to rest up, before confronting the older brother alone, in front of his house. One black eye and two missing teeth later, Slugger had his face in the mud and blood, telling him this Nigger would beat him any time he wanted, and to tell his Dad to come on out of the house, where he was standing watching his oldest son getting beaten, and he could get some too.

"Please tell me you won't go home on your own, Donny," said Slugger, getting angry again despite himself at the memory of it, like so many of his memories, of having to fight every kid in town just to be able to walk down the street.

Donny stood silently, not moving. Slugger grabbed his neck again, turned him around, and began marching down the alley. After dragging his feet for a few steps, Donny started walking, and after trying to jerk away a few times, decided it would be better to walk straight. They rounded the corner, and as soon as he was out of the sight of Jimmy and Joe, Donny started to cry.

"So now you're crying?" asked Slugger. "Make sure to tell your brothers what happened. Please. Ask them about the last time they messed with me."

It was only a two-minute walk to Donny's house. To Donny it seemed like an eternity. Like all little boys, he was starting to learn life may not turn out in the way it was described in his house growing up. The thought that this black boy was not afraid of his brothers was not something he thought was possible. He had been taught all black men were cowards and they would never stand up to a white man, let alone be unafraid to be outnumbered. By the time Slugger knocked loudly on his front door, ignoring the door bell, Donny was beginning to change his world outlook.

When his father came to the door he remained inside the house, behind the screen door. Donny tried to run into the door, but Slugger was still holding him fast. Slugger smiled the sick smile again. He had been hoping one of the brothers would come to the door, but this, he thought, would be even better.

"I had to bring Donny home because he wouldn't leave when he was told," said Slugger, pausing to give the man staring at him in shock time to respond. He didn't. "If I ever hear of him messing with my little brother again, I'll be coming back."

Another pause, another silent response. "And I like to start at the top," Slugger finished.

With that, he let Donny go. Donny's dad opened the door to let him in, and quickly closed it again and locked it.

CHAPTER
Fifteen

H arry Williams was not known for his sense of humor. He was not pleased the gravel he had paid for, transported, and spread out so carefully in his driveway was piled into an old baby carriage. But he couldn't help chuckling to himself as he walked into the house with his wife. The things his young son did were constantly amazing to him. He was always thinking of things no one else did, and somehow, he made a lot of them work, sometimes the least likely of them. Harry was filled with the promise of his future. Maybe he would get the opportunities denied to Harry and his generation, and so many generations before him. Maybe he would get the degree and become the professional Harry could only dream of being.

In the warped world that was American Apartheid, black people saw no benefit in sending their sons to college. It was much better for them to be trained as carpenters, plumbers, porters, factory workers, any kind of work which was at the time called 'skilled labor'. That was the top of the career ladder for most black men. Unskilled labor was the common beginning and end of the career of most, and staying steadily employed at any level was a supreme struggle. Even if a black man could find a college to educate him as an engineer or accountant, finding a job would be nearly impossible in the segregated workplace of the office. Girls, on the other hand, could get jobs as nurses and teachers which required college degrees, so Harry had sisters who graduated from college. Even that was quite an accomplishment for a black family, to have multiple college graduates in the 1940's and '50's.

Harry was smiling at the thought of Jimmy being able to do it. Harry had gone as far as he could go, a skilled factory union job with good benefits, which was farther than his father had gone, who had swept the floors of the same factory. But that father had put children through college sweeping floors.

He was deep into this revelry as he entered the bedroom behind his wife and she closed both doors behind them and walked to and sat on the bed. She looked at her husband, lost in thought, at his dresser. She took a deep breath and said to her husband, "We need to talk about this...." and her voice trailed off as she heard the back screen-door open and slam shut.

It was Jimmy, coming in after he and Joe dumped all the rocks back in the driveway. Jimmy saw the short route to his bedroom, through his parent's room, was not available, and since he had learned long ago not to disturb his parents when the door was closed, he took the long route, through the family room, kitchen, front room, and down the hall past the 'kid's bathroom' and into the room he shared with Slugger. The long day had worn him out, and so instead of joining his sisters in front of the television he went into and sat on the floor of his room, next to the bunk beds, with his back against the lower berth. He had also learned long before if he wanted to be left alone he had to remain as quiet as possible and not attract unwanted attention, so he sat there silently, listening to the air flow in and out through his nostrils. The walls of the house were thin, and the distance which separated Jimmy from his parents on the other side of the door was six feet at the most. Unless they were whispering, he could easily hear them talking. That came in handy when they were discussing his punishment, or better yet, one of his siblings' punishments, behind closed doors. As he did not know whether his father would be calling him in the next minute to dole out whatever he had coming for the rock fight, he leaned in to listen closely.

His mother started softly, trying to stay calm at a time that was to her one of the most frightening of her life. "You know that I made a vow before God to always obey you."

The hair on the back of Harry's neck started to stand up. He was instantly ripped from the happy future he was imagining. That future may still happen, but he had some more immediate issues to deal with, or so his neck hairs were telling him. Before she could say anything else, he reflexively said, "Yes, dear."

Her voice rose and hardened as she continued. "Well, this is one time you are going to have to obey me."

Jimmy, when he heard this, crawled over to the door and put his ear against it. This was something he had never heard coming from his mother's mouth. Strange moaning while his father giggled was the most fascinating thing he had heard before, but this was even more unexpected. He had never heard his mother say anything remotely close to this to his father before.

Harry didn't answer, but turned to face his wife.

Her voice trembled as it rose in strength and anger. "You know how, when Slugger gets in a fight, or gets a bad report card, or gets accused of something whether he did it or not? You know how you say 'Your son did this, or Your son did that?' Well, let me tell you something. My son, yes, MY son, IS NOT GOING TO VIET NAM!!!!"

She paused to collect her breath. She was not talking loud enough for anyone in the family room to hear over the roar of the television, but of course she did not know Jimmy was just a few feet away, with his head against the thin door.

"And YOU are going to tell him," she commanded.

Harry stared at her in shock. All Slugger ever talked about wanting to be was a soldier, in the Army, since he was a little boy. It never changed, except for a short period when he wanted to be a cowboy. It was the one thing he agreed with Slugger, the one thing he thought he could use to fuse the bond between them that had never quite been fused. He had always had to deliver the beatings, impose his will, to provide the family discipline. He had done what was necessary to get control of Slugger, to make it possible for him to make his family work. But he had not been able to overlook the boy's flaws, and his wife was not fabricating the taunts from the past. It had never erupted openly like this before, but it had always been there, just below the surface.

As Harry looked at his wife staring at him, he knew he would not sign the paperwork allowing Slugger to enlist at age eighteen. He knew he had to do what she said. The hairs on the back of his neck were screaming at him that his very life depended on it.

"You know I was in the Army too," he answered softly, his mouth not quite up to speed as his neck hairs were. "It might do him some good."

"It will also do him some good to go to college," she said, and now she was becoming quieter, as if she was marshalling her energy to strike.

Harry's mouth now got the message. She would risk her life before she would let her son go to Viet Nam. If he signed those papers he would need to find a safe place to sleep, and food from a secure source as well. He paused as he thought of a few futile things to say but decided not to waste his breath and further enrage her. He ended the conversation as he had started it. "Yes, dear. I'll talk to him tomorrow after work."

Jimmy heard the distinct sound of a kiss. This was when he stopped listening and crawled away from the door. He put on his pajamas, which was the original reason he sat on the floor, and climbed into the top bunk. He had stashed the encyclopedia volume B under his pillow and read himself to sleep preparing for the next day's adventures.

CHAPTER
Sixteen

When Jimmy woke up the next morning, it was to Slugger's smiling face about two inches away from his. If anyone ever asked Slugger what his little brother's favorite thing to do was, he would answer "sleeping" without hesitation. Jimmy did love to sleep. Each night was a new adventure of dreams and not infrequent enough nightmares, an escape from the squeaks and rumbles of the darkness and the thoughts of death that accompany insomnia. He hated to go to bed because that meant turning off the lights and laying in darkness, but once he had escaped the darkness by falling into his dreams, the fact the sun was back up didn't make any difference.

"Time to get up, Jimmy," ordered Slugger firmly, but happily. "You need to eat breakfast before you go to practice."

Jimmy tried to pull his eyes open, but could only manage to open the right one. The left was fused shut. "Go wash your face and get all that eye slobber off it," continued Slugger, and with that he yanked the covers off Jimmy, leaving him curled up, fetal style, his bare feet cold and exposed. He had no choice at this point but to sit up with his feet dangling over the side of the top bunk. Slugger turned and left the room.

He was still in that position a few minutes later, with his eyes closed, trying to fall back into the last dream he hadn't finished when Slugger returned to the room. "JIMMY!!" he shouted.

Everyone else in the house was already awake, but the girls in the next room didn't appreciate the abruptness of it, so they yelled back, in unison, "SHUT UP, SLUGGER!!!"

Slugger, who had anticipated such a reaction, yelled back "YOU SHUT UP!! WHY DON'T YOU COME IN HERE AND TRY TO WAKE HIM UP?!?!"

Jimmy had mastered a half smile of resignation by this early stage of his life. He used it in all his class pictures, and he used it as he sat on his bed listening to the loud voices of his siblings. As he rubbed his eye to open it and slid off the bunk and down to the floor, he realized that none of his siblings ever appeared in his dreams, and he also realized why. His dreams had no soundtrack. He walked a few steps toward the bathroom, and the door to his sisters' bedroom swung open and JoAnn ran out and into the bathroom before Jimmy could get there. Another typical day, thought Jimmy, and then he realized that no, it wasn't. Slugger woke him up because today was his first day of baseball practice.

He stood leaning against the wall in the hallway, waiting for his sister to finish doing whatever girls did that took so long in the bathroom, and contemplated what practice would be like. When the bathroom door finally opened, Jimmy had managed to half drift off to sleep again.

"Only you could fall asleep standing up, Jimmy," said JoAnn as she saw Jimmy startled back to reality by the opening of the door.

"How bad does it smell in there?" he responded. In this house, you had to wake up on your game.

JoAnn did not answer and returned to the girls' room and closed the door. When he had finished in the bathroom he came into the kitchen where his mother was standing by the stove, mixing eggs in a bowl. She had placed a plate with two slices of bacon at Jimmy's designated position at the table, and milk in a tall glass. Jimmy sat and drank the milk in steady gulps, leaving only a small portion to drink after he had finished his eggs and bacon.

Slugger came into the kitchen and said "Hurry up Jimmy, we don't have all day. Practice starts at nine."

Jimmy felt a surge of absolute fear. He had not considered who would take him to practice, but he did not want it to be Slugger. Slugger was too unpredictable. He turned to his mother with his eyes wide. "You're taking me, aren't you, Mom?"

His mother looked down at her youngest son and saw the look in his eyes. Of all her five children, Jimmy was the only one she came close to losing. Overcoming his medical problems had been the cause of more prayer than all her other children put together. In fact, her faith in God was permanently cemented when he answered those prayers. And what blessings God had given the boy. What he lacked in size and strength physically he more than made up for intellectually. All the other mothers would talk about the things their sons did, the fights and broken furniture. She talked about report cards, the glowing words of his teachers, the constant questions. She, like her husband, saw a future for her son she saw for none of her other children. With Slugger, she would send him off without a second thought to his safety around other boys, he could fight for himself. But with Jimmy, she would keep a close eye. No one would break him, physically or emotionally, while on her watch.

"OK, I'll take you this time," she said.

Jimmy finished the last gulp of milk in relief. He didn't even see Slugger from the time he left the table to the time he got in the car with his mother. Not that Slugger would admit to having his feelings hurt anyway, because the first practice was when they passed out schedules and other official stuff, and his mother was the best one to be there for that, but it did strike him as Jimmy's being a bit ungrateful. He watched from the window as the car pulled out of the driveway and down the alley. When it was gone, even though he had other things to do, he almost couldn't help himself but to follow, but he swallowed hard and went about his other business.

Jimmy loved riding in a car, looking out of the window as the world went by. He noticed the wind bending the trees, which were covered with the half-grown leaves of late spring, and the ground was wet. It must have rained the night before while he slayed the dragons behind his eyelids. Jimmy was glad his mother had made him wear two sweatshirts over his mandated tee-shirt, and he hadn't worn his old jeans with the holes in them.

The drive to the park took the same path as to the junior high building, but instead of turning left on Maple she went to the next block and turned left on Walnut. The route they were taking seemed very familiar, and Jimmy, who had remained quiet for the first few blocks, commented as such when his mother made the left turn off Main Street.

"Yes, you are right. The park is very close to your Aunt Emma's. You've played on the swings in that park before." None of her other children would be so observant, but this was everyday Jimmy. "I'm going to visit her during the practice."

As soon as she said it Jimmy remembered. Once on Walnut they would pass the hospital, Graham Hospital, where Jimmy had come into the world. Then down a big hill and at the bottom was his aunt's house. They continued past it, and at the end of the block was the start of the park. It was small, one block wide and about three blocks long, with one side bordered by a small stream, which was named, ironically, Big Creek. The ball field was along the street as the coach had promised, and there were places to park next to it. It was placed in the corner of the park formed by Walnut Street and Big Creek, with a chain link back stop in the corner. The street continued after passing over the stream, but the park did not.

As Jimmy's mom pulled the car over, he could see several disorganized looking boys running around, shouting, and generally acting like boys. With the exception that most were wearing baseball gloves, it was like being dropped off at school next to the playground. A very large white man was standing near the row of cars, talking to a few adults. He had a large square head; short, buzz cut hair, and horn rimmed glasses. Jimmy's mother walked over to him, with Jimmy in tow. Jimmy noticed he had a stack of papers, just like a teacher, and he handed one to Jimmy's mom. Then he realized it was the same man who was standing in line in front of them at the junior high.

"I'm Coach Schmidt!" the man said cheerfully. "If you are here for the first practice of the Minor League Cubs, you are in the right place! Here is the schedule."

Jimmy craned his neck to see the paper through his mother's fingers, but he could only see the top part. On it, at the very top, the very first line, were the words:

Cubs V Cardinals 1PM   June 24.

As he tried to look further, he felt a tug on his sleeve. Jimmy turned to see a boy, about his height, but of course much bigger, as were all the boys Jimmy could see as he looked around. Some were taller, some were shorter, but none were as skinny as Jimmy. The boy doing the tugging was the same one Jimmy had seen at the sign up.

"Let's play catch!! I have a ball!!" said Brad Schmidt.

Jimmy looked up at his mother for guidance, and saw the big white man roll his eyes and let out a laugh. "That is my son, Brad," he said to Jimmy's mother.

"This is my son, Jimmy," she responded.

"Welcome, Jimmy," said the man, and turning to his mother, "You can come back in an hour and a half. We'll take care of him."

Brad could not wait any longer, and grabbed Jimmy by the arm and dragged him away from his mother. When she didn't say "stop", he trotted off with Brad.

"Wait here!" said Brad, and took off running with the ball. When he was about twenty steps away, the proper distance, thought Jimmy, he turned, and with some deliberation threw the ball to Jimmy. It was off line, which Jimmy thought was funny with all the motions Brad had gone through to throw it, but not so far off line Jimmy couldn't catch it. He threw it back and so it went, but not that simply, as other boys would crowd in and steal the ball, other times the ball would roll into someone trying to play catch, and then there were boys playing tag and tackling each other and wrestling throughout it all. So much was going on Jimmy didn't even notice his mother's car as it pulled away.

"OK, LISTEN UP, EVERYBODY!!" boomed out Coach Schmidt. Jimmy and the rest of the boys were startled and turned their heads, at least most of them. Two boys had gotten into an intense wrestling match and had to be separated by two older boys, who as it turned out were the older sons of Coach Schmidt who had been volunteered to help him coach the team.

"I WANT EVERYONE TO FORM A LINE, RIGHT HERE." He pointed to a line in the grass that started at third base and extended out to left field. The boys ran to the line to see who could get there first, even though it wasn't a race. That is, everyone except Jimmy and the two wrestlers, who had used the opportunity to start fighting again. Jimmy didn't see the point of running. In school, they always made the children line up in alphabetical order, so what was the rush? The two older boys grabbed the fighters again and physically carried them to opposite ends of the line. Jimmy went to the end where he thought the W's, Y's, and Z's would be.

Instead, the man said, "When I call out your name, step forward!"

There were twelve boys in the line, and as their names were called, Jimmy tried to remember them all but couldn't. The ones who had a unique feature, or personalities, were the ones he could. All the faces were white faces, so that did not help. There was one kid, when he stepped forward, who was wearing slip on shoes instead of tennis shoes. His name was Ken Ferry. There was another named Derek who walked and talked in such a feminine way Jimmy at first wasn't sure if he was a boy or a girl. He had the same last name as Brad, Schmidt, but he was not Brad's brother, and Brad made sure everyone knew it. Maybe he was a cousin. There was the boy standing next to him, named Scott Michaels. The red headed boy was named Kevin Morgan. When the roll call was finished, Coach Schmidt introduced his assistants and explained what he expected. Jimmy did not remember any of their names, but since they all started with 'Coach', he addressed them all as 'Coach'.

"First thing, no fighting," said the oldest Coach. This wasn't on his original list, but recent events had prompted the addition of this rule. "Next, always do what the coaches tell you to do."

"Don't worry about making a mistake," he continued. "We are here to teach you how to play, and we expect you to make mistakes."

"Last," he said with a smile, "We are here to have fun."

"Now, I want you all to run across the field, to where the other coaches are standing, and then run back," he said. Some of the boys started running immediately.

"Wait!" he said, "Come back! I haven't told you to start yet!"

This was a race then, Jimmy thought, and he knew he had better try hard so he would not finish last. He knew from past experiences on the playground most boys his age could run faster than he could, so winning the race was not within the realm of possibilities in his universe, but finishing last was if he didn't do his best.

"Go!!" shouted the coach, and off they went, some blasting away instantly and others, like Jimmy, hesitating for a fatal half-second.

Jimmy looked around when he reached the coaches at the other end, and as expected almost everyone was ahead of him. As usual, the boys farthest ahead had turned and were coming back toward him laughing when he reached the turning point. He saw a few of them cheated, as always, and turned before they had reached the line, but there was no time to stop running to accuse them. He felt great relief when he made his turn and saw two boys behind him, one of those being Derek Schmidt.

Next they played catch again, but this time it was organized, with the boys throwing to a definite partner, and with the assistants watching and correcting the boys if they weren't throwing it properly. Jimmy's partner was Scott Michaels, and that is why he remembered his name. He was a blond haired, blue eyed, happy faced kid, eager to be alive and out in the sunshine. Jimmy noticed Scott, and most of the boys, were as erratic at throwing and catching the ball as Joe was. In fact, when it came to throwing a ball the other boy could catch, Jimmy saw that he was better than almost everyone, except maybe Brad Schmidt and a couple of others.

The next thing they did was split into two groups, each going to a different part of the park. Jimmy's group went far out into the grass, away from the backstop, where one of the assistants had a bat and ball. He told the boys to spread out and began tossing the ball into the air and hitting it with the bat, sending it arcing through the air toward one of the boys to catch. The boys did as well as could be expected, which means boys were running away from the ball, running in circles around the ball, tripping and falling as they ran toward the ball, reaching up to catch the ball and it hitting them in the arm, back, or leg, directly or after having bounced off their glove because they forgot to open it; and the occasional catch. Sometimes the kid who caught it had his eyes open at the time, but more often they were afraid to look at what was about to happen and closed their eyes at the last second, and it luckily happened anyway. The most frequent result was the ball would drop, and the kid it dropped right in front of would pick it up or go chasing after it. At the beginning, all the boys would run after it when it bounced past them no matter to whom it was hit, but before too long the boys would just laugh at the kid who was supposed to catch it and let him go running for it himself.

If the ball was hit more than two steps away from him Jimmy couldn't run far or fast enough to catch it, but if it was a step or two away and not hit straight at him, he could usually catch it from the side. When it was hit straight at him it made things much more difficult, because he was more worried about getting hit with it than catching it and so he had to dance away from it while reaching back to catch it. That was trickier. But after having to run for what seemed a mile to fetch a ball he had side stepped, he began to realize if his side was going to ache from running after it he might as well stand still enough to stop the ball at least, even if he couldn't catch it.

After what seemed an eternity, the coach called out to the assistants to change positions. Jimmy's group came running in, and the other group went to the outfield. The coach stood at home plate with a bat and ball, and he had the boys spread out around the dirt quarter circle which made up the infield. He then started hitting them the ball, except this time bouncing it off the ground instead of hitting it in the air. This, Jimmy knew from playing catch in the alley with Joe, was inherently more dangerous. A bouncing ball could go anywhere. It could bounce left, right, or the worst of all, up, and you had to look down to catch it. It did not take long for the first blood of the practice to be spilled because of that fact. Kevin Morgan, who obviously had not played much catch before, was bending over to catch a ball and it hopped up, catching him square on the nose. As the blood poured out and mingled with the soon to flow tears on his shirt and pants, Jimmy was thinking he couldn't let that happen to him or his mom would be mad. Bloodstains on Slugger's clothes had always led to trouble, from what he remembered.

Amazingly, practice did not end with the nose bleed, as playtime had always been ended by the grownups in charge when blood was shed in Jimmy's past experiences on the playground. Coach Schmidt calmly trotted over and pulled a handkerchief out of his pocket and tilted the boy's head back. He squeezed the boy's nostrils with the handkerchief, and told him to go sit down on the bench beside the backstop. Then he went back to his position as if nothing had happened, and started hitting balls again.

Despite this, or more probably because of this, Jimmy didn't do very well with the ground balls. He wasn't getting a bloody lip or nose if he could help it. And he found he could help it by moving out of the way of the ball, which was easier to do without the ridicule of the other boys which accompanied missing a pop up. When the coach finally called a halt to this drill, Jimmy's heart surged. He had survived without bleeding.

The coach called the boys together, and said the next drill would be a batting drill. He told each boy to take a position in the field. Five boys went into the outfield, and five spread about the infield, and as one boy took his turn at bat, another would stand to the side, swinging a bat at imaginary pitches. An assistant stood on the pitcher's mound and another behind the plate. Each boy had to pick a bat from the pile next to the backstop, and after each one's turn they were sent into the outfield or infield to be replaced by one of the boys standing there.

The coach let each boy first stand as they thought best, but then he moved their feet and positioned their hands to what he knew to be better. Some would listen, some would not, and almost all the boys chose the biggest, heaviest, bat they could lift. Just like catching, most of the contact that was made was with their eyes closed. Once again, a couple of the boys looked like they knew what they were doing, the ones who had older brothers. They knew how to stand, how to step into the pitch, and how to keep their eyes open, sometimes, but Jimmy noticed even they would most times close their eyes just before contact.

Jimmy understood how closing their eyes made it easier to imagine they were going to hit the ball. It had to first be a dream for it to become a reality. But Jimmy also deduced closing his eyes made it harder to do whatever he was trying to do, and it was obviously best to always watch the ball, as it could be headed straight toward his face. So, when his turn came to bat, he vowed to keep his eyes open. His main concern was whether there would be a bat light enough for him to not only pick up, but to swing, which occupied his mind more than getting hit with the ball. He could hear all the boys laughing at him for not being able to bat with anything heavier than a plastic bat because that was the only bat he had ever managed to swing before this day.

By the time his turn came, he had seen three boys hit the ball hard enough to barely clear the infield, many that rolled it back to the pitcher, and a few that made it to the boys in the infield, but no one had done anything spectacular. Despite the boy in front of him telling him to use the bat he had used, the heaviest one, Jimmy looked for and selected the smallest bat in the pile. It was well worn, not shiny with new paint like some of the others. Jimmy worried there was a risk of splinters just grabbing it too tight.

He stepped to the plate and the catcher asked, "Right or left?"

Jimmy, having heard this question asked to the boys ahead of him, said "Left," and the coach showed him where and how to stand.

The first pitch was higher than his head, so Jimmy didn't move the bat from his shoulders. Some of the boys swung at every pitch thrown, but Jimmy couldn't see the point if he couldn't hit it anyway.

"Good eye," said the assistant behind the plate.

Another pitch came in, and Jimmy swung as violently as he could, which meant he was barely halfway into it when the ball smacked the catcher's glove. The bat curled around his body and hit him on the back of his leg.

"Just put the bat on the ball. Don't swing it too hard," was the next instruction.

Jimmy had no clue what the coach was talking about. Just put the bat on the ball? If he had swung any less hard, the bat wouldn't even have crossed the plate. The next pitch was perfect, but to Jimmy it was too close, and he stepped back to avoid it.

"That was a perfect pitch. What do you want?" called out the coach who was pitching, as if annoyed he hadn't hit it all the way to Jimmy's aunt's house.

The next one wasn't nearly as perfect, but Jimmy took a swing at it anyway, an eyes-closed, full strength, hack.

"You'll never get a hit that way. Just stick your bat out," said the coach behind the plate. "One more, and then it's the next kid's turn, so run this one out if you hit it."

Jimmy did not care for the tone, but he had to admit he would probably never get a hit swinging as hard as he could with his eyes closed. He decided to do what he often did when he couldn't figure something out. That is, do the opposite of what seemed to make sense. Try to catch the ball with the bat, not hit it. At least he wouldn't miss it completely. The next pitch, his last chance, came and he did just that. He watched where he thought the ball was going, and instead of swinging hard, he swung just hard enough to put the bat where he thought the ball would be when it got closer.

The most amazing part of what happened next was the sound. It was like a pop! Jimmy had been so nervous throughout most of the practice he had been shivering the entire time. When the ball hit the bat Jimmy's hands stung so badly he thought he had squeezed a bee between his fingers. It was cold, he thought, too cold to be playing this long outside. But as that thought crossed his mind he saw the ball rolling along the ground, just fast enough for the pitcher, who wasn't trying very hard, to let it roll past his glove toward the boys clustered between 2nd and 3rd base. Jimmy stared for a fraction of a second, in wonder he had hit the ball at all. The boy waiting to bat, and the guy catching, startled him out of his daze.

"RUN!!!!" they yelled. Jimmy dropped the bat and ran to first base, as he had seen the other boys lucky enough to hit the ball do. The boys had not been instructed to throw the ball to first base, so Jimmy didn't know whether he would have gotten a hit or not, but it did not matter that much. He had made contact at least once, which was more than he had expected. He went back to the where he had dropped his glove, next to the backstop, and trotted back to his previous spot in the outfield.

As he did the rain drops started to fall and the temperature, which had been dropping throughout the morning, became the only thing Jimmy was thinking about. The last thing he wanted to do was catch a cold. The other boys jeered and cheered as their teammates took their turn batting, but Jimmy could only think about when his mother would come back and he could get out of the freezing air. His teeth chattered as he stood there, and he could hear a few of the other boys laughing. One of them said, "If we have to play with one of THEM, why does he have to be so skinny and slow?"

Jimmy pretended not to hear it, but Scott Michaels didn't. When the boys were called together after the last one had his chance to bat, he came up to Jimmy as they walked off the field. "Jimmy," he said as he trotted alongside him. "Don't let those guys bother you. I think you'll do good!"

Jimmy smiled at Scott, not nearly as convinced as he was. The coach gave a short talk, advising the boys the next practice date and time, and letting them know each one's position for the first game would be selected then, and after the next practice would be the first game. While Jimmy thought about this he saw his mother drive up and park, along with many other parents, as the designated time for the end of practice had come. As they walked to their cars Scott waved to Jimmy.

"See you later, Jimmy!" he said with a smile.

Jimmy looked back at Scott as he opened the car door. "OK, see you later."

CHAPTER
Seventeen

"How'd it go, Jimmy?" asked Slugger later that day, the next time he saw Jimmy after watching him leave for practice.

"It was alright," said Jimmy, which was as noncommittal an answer as he could come up with.

It was also the truth. He liked some of it and he didn't like some of it. Mainly he did not like how cold it was. But rather than explain it to Slugger in any more detail, he stopped after three words, and Slugger did not press him for more as he had more important things on his mind.

His mother had told him to be sure to be home when his father returned from work, because he needed to speak with him. Slugger could barely contain his excitement, as he knew it had to be about his upcoming enlistment. He had already started counting down the hours until October 6th, the day he turned eighteen and could join the Army with parental consent. It would be the last one he hoped to spend in Canton, Illinois. He had graduated a few weeks before from high school, which was all he thought he owed his parents, and now he could start living the life he was born to live. What a day it would be when his chains were finally unshackled! He could not ever remember being so eager and nervous for his father to turn into the alley. The fact his father came into the house quietly, solemnly retreating into his bathroom without a word, did not give Slugger any warning of what was coming next.

He sat on the couch in the living room, smiling and dreaming. Patience, never a virtue Slugger aspired to, was in abundance.

Harry lingered in front of the mirror after his normal routine of washing his face, arms and torso to the waist. He felt the psychological need to cleanse himself of his factory smell. Working in the environment of the shop floor was not healthy for him physically. The dust invaded his sinuses and caused him difficulties in breathing, and he had hurt his back years before lifting and twisting in a way his spine could not accommodate, but the main hurt was psychological. It was the constant sameness of the work. It was his constantly changing supervisors and their demeaning assumptions and rules. It was the intimidation by both sides in the labor-management battles. It was the reality that no matter how well he did his job it would not lead to anything more than what was agreed in the latest contract. It was the frustration at the mental frailty and lack of discipline of his co-workers. He needed to wipe all that away before he faced his family.

The girls were in their room, as usual, with the record player on. Jimmy was allowed in, if he kept quiet, but of course he didn't have to stay quiet once he got in, as far as he was concerned. Many times, in fact most times, Jimmy was kicked out of the room after listening to a few songs and being as obnoxious as possible if they put something on he didn't like. The girls had what was called a "close and play" record player, which played 33 RPM or 45 RPM records, but they only bought the cheaper 45's. The close part didn't work, and they had taped a nickel to the needle arm to stop it from bouncing and causing the record to 'skip', but music was a requirement. Since they talked even louder than the records, it was nearly impossible to hear a conversation on the other side of the wall from the bedroom, which was the living room where Slugger was happily waiting for his father.

When he walked into the living room and saw Slugger sitting there, he was at a loss for words. How could he tell the boy what he had to tell him? The sound of the pots and pans clanging in the kitchen around the corner as his wife noisily measured the flour and sugar, making her presence known without being seen, kept him rooted to the middle of the living room floor instead of fleeing as he might have without it. Now Slugger, sensing his father's unease, felt his stomach knot. Being a man of few words anyway, Harry Williams stayed true to his universe by speaking the minimum necessary.

"Slugger," started Harry, "I'm not going to sign the papers for your enlistment."

Staying true to his universe as well, Slugger rocketed off the couch and into the air, screaming "WHAT??" at the top of his lungs.

This was a betrayal beyond any Slugger had ever conceived possible, while at the same time being the only result he knew he should have expected. What a miserable fool he was, what an emotional orphan, to be still clinging to the idea that his life could be anything beyond constant rejection. He landed standing in front of his father, nose to nose.

"Your mother and I..." continued his father, his voice trembling, but Slugger couldn't hear him anymore. His mind was too full of his screeching emotions to hear another word.

"WHAT?????" screamed Slugger louder, as if the sound could drown the demons swimming in his brain. This man standing in front of him, who had come into his life so many years before Slugger had almost forgotten what life was like before him, was once again proving to Slugger he did not love him like he did the other children, his children. He couldn't love him if he wouldn't do this for him. It was all he had ever wanted. All he had to do was write his name on a piece of paper. It proved to him once and for all he was just part of the bargain, the unwanted piece of a package deal his father had to agree to before marrying his mother. He had never, not once in the more than fourteen years that had passed since that day, told Slugger he loved him. He had beaten him plenty, but not once said he loved him. Slugger instinctively balled his fists and stepped back, in a classic boxer's position.

"I HATE YOU!!!" he shrieked, and then started bouncing on his toes as if looking for an opening to strike, like Muhammad Ali.

Harry's universe had also taught him his instincts, and the instinct of a man of his generation was children did not step to their father with balled fists. In his universe if your son did so, you dealt with him in the same fashion as you would any other man. And Harry, who did not have the fighting nature or ability of the boy standing before him, still had the forearms and wrists and hands of a working man. He had the strength that came from carrying a heavy load for decades, forged in the heat of frustration and struggle. Harry unleashed a left and right combination to the sides of Slugger's head before he could move. He pulled the punches, but they still landed with such force and fury Slugger was shocked at the impact. Slugger knew instantly fighting back in his normal fashion was not the answer this time. He slumped down to the couch and covered his head with his arms. His father leaned over the boy with his fists still balled, breathing fast and hard like a raging bull.

All this commotion overcame the music and loud talking ringing in Jimmy's head, and he bolted out of the bedroom. When he came around the corner, he saw his father taking his last swing. He stood there transfixed as his father loomed over his brother, cowering on the couch. His father's anger was overflowing, his chest heaving. He pointed his finger at Slugger and said, "Get out of my house!" with a threatening snarl. He did not want this to escalate, he did not want to hurt his son, but his house was indeed his house, and he would maintain order in his house. Slugger looked at him, uncovering his eyes, incredulously, and then steeled himself, stood up, and ran out of the front door of the house without another word.

By this time the girls were crowded around Jimmy, watching the scene. Their mother was at the other end of the room with a towel in her hands rubbing a glass, even though it had been dry for a while now. Her husband stood in the living room, transfixed on the front door that had slammed closed in Slugger's wake, and then he turned, walked toward his wife, and brushed past her as he exited the room opposite his other children. She saw the wide-eyed looks on their faces, and Belinda burst out in uncontrollable tears.

"Sit down, all of you," their mother said. She knew this was all her doing, but held fast to her conviction that in the end, this was for the best. Despite what had just happened, she tried to exude an air of calm.

"Your father did not want this to happen," she said. JoAnn sat next to Belinda, and hugged her as her tears flowed into JoAnn's blouse. Jaqueline looked on skeptically. Jimmy listened and wondered, why was it everyone around him always got so emotional? Why couldn't they anticipate what they should and should not do and what they should and should not say to avoid this happening? It was obvious to him. Of course, this was obvious to Jimmy because he always had to stay calm and watch what he said, or he'd get beaten up every day.

A tear fell from his mother's eye as well, and she wiped it away with her apron. She began to talk again, to help herself from completely breaking down. "We want Slugger to go to college. We want ALL of you to go to college. If Slugger would just have listened to what your father was trying to tell him this wouldn't have happened." She tried to continue, but the words could not get past her throat, and silence enveloped the room like a stifling blanket.

As always, Jimmy thought of a question. "When can Slugger come back?" he asked. He was practical to a fault, and he knew no matter how emotional those around him could be, they always calmed down eventually. He was just thinking ahead.

Jaqueline said, "Maybe he'll never come back. I bet he doesn't want to come back." She said it as more of a threat to her mother than something she feared. In her mind Slugger, despite all his shenanigans, was more loved by her mother than she was. If she was the one who left her mother may not even notice, and she wouldn't bother to cry if she did notice.

Jimmy stared at her wide-eyed. He wondered why she would want to scare her mother even more. No one had kicked her out of the house. Besides, this wasn't the first, second or third time Slugger had run away, and he had come back all the other times.

"He can come back in an hour. Your father just wanted time to cool off first," her mother responded, ignoring Jaqueline, glad Jimmy had broken the spell.

With that the girls fled into their room before their mother could continue the conversation, and Jimmy retreated to his. Belinda was still sobbing, but at least her nose wasn't running any more. They only came out of their rooms again to eat the most silent dinner in family history. As soon as the dishes were washed and dried the children withdrew to their rooms for the remainder of the evening. Jimmy tried to stay awake until Slugger returned, but he couldn't. When he woke up the next morning, Slugger's bed was still made and he was nowhere to be seen.

CHAPTER
Eighteen

It was almost a week later when the Cubs had their second base-ball practice. Slugger had still not returned home from what Jimmy had seen. He was hoping Slugger would take him to prac-tice this time, because this was the one when each player's position would be selected. They had been told to make a first, second, and third choice, because no one would be guaranteed to get their first, but the coach had promised by the end of the season all the boys would get to play all the positions they wanted to. Jimmy had picked pitcher, then first base, then outfield. It was easy for a lefthander, be-cause those were the only positions a left hander could play unless he counted catcher, and Jimmy vowed never to catch. That position had the highest chances of getting hit, either with the ball or the bat or someone running him over, and to Jimmy, getting run over was worst of all, even worse than getting hit with the ball.

It was left to Jimmy's mother to take him, just like the first practice. Jimmy noticed she took a different route this time. In-stead of turning right out of the alley, she turned left, then turned left again past Donny Gomes' house and up Maple Street to Fifth Avenue. There she turned right and continued down Fifth until reaching Ash Street, where she turned left. Jimmy wondered if she was looking for Slugger, as her eyes wandered left and right, watching the people walking up and down the sidewalk.

"Is practice someplace different this time, Mommy?" he asked, to distract her.

She smiled and responded "Yes, it's at Big Creek Park."

Jimmy knew of this park. It was the biggest and best park he had ever been to, located on the north end of town. The entrance was across the street from the high school. Jimmy's mom turned off Ash to Main Street, as he knew she would, and traveled the six blocks down Main to the high school, which was the last building on the north end of town. He could see the tallest structure in Canton behind the high school, the water tower, which he always looked for when he travelled so far from home.

Big Creek Park was a big park, even though the creek wasn't so big. Jimmy could play in the park all day and never see the creek. Jimmy's mom turned left onto the main park road off Main Street, which led to the south entrance of the park. The road looped through the park and returned to Main Street at the north end via the aptly named North Park Drive. Starting at the south end it then meandered west past a large, concrete, above ground swimming pool which was only open during the summer months, and then down a steep hill to where the creek was, behind a stand of trees. At the bottom of the hill the road curved north, and as they drove through this section of the park Jimmy could see the picnic tables off to the left and to the right a valley sloping upward to the east. The playground located in the valley had the tallest sliding board and highest swings Jimmy had been on in his life, and next to it an area with metal posts sticking out of the ground where the adults played horse shoes during the annual summer church picnic.

Jimmy did not like the swings. During the last church picnic, or maybe the one before, Jimmy couldn't quite remember, Slugger had made him cry by swinging him as high as he could push him, until the swing almost flipped over the top bar, and Jimmy had almost fallen out. Of course, Slugger wouldn't let him off despite his begging, and started pushing him higher and higher again, until Jimmy calmed his panic long enough to time it and jump off when he was near the ground on the upswing. The momentum caused him to tumble to a stop scraping his knee, the blood drooling out hot and stinging while his brother laughed. Even church picnics held memories of terror and blood for Jimmy.

Past the playground, the road rose again and curved east and up the hill to the north of the valley. At the top of the hill was a narrow road leading south, and the baseball fields were on this road. The main park road continued out of the park, past a row of houses just outside it, and where the houses started and the park ended, the road became North Park Road.

Jimmy's mother turned at the narrow road to drop Jimmy off at the first ball field. On the corner was a strange and wonderful little shack, which Jimmy knew from picnics past was the called the Concession Stand. He had seen kids getting snow cones and popcorn from it during past picnics, even though Jimmy was never given any money to buy anything from it himself. On this morning, it was boarded up, probably because it was so cold, Jimmy thought. Jimmy's mom drove past the Concession Stand and parked on the left side of the road. There were two ball fields along that road, the closest to the stand had its backstop just beyond the stand, and bleachers ran down the third base line. Those bleachers, made of wood and painted dark green and five rows deep, had enough wear to discourage much scooting around, as splinters were sure to follow such activity. Ruts in the ground along the left field line were testament to the fact cars parked beyond where the bleachers ended, which was about third base, perpendicular to the left field line. Spectators pulled off the main park road and drove across the grass.

No bleachers were on the first base side of the first field, only a long bench for the players to sit on. There was no outfield wall. Left field ended with some trees far in the distance, at the boundary of the park, and right field sloped downward once it got beyond the reach of any Minor leaguer's batting strength, but a ball could roll down it to the next ball field, which was located further down the road at a few feet lower elevation. That field was positioned with its backstop in the southeast corner of the field, such that its left field merged into the right field of the first field. Any boy playing on the second field who could hit the ball in the air past the slope was given a home run. That field had no bleachers at all, only benches for the players.

Jimmy could see most of the boys were already there, and had paired off playing catch. Jimmy looked for Brad Schmidt and Scott Michaels, but he could not find them. He waved goodbye to his mother, who pulled out of her parking spot and called out, "I'll be back when practice is over." As there was no one to play catch with, Jimmy walked toward the bench to sit down.

"Hey!!" called out a voice, causing Jimmy to turn around. It was Kevin Morgan. "I just got here too!!" Jimmy could tell Kevin had been looking for someone to play catch with.

"Want to play catch?" asked Jimmy.

"Sure!!" Kevin answered, then both realized without a ball that would be difficult. They looked at each other to figure out the next step. Before they could solve it, they heard Coach Schmidt's voice booming out over the chirping boys.

"OK everyone, gather round." He was standing on the first base line with a clip board in his hands and a pencil stuck behind his ear. The boys, who were happily scattered about the field the moment before, quickly condensed around the coach. "All of you sit down on the bench," he commanded.

There was a struggle and an immediate game of Musical Chairs erupted. A couple of boys, Jimmy included, got pushed out of their first attempt at a perch and had to circle around to find a place, but Jimmy finally secured one at the end of the bench, next to Ken Ferry, and stared at his slip-ons. Jimmy could not believe he didn't wear tennis shoes this time either. From Jimmy's vantage point he could count eleven teammates, not including himself. That was a relief, since he knew they needed at least nine for a team.

"Today we are going to pick which player will play each position. You will each get to try a couple of field positions, and I want everyone to try to pitch," the coach continued.

Jimmy was sad to hear that, calculating if everyone had a chance to pitch someone would for sure be better than him and he would have to play another position. Instead of each boy selecting where they would play, Coach Schmidt, his assistant, and his two older sons would decide who would play where. They started by telling their little brother, Bradley, he would be the catcher. He didn't seem too upset, not like Jimmy would be, but he didn't seem too happy about it either. Jimmy could tell Brad didn't have much choice about it in any case, so he was making the best of it. Ken Farris ran to first base before they could stop him, and they could tell by the look on his face it would be best to keep him there. The other boys were seemingly chosen at random for the other positions by where they were sitting on the bench, and since Jimmy was at the end, all eight positions, minus the pitcher, were selected before they got to him. Kevin Morgan, Scott Michaels and Andy Peters, who told everyone to call him A.P., were at second, short and third base. The trio of boys who had laughed at how slow he was and had made sure he had to sit at the end of the bench were in the outfield; Mario Bruno, Johnny Mars, and Buddy Hoffman.

That left Derek Schmidt, Donny Demoss, and Steven Albright still sitting with Jimmy. Derek and Jimmy weren't too upset, as Derek didn't want to be there anyway, he had dolls he could be playing with, and Jimmy wanted to see what the other boys had to do before he had to do it himself. The coach may have expected mistakes, but Jimmy would gladly let others make them first. But the other boys weren't happy. "So what are we going to do?" asked Donny, as the other boys trotted off to their positions on the field.

"We'll start you boys pitching," responded the Coach. "Take them over there, son," he said to his oldest, pointing to a grassy strip across the road from the bench. Now Jimmy was wishing he had been chosen for a position. He wanted to be a pitcher, anyway his brother had told him he wanted to be a pitcher, but fantasizing about it and doing it in front of these other boys were two different things. He walked dutifully with the others toward the grass where they had been directed. The assistant coach came along too, and stood at a point there and dug a line into the ground at a level spot. The son then marched off several paces, as Jimmy had seen Slugger do, but he had a tape measure in his pocket which he used to mark the exact distance boys this age pitched from. Jimmy tried to gauge it against what Slugger had done, but was not sure whether it was farther or closer than he was used to in his backyard. As he knew what was coming next, he made sure not to be standing where he thought the line would form.

First, all the boys were told to stand in a row and watch as the assistant coach demonstrated how to wind up, something Jimmy had been practicing for weeks now.

It was obvious the other boys had not practiced a proper windup before when they were asked to copy the motions without the ball, as Slugger had first taught Jimmy. To the coaches' surprise, and their relief, left handed Jimmy already knew how to do it, so they didn't have to show him opposite the other boys. After a few minutes of this the inevitable line was formed, and no matter how hard he tried to be last, Jimmy ended up next to last.

The coach's son squatted into the catcher's stance, and Donny Demoss toed the line and went into his windup with live ammo. Not to Jimmy's surprise, Donny had not grasped the nuances of how to keep his balance during his windup. You could tell he had seen a windup, but never been instructed to do one correctly. By the time he had finished twisting, turning, and contorting his way to the delivery, he was so hopelessly unbalanced the ball flew beyond the catcher's desire to attempt to catch it. He looked over his shoulder as the ball sailed off into the trees.

As Jimmy tracked the flight of the ball into the woods he thought he saw someone crouching in the shadows. Jimmy was always imagining seeing things in dark places, so this was not that surprising, but what was surprising was this time it looked like Slugger and not some other scary monster. Jimmy looked harder, but whoever or whatever he thought he saw there was gone.

The coaches had thought of the probability of the pitchers' inaccuracy and had extra balls at the ready. Donny continued throwing as the next boy in line ran off to retrieve the first ball. Jimmy didn't volunteer to help in the chase. If it was Slugger, and Slugger did not want Jimmy to know he was there, Jimmy didn't want Slugger to know he knew he was there. Plus, it was probably just his nervous imagination.

"Keep it down!!" shouted the catcher.

Donny tried to comply, and the next pitch bounced into the ground. After ten chances and not putting any of them where he had tried to throw them, Donny had to turn the task over to Steven Albright. Steven was better, slightly. The running and searching through the brush to find the ball Donny had thrown had taken the edge off, so he wasn't trying to throw it as hard as Donny had, but still, keeping his balance through a windup was not that easy. By the time he had finished his ten, he had thrown a couple which could be considered strikes, but there was no hint of consistency on the horizon when he handed the ball to Jimmy.

Jimmy was startled out of his imagination when the ball was placed in his hands. He took a deep breath and toed the line. As he went into his windup, all thoughts of Slugger, how cold it was, and the other boys staring at him, went away. His only thoughts were on making sure he placed his foot in the right place, his leg in the right place, his arm at the right angle, and taking the final step directly toward the target. He let it go and it wasn't perfect. It didn't sail away, or bounce away, in fact the catcher didn't have to reach that far, but Jimmy wasn't happy. His unhappiness caused him to nail the next one. The catcher did not have to move his glove.

"Good pitch," the son said. Jimmy hadn't heard that when the first boys pitched. It re-enforced what he already knew. When it left his hand, he knew it was the best pitch to be thrown that day. Jimmy smiled. He'd make it through, he thought. On the next pitch, he went all out, lifting his leg like Juan Marichal, the master, did. Jimmy had never thrown a ball as hard as that pitch. And when he let it go, he knew it was bad. This pitch would have been a window breaker in his garage. Because of the windup he had just seen the catcher was not surprised at what was coming and was ready to spring up and catch it with some confidence.

"You don't need to throw it that hard, Jimmy," he said at the identical time Jimmy was thinking it. Except Jimmy wasn't so sure he wouldn't need to throw it that hard if someone was swinging at it. Jimmy remained calm enough to not go overboard for the next four or five pitches, and all were close to the target, even though Jimmy wasn't happy if the catcher had to move his glove an inch to make the catch. In Jimmy's universe, he shouldn't have to, or so he had been taught. On the eighth and ninth he focused as hard as he could, and the glove did not move. He felt so good about it he was careless on the tenth and bounced it in, which surprised the catcher so much he forgot to put his glove down in time and it bounced off his knee.

"Aaaooow !!" he yelled as he hopped up and down to take the sting out of his kneecap, which had received the blow perfectly, if the intent had been to maximize the pain.

Jimmy's confidence, at an all-time high the second before that pitch, quickly plummeted to an all-time low. Not only had he thrown a lousy pitch on his last chance, he had hurt the assistant coach catcher who would probably tell his dad, and that was that as far as Jimmy being a pitcher. In fact, he didn't have to tell his dad, as his howl had been heard by everyone and his dad and brothers were already doubled over in laughter.

From there, Jimmy's transgressions and triumphs were quickly forgotten by the next pitcher's performance, Derek Schmidt. Jimmy's first thought was 'he throws like a girl' but then realized what an insult that was to the girls he had seen throw before. Most if not all could do much better than Derek. Deeper still was the fact in Jimmy's universe it was one thing to not know how to throw a ball and it was quite another to not know how to throw a ball and not care; but in Derek's universe there was obviously no such distinction. Derek didn't attempt to wind up, or even turn his body to make a regular throw, or step toward the catcher. He just flung it, and it didn't seem to matter to him if the catcher caught it in the air or rolling. At least there was no chance of the ball going past the catcher, since the ball was never thrown hard enough. The other boys were too shocked, too embarrassed for him, to even tease Derek about it. Jimmy wondered how long that would last.

After Derek was finished, the four boys were sent to the main field. Jimmy was sent to right field, replacing Johnny Mars. As Johnny trotted off to take his turn pitching, he said to Jimmy, "You can have right field. I'll be the starting pitcher anyway!!"

Jimmy didn't mind Johnny's taunt. What he did mind was the cold breeze he suddenly noticed once he was alone in the outfield. The Coach was hitting the ball to each player at each position, and stopping to explain where the ball should be thrown. Since a right fielder doesn't need to do much, Jimmy stood there and shivered. When the ball was eventually hit toward him he wasn't ready for it and it bounced past him and rolled down the hill. It rolled so far Jimmy was tired of running before he reached it and walked the last few steps.

When Ken Farris took his turn to pitch, Jimmy was called into the infield to play first base. The coach hit ground balls to each of the other infielders, and they threw the ball to Jimmy instead of the coach. Jimmy was told to stand on the base and stretch out toward the ball so he could catch it as soon as possible. He had to keep his foot on the base though, or the coach would yell at him. Even when they threw the ball and it bounced, he had to keep his foot on the bag and try to reach and catch it. Once the ball was thrown so far away Jimmy couldn't keep his foot on the base and still catch it so he let the ball sail past, even though he might have caught it if he had taken a step or two. The coach yelled at him for that too. The result was he came to understand the first option was to catch it with his foot on the base, and the second option was to catch it with his foot off the base, but he should try to catch it no matter what.

Next thing he learned was he wasn't supposed to stand there with his foot on the base when the pitcher pitched it, he was supposed to stand a couple of steps away to be able to catch a ball hit on his side of the infield, and then run to the base and step on it if the ball was hit to someone else and they threw it to him. Now that added another dimension to what had seemed a fun position to play. He didn't have to run much, and he got to do what he thought he was best at, which was catch the ball, and it wasn't boring because he had to do something almost every time the ball was hit. Right field, he decided, was more boring and more frightening, and potentially more tiring, as running after the ball had shown him. He figured catching a ball hit by someone would hurt more than catching a ball thrown by someone, at least someone as small as he was, not someone as big as Slugger.

Jimmy was content as the practice came close to the end and he was still playing first base. After the last boys finished their turns pitching, the Coach gathered them together on the field. He spoke to them about the first game, which would occur that very Saturday, and they had to pick up their uniforms between now and then. He told them when they needed to be at the park, and the game would be played right here, on this diamond. And then, as Jimmy's mind drifted back to the cold wind, and the hope his mother would be there to pick him up soon, the coach continued, "We've narrowed it down to three boys, as far as who will be the starting pitcher. Johnny Mars, Scott Michaels, and Jimmy Williams. You three come with me, and the others take a position and we'll have batting practice."

The three boys trotted back to the spot they had pitched from before. Jimmy was nervous, yet somehow calm. If he didn't get to pitch, hopefully he would get to play first base, so he was content. As they walked across the road, Johnny elbowed Jimmy in the side, not too hard, but hard enough for Jimmy to feel the intent. "You don't stand a chance, boy," he said, emphasizing the word boy in a way he had heard his father called boy. Slugger had long ago added that word to the list of words that got any white boy beaten up if uttered in his direction, but his dad did not react to it. At this point in his life Jimmy hadn't decided what his go-to response for this word would be, and he was still a boy by any measure so he didn't have to have a go-to response yet, but he knew at that instant he wanted to beat Johnny at pitching more than he wanted to be the starting pitcher. His nervous calm was replaced with anger and a quiet resolve.

Johnny Mars went first. He could throw the ball harder than Jimmy; that much was clear, but accuracy was not his strong suit. He was bigger and faster and stronger, but maintaining the proper balance throughout a windup took more than that. Maybe three of his ten chances were strikes. Three more had to be shagged, as the catcher had no chance to stop them.

Scott Michaels did better, maybe half of his were strikes, but when he missed, he missed wildly. Five strikes, five shags.

When Jimmy's turn came, he was confident he could do better. The door was open for sure. But on his first pitch he didn't take his deep breath, didn't focus on his steps, and when he delivered he was slightly off balance. He tried to compensate, but the ball bounced before it reached its target. But just as Jimmy's confidence started to wane, he heard Johnny giggle. He turned to Johnny and stared, pressing his lips together, and out of the corner of his eye, he thought he saw a shadow moving in the trees beyond. This time he was sure it was Slugger.

Jimmy turned back to his pitching position, toed the mark, took a deep breath, and went into his windup. It was perfect, that delivery, perfect. The glove did not move. Johnny stopped giggling, and Jimmy turned and glared at him again. Then he repeated the process. The glove did not move. Then he did it a third time, a fourth, and a fifth.

"I think this kid's got it," said the catcher to his father.

Jimmy stopped, staring at the boy catching and then at his father, then went into his windup. Again, he did not focus, and the ball bounced in again.

"That's enough, we don't want him getting too tired," said the Coach.

"OK, it's enough for me too," said his son.

"Wait," said Johnny. "I want another chance!"

The Coach looked at him, rolled his eyes, and said, "Son, before this season is over, everyone who wants to pitch will get to pitch. But for the first game, it's Jimmy."

Jimmy forgot to look again for Slugger hiding in the trees. He was never sure if it was him or his imagination. But when they rejoined the rest of the team on the diamond, and the coach told Jimmy to go to the pitcher's mound, he knew something was real.

The other boys were sent to where they would start the first game. The coach gave them some final fielding practice and each got a chance to hit if they hadn't before, but Jimmy spent the rest of the practice in the clouds. What an unexpected miracle it was that on this day he had expanded from a skinny kid who everyone could beat up, including his sisters, to being the starting pitcher on his first baseball team.

When he saw his mother in the car, and saw his sisters in it with her, he knew if it was hard for him to believe what had just happened, it would be impossible for his sisters to believe. It took all the discipline he could muster, years of practice went into this moment, to be able to state calmly, in a matter-of-fact way, he would be the starting pitcher in the first baseball game of his life and all the other boys' lives on this team. He was the only boy on his team who could utter those words when their sisters asked them how practice went.

"I'm the starting pitcher!!!" he screamed as softly as he could through his excitement, which wasn't close to being soft. He barely had the car door open before the words tumbled out of his mouth. His sisters didn't have a chance to ask him anything.

"Sure you are," said JoAnn.

"It doesn't matter if you believe me," said Jimmy, so joyfully and confidently she had to begin to believe him. "I'm still going to be the starting pitcher."

CHAPTER
Nineteen

J immy's great grandmother, who everyone plainly called Gramma, lived on the corner of Seventh Street and Anderson, the same street as the Williams family. Five houses, plus Seventh Street, stood between her house and theirs. She lived by herself, as both her husband and brother, who Jimmy remembered vaguely, had died years before. She was so old Jimmy couldn't conceive what her age could be. He had never asked her, which was very odd for Jimmy, but since Jimmy's mother had made it clear her grandmother was not to be pestered by too many questions, on promise of severe pain, maybe it wasn't that odd.

As the years passed since Gramma had lived alone and Harry had purchased the house nearby, Hazel Williams provided a greater and greater portion of her former nurturer's daily care and feeding. Jimmy was too young to understand it, maybe even Slugger didn't understand it, but Gramma was slowly, softly, slipping into a happy state of dementia. It would take another ten years for it to completely take her mind, but she was already missing meals and she had fallen down the stairs at least once. Hazel was in the habit of sending her dinner every day by way of one of the children and sometimes Slugger or Jaqueline would even spend the night in her spare bedroom. In the not-too-distant future, this would be a task Jimmy would take over from his brother, as someone would have to spend every night with her.

But on this day, after Jimmy had finished his dinner and washed his face and hands, his was the task to take his Gramma her portion of the family meal. His mother used aluminum trays, the kind in which frozen dinners were packaged in those days, placing each food item in separate sections as her Gramma liked it. She then slid the food filled tray into a paper bag. When that bag was handed to Jimmy, he was under strict orders to not only go straight to Gramma's house without stopping, but to keep the tray level in the bag or risk his mother's wrath. If Gramma's food got mixed, his mother, and then he, would hear about it.

Out of the house and down the front sidewalk he marched with the tray, hoping he didn't see Joe along the way. He of course was bursting to tell him about the upcoming game, but in his universe, that would lead to quality problems with the food delivery he had been charged with, and Jimmy knew it would be better to let himself burst than to let those problems happen. The tray needed to be out of his hands as soon as possible, as the danger of spilling it was directly related to how long he had to hold it, so he scooted down the main sidewalk past the one-armed man's house and his almost always barking dog, which was oftentimes tied to one of the poles of the clothes drying line that ran along the side of his house. It wasn't always barking, but it always was when it was tied to the pole and Jimmy walked past. After clearing that obstacle, he slowed to a tiptoe in front of Joe Gurnsey's brother's house, preparing to silently pass the next, which was Joe's house. As he bobbed from toe to toe he peered into Joe's front door, through the screen, and thought he saw Joe at the kitchen table so he ran a few steps to make sure he wasn't seen. Then he passed the last two houses on the block, small tidy white houses with bright white fences so short even Jimmy could jump over them, even though he never tried it. There were no children living there, so to Jimmy the houses may as well have been occupied by ghosts or space aliens, and the contrast between them and the unkempt, dirty shacks of the Gurnseys' was completely lost on him, even though his mother never failed to complain about it. Then he came to Seventh Street, paved with tar and gravel, barely worth looking both ways before crossing, as a busy traffic day might bring twenty cars down it between sunrise and darkness. Jimmy managed it without incident.

Gramma's house was much older than Jimmy's. Unlike Jimmy's house, which had a small concrete pad as its front porch, Gramma's house had stairs leading up to a long wooden porch, as wide as the house, big enough for a love seat sized swing. In the summer, Gramma would sit in that swing and holler across the street at her neighbors and wave at the passing cars. The stairs creaked as Jimmy climbed them. He opened the never locked door and stepped in and saw his Gramma sitting in her chair near the front door, watching television. The television was placed just inside the front door, to the right as he walked in, in the living room. As was her custom, she was watching Gunsmoke.

Jimmy, after greeting his Gramma, strode past her into the kitchen and put the tray on the table, and with that mission accomplished he breathed a sigh of relief. Needing even more relief, he walked around the table which dominated the small space and entered the small powder room located in the corner. He loved to use this bathroom because it was where Gramma kept her razor strap hanging from the wall. The family legend was she used to whip Slugger with it when he was small and lived with his Gramma and mother there. Jimmy couldn't see how someone so tiny, and slow, and rickety could even catch Slugger to whip him, but the razor strap was a fearsome looking weapon and the thought Slugger had taken some licks from it made Jimmy smile every time he saw it.

The razor strap was made of leather, a foot long, three inches wide and a fraction of an inch thick. Three such straps were tied together by means of a hole through each and a cord. Jimmy couldn't figure out how it could possibly be used to sharpen razors, but it was obvious how it could be used to smack someone across their bare legs and butt. And since he had never felt it, as it had been retired when Slugger and his mom moved out, he had no painful memories of it himself.

After coming out of the bathroom, he headed for the door, but his Gramma stopped him and asked him to sit down on the couch on the opposite wall from the television. She had not risen from her chair while Jimmy was in the bathroom, so it couldn't be a scolding for mixing the meatloaf with the fried potatoes. Jimmy sat down and waited for his Gramma to speak.

"I hear you are going to play your first baseball game tomorrow," said Gramma, smiling.

Gramma wore her hair in a bun, on top of her head, whenever she left the house. But at home she would take it down and brush it as she sat and watched TV. It was long, all the way down her back, and gray, and bone straight like that of a Native American. She was just as light skinned as Jimmy's mother, maybe even lighter, and had high cheek bones and what looked to Jimmy to be gray eyes. Every person who saw her thought she was a Native American mixed with African, and that is what she claimed. This was long before anyone had heard of DNA, which disproved this in almost all cases, but she was undoubtedly mixed with some tribe, be it Native American or European, which had straight hair and fair skin. It was far easier for her to claim herself part Indian than part White.

Having been born in the 1880's, she was a walking history book. She was born before cars were common. Her mother and two older sisters were lost to a fever when she was thirteen, so she was forced into an early start on wisdom by having to take over the care and feeding of her younger siblings from that time. To her the Big War was World War I, not II, because her friends and family died in that one, and then she lost even more of them to Influenza than the Big War. She married and buried two husbands, and bore and buried three children. She had cared for and buried all her eight siblings except the one who still lived by Wallace Park. When it came to the practical knowledge which goes by the name of Common Sense, but wasn't very common in Jimmy's universe from what he had observed so far, Gramma had more than anyone Jimmy knew.

"Yes, Gramma," Jimmy responded.

"You know, your grandfather, your mother's dad, played baseball," she mused.

Gramma was always telling stories, the same stories, and by this time in his life Jimmy thought he had heard every one of them, but he hadn't heard this one, and he was sure he was about to hear it now. He waited, but his Gramma did not speak, instead staring at Marshall Dillon lecturing Festus and pulling the brush through her hair in long, slow, strokes. Jimmy finally stood, his fidgeting having expanded to the point it would not accommodate sitting any more.

"Jimmy," she said as she saw him rise, diverting her eyes from the screen to stare up at him, "Always remember, sticks and stones may break your bones, but words will never hurt you."

Jimmy stopped, his mind stopped, and he looked at his Gramma, puzzled. "OK, Gramma," was all he could say once he started thinking again. "You should eat your food before it gets cold. You want me to bring it to you?"

"No, Jimmy, leave it on the table. I'll eat it after Maverick goes off," she said with a smile, her eyes now back on the television.

Jimmy thought to correct her as he reached for the front door screen, but decided not to, instead saying, "OK, I'll see you on Sunday, Gramma."

"Don't forget what I told you, Jimmy," said Gramma, again staring up at him sternly.

"I won't, Gramma," said Jimmy as he smiled and walked out the door.

As soon as he crossed the street he could see Joe standing in the sidewalk in front of his house waiting for him. He had been sitting at the kitchen table when he saw his friend walking past his house, but he wasn't in a hurry to stop him, knowing he'd be back in a few minutes, as this was a routine everyone on the block was accustomed to by now.

"Hey, Jimmy!!" he shouted as soon as Jimmy stepped past the second white picket fence, "Guess what?"

As Jimmy had news for Joe he thought more important, he was too annoyed to guess. "What?" he said.

"I'm on the Cubs!!" said Joe.

"What do you mean you're on the Cubs?" asked a startled Jimmy.

"You know, the baseball team you're on," Joe explained with excitement.

Jimmy was not prepared for this, and at first the idea of Joe being on the team was unsettling. Jimmy did not like being followed, the concept having led to so many uncoverings and mounds of ridicule in his past even sincere followers like Joe were suspect. Plus, it made no sense, as he hadn't come to either practice. All Jimmy could say was "What?"

"My brother took me down to the Park District and they told us it wasn't too late to sign up, so I did. They said your team was short on players and they let me join," explained Joe.

Jimmy remembered they already had enough players, so he wasn't sure about Joe's claim. "Did you get a uniform?" asked Jimmy, as a test. Jimmy and his mom had picked up his jersey and hat the day before.

Joe disappeared into his house. He returned with a purple jersey which had CUBS on the front, just like the one Jimmy had, except the letters looked taller and thinner. "I got this, but they'd run outta hats. Good thing my dad has a REAL Cubs hat I can wear."

"A real Cubs hat?" Jimmy asked.

"You know, from the real Chicago Cubs baseball team," responded Joe.

This was the first time Jimmy considered there was a real Cubs baseball team. When Joe went into his house and returned with the blue hat with a red and white C on it, Jimmy realized he had seen this hat being worn many times. He had assumed it stood for Canton.

"And you know what else? The biggest rivals of the real Cubs are the Cardinals, from Saint Louis. Almost everyone in town is either a Cardinals fan or a Cubs fan. And that's who we play first!!" Joe exclaimed.

Jimmy thought about it. The hats with the red bird on them were Cardinal hats. He had seen about equal numbers of them around town. Jimmy had his first inkling of the sports rivalry which divided the town of Canton in two. Half of the people in town were Cardinal fans and half were Cubs fans. No other team even rated. You had to choose.

The city of Canton, Illinois was located nearly midway between the cities of Chicago and Saint Louis. Saint Louis was the northernmost Southern city in the US, while Chicago was as Northern a city as any, and they were only a few hundred miles apart. The Cardinals had fans all the way from Louisiana and Mississippi in the south to Colorado in the west. Good country folks were Cardinal fans. Good country folks felt safe going to Saint Louis for games. Good country folks knew Chicago as an evil, unsafe place, full of unruly dark skinned people and foreign languages, and the Cubs represented Chicago. They still knew how to keep those people in line in Saint Louis. Add to that the fact the Cardinals were average during the bad years and great during the good years; and the Cubs were normally terrible, occasionally decent, and always, always, disappointing in the end; and the result was an uneven rivalry in results, but an intense one in its day-to-day dealings. Cardinal fans felt superior and their team, in fact, was. The Cub fans main delight was in spoiling the Cardinals seasons more so than winning championships themselves, because that was a delight they had never felt.

"I'm the starting pitcher," said Jimmy matter-of-factly to change the subject, plus he couldn't wait to say it any longer.

"No, you're not. You can't be," said a now even more startled Joe.

Jimmy shrugged, knowing he could prove it later.

"Are you serious?" asked Joe, seeing Jimmy seemed serious.

Jimmy did not answer. He had spent enough time in this conversation, and his mother would be walking down the front walk of their house to look for him any minute. Jimmy had a sixth sense about these things. He turned away from Joe and continued down the sidewalk toward his house, and true to form, just like Haley's comet, his mother was stepping out of the house when he turned off the sidewalk and up the walk to his front porch.

CHAPTER
Twenty

The morning of June 24, 1967, promised to evolve into the most beautiful day of the year in Canton Illinois. Before he could even open his eyes, Jimmy was brought into consciousness by the smell of freshness blowing in from his bedroom window, and the harmonious singing of a passing flock of birds. When his eyes popped open, the light flowing into his room confirmed the day would be sunny and warm. Because of his developing morbid sense of humor, he laughed at the thought of all the days he wouldn't mind it raining, the weather was perfect. He imagined himself waking up on the day of his execution, like the guy in the book about the French Revolution, and everything would depend on the weather. If it rained it would be postponed and if it was sunny the beheading would go forward, in the public square in front of a cheering crowd.

But the smell of bacon broke his sinister mood as he dropped his legs over the side of the bed and slid down to the floor. He had a happy smile he couldn't explain as he walked into the bathroom that wouldn't wipe off as he washed his face, but as he looked at it in the mirror, he realized he had to before his sisters could see it. Today was serious and he had to act like it.

When he came into the kitchen and saw there was not only the standard eggs and bacon, but also fresh, homemade biscuits, the smile returned and he could not hide it. His mother was standing with her back to him, running water in the sink over the still steaming skillet she had scrambled his eggs in.

"Good morning, Mom!!" Jimmy said with much enthusiasm.

His mother turned and smiled, but did not answer. Jimmy was a very sensitive little boy. That's where his ability tease his older siblings so effectively and mercilessly came from, when he realized something bothered them, he could zero in right away. Instead of sitting down he stood beside his mother, and stared up at her.

"What's the matter, Mommy?" he asked.

She turned to him, shutting off the faucet and wiping her hands on the apron she was wearing, and tried to change the subject. "Sit down and eat, Jimmy. You have a big day ahead."

Jimmy did not like to see his mother in this kind of quiet mood. When she was happy she was never quiet. Even when everyone around her was sad, or depressed, she would still be bouncing around and singing, trying to be the one to raise everyone else's spirits. When she was sad, she could never hide it from Jimmy.

Knowing her son, she knew he would not stop asking questions and leave her alone with her thoughts until she told him what was bothering her.

"It's your brother. He hasn't called or anything," she said.

The worry had been growing in her every minute since he had run out. Slugger had run away before, so many times she had lost track, the first time when he was three years old. He ran out of the house to avoid a spanking his grandfather was about to administer for the offense of pulling every leaf off his mother's favorite house plant, the very one he had told the boy to stop touching just hours before. He hid behind a bush in the back yard, shivering in the cold, as the adults in the house could not contain their laughter. Despite how cute and funny it was, however, Slugger still had to take his licks when he finally came back in the house. She was thinking maybe this time he wouldn't come back. Maybe he would find an Army recruiter not worried about the birthdate he put on his form being correct, or the name for that matter, the quota being the quota. Maybe he had been arrested, or hurt. Maybe he was somewhere right now, in a ditch…

"He'll come back soon," said Jimmy with absolute confidence. Jimmy had no means to be sure his brother was coming back, but he knew what his mother needed to hear. He was an A student. He always figured things out before anyone else. Maybe his mother would believe he had his brother figured out too. Maybe he could make her believe they had been in contact, and Slugger had sworn Jimmy to silence about where he was.

To make his act seem more believable, he sat down to his breakfast and began to eat like all was well with the world. And when he started to chew on the bacon, it was. Bacon was comfort food for Jimmy, his favorite thing in the world to eat. When he smelled it, it reminded him of the sound of his mother and father in the kitchen, while he lay awake in bed, laughing and talking as his father ate his customary late-night snack, a bacon sandwich and a bowl of vanilla ice cream.

"Where are the girls?" Jimmy asked, for the first time aware his sisters were nowhere to be seen, and could not be heard.

"They are at your Gramma's," his mother answered without further elaboration.

"They aren't coming to watch my game?" asked Jimmy. At this point, he was hoping he had gotten her mind off Slugger. His certainly was. Jimmy was sensitive, but he couldn't wallow in it. The bacon had reminded him of the great, fantastic world all around him. It reminded him of what he had to do that day.

"No, your dad is taking you. I'm going to Gramma's myself, as soon as I clean up after breakfast. We are helping her with her cleaning today," she said.

That was a shock to Jimmy. His father would take him? His father had shown no interest in the fact Jimmy had joined the Cubs. He had never even played catch with Jimmy, ever in his life Jimmy could remember, it was always Slugger. He hadn't taken him to sign up, to get his gear, to practice, or anything. He knew the money for his entry fee, his hat, and his jersey had come from the thick, black wallet his father kept on top of his dresser when he was at home, but that was the extent of his involvement. Jimmy hadn't even bothered to tell him he would be the starting pitcher!

Jimmy was still sitting there, deep in thought after eating the last bite on his plate, when his mother broke the silence as she walked out the front door. "Make sure you put your Cubs shirt on and don't forget to tie your shoe laces!!" she called out, ending his day dream as the door slammed shut.

On most Saturday mornings Jimmy's dad worked part time, cleaning the offices of small businessmen. He did the same in the evenings during the week, after coming home and eating dinner with his family. When Jimmy finished putting on his best blue jeans, his PF Flyers, and his Cubs shirt, he found himself alone in the house, sitting on the couch in the living room waiting for his father to return. Despite the fact this was one of the rare occasions Jimmy had the television to himself and cartoons might be on, he did not flip the switch. As he tried to sit there in silence, he felt a warm glow in his stomach he had never felt before, and he couldn't sit still and started pacing the room. That led to the terrible thought his father would be late, and he would miss the game, and the horror grew as the clock softly ticked on the wall behind the couch. By the time he heard the familiar sound of the car crunching the gravel as his father drove up the alley, Jimmy burst out of the backdoor running to greet him.

"Hi Dad!!" cried Jimmy, running and skipping. "Are you ready to go?" His father had not even rolled to a stop yet, and Jimmy had to jump out of the way to avoid getting knocked down by the car door when his dad opened it.

"Give me a few minutes, Jimmy" said his dad, who walked slowly, to Jimmy anyway, into the house.

Jimmy followed him and was met by a closed bathroom door. He stood outside and waited, not too patiently, while his father washed and changed. After what seemed like an eternity, his father emerged, smelling like talcum powder and after shave, wearing a casual short sleeved shirt and pants, slip-on leather sandals, and dark socks. Jimmy thought he was overdressed for the park and if he wore something like that he would get it dirty or torn and would be in big trouble, but his dad would be OK. Jimmy never saw him do anything like swing on the swings, or run through puddles.

"Let's go, Jimmy," said his father, and off they went, out the back door and into the future.

CHAPTER
Twenty-One

Jimmy and his father didn't talk much. It wasn't that they were distant, his father was always a positive presence in his life, but they just didn't talk much. His father had passed down to Jimmy his delicate physical nature and was seldom well enough to be talkative at the end of his long days of work, and Jimmy's grandfather had passed down to his father his quiet manner and lack of emotional expression. Jimmy didn't get much of his personality from his father, other than his analytical skills he was more like his mother. They were the ones constantly trying to find something funny to say.

Jimmy stared out of the car window, wearing his barely broken-in baseball glove on his hand as if a ball might fly through the window at any second for him to catch. The clouds were puffy and the air rushing in was warm on his face, and he could hear the familiar sound of an ice cream truck somewhere in the distance, the thought of ice cream making him slightly nauseous. As was his usual practice, Harry gauged his speed so he could make every green light between Anderson Street and Big Creek Park, all three of them, and sped past the park entrance his wife used to the second entrance, North Park Drive. As they turned into the park, Jimmy's peaceful ride turned to chaos.

Instead of the smooth ride down the lane past the bleachers he expected, there was a mini traffic jam. Cars were pulling off the road from both directions, and parking along the left field line beyond the bleachers, forcing Harry to wait before proceeding. Jimmy could see people sitting in the bleachers, and children, smaller than Jimmy even, running up and down. As they inched along, he could see the boys on the other team, the Cardinals, playing catch in their bright red uniforms. Beyond that, they came to the corner where the Concession Stand stood and Jimmy saw four or five people impatiently peering over the counter. As they turned the corner Jimmy could smell his second favorite food, popcorn, flowing out from the open stand. The cotton candy was on the wall behind.

Cars were also parking along the road on the first base side blocking his path, so Harry stopped the car in the road next to the bench where Coach Schmidt was standing with his son Brad to let Jimmy out. When he jumped out of the car, he saw most of the team was already there, playing catch and running around in a much more disorganized fashion in their purple Cubs jerseys than he had seen from the boys in red. He waved to his dad as he drove further down to find a place to park.

As he walked away from the car toward his coach, the first thing he noticed was the funny look on Brad's face. The second was the white cast on his right arm, and the blue sling it was held in. Before he could ask, Brad blurted out, "I fell out of a tree and broke my arm."

Jimmy had never tried to climb a tree before, and at that moment he realized what a good decision that had been. He never tried to climb a tree after this day either.

"Glad to see you, Jimmy. I was beginning to worry," said Coach Schmidt. "With my son, here, not able to play, we are really short on players."

"We don't have nine, Coach?" asked Jimmy.

"We should. We just have to make some changes," said the coach.

Jimmy was crestfallen, because he assumed this meant he wouldn't be pitching. On the other hand, as he looked around and saw how many people were coming to watch the game, maybe it was better he didn't pitch. All these people and noise were making him extremely nervous.

Coach Schmidt turned from Jimmy, and called out to one of the boys playing catch, "Bruno, come over here!!"

Mario Bruno came running, and Jimmy could see he was wearing a catcher's mitt. "I need you to warm Jimmy up," Coach Schmidt said, and turning to Jimmy, "Bruno will be catching now that Brad can't," with some disgust, as he also did not see much wisdom in climbing trees.

The coach took Jimmy to a spot behind the bench where he had drawn a line, and had Bruno stand in another. They started by tossing the ball to each other, and then Bruno was told to take a step back and they tossed more, then another step back, then another, until Bruno reached the second mark the Coach had drawn. Jimmy was then instructed to wind up and throw at "half speed," whatever that meant, to Bruno in a crouch. He focused on slowly and deliberately performing his windup and his follow through, and after a few throws, none of them too accurate, he saw Slugger.

Slugger had emerged from the same trees Jimmy thought he had seen him at practice, but this time he was not attempting to hide. He had been waiting in the park for Jimmy to arrive, and when he saw his father, not his mother, in the car he had not known what to do, so he stayed in the trees. As he contemplated finding another vantage point, where he could see the game and not be seen by his father, watching his brother struggle to warm up overcame that thought process and he stepped out.

Harry had in the meantime parked the car and walked to the bleachers behind the backstop. He could see Jimmy throwing and when he saw Slugger he gritted his teeth, but did not move. Sitting stoically, he waited for what would happen next.

Slugger walked over to Coach Schmidt and nodded, and they both watched Jimmy's next effort. Jimmy stepped too high, nervous about his brother's eyes on him, and sailed one over Bruno's head.

"Just relax, Jimmy, and keep your eyes on the target," commanded Slugger.

Harry leaned over in the bleachers, staring at the scene intently. He wondered if he would need to get up and go over there. It was not in his nature to make a scene, but he would if that was what was called for. His jaw clenched. Jimmy took a deep breath after the ball had been retrieved, went through his motion, and hit the target. All the weight was off his shoulders, if only for a moment, as he repeated the process three more times. Harry's jaw unclenched.

As Jimmy wound up again he saw a man emerge from a car wearing all black and carrying a bag which looked like the one Santa used at Christmas. He walked to the backstop and dumped the contents onto the concrete behind it. In it were the three bases, white and puffy, containers of brand new balls, and a curious looking brush.

A large black pad was also inside, and he stuffed it into his shirt before proceeding to the field to set the bases in their holes, which he verified with a tape measure pulled from the bag as well. He then strolled over to the Cubs' bench and asked "Who's the coach?"

The answer seemed obvious to Jimmy, but Coach Schmidt raised his hand anyway and started to walk toward the man.

"I'm Bill, the umpire," he said with the kind of slow Midwestern drawl any movie cowboy would be proud of. "I need your line-up card. Bring it to me at home plate and we can get the game started. You are the visitors, so your guys need to come off the field so the Cardinals can take their positions."

"I've got it right here," said Coach Schmidt, pulling a piece of paper from his back pocket.

Bill the Umpire did not care to notice. He had given his instructions, and he expected them to be followed. He walked as slowly as he talked to the backstop, and he motioned to the Cardinals coach to meet him there as well.

Coach Schmidt hesitated, then called out to his troops, "OK, everybody in!!"

As Jimmy sat there he counted eleven boys, not including Brad. Instead of speaking to them, the Coach walked to home plate, where he shook hands with the Cardinals coach, and they exchanged pieces of paper, the lineup cards. Coach Schmidt walked back with his pieces of paper, and finally addressed the squirming, laughing, excited kids all around Jimmy. Jimmy himself was too queasy to squirm. The moment he sat down and stopped moving, a rush of nausea had flooded his guts and he didn't know whether to run or cry, so he did neither. He just sat there to let whatever was about to happen, happen.

"OK, boys," said the Coach. "The game is about to start. We are the Visitors, so we are up to bat first. I'm going to tape the batting order up on the end of the bench. You guys need to make sure you know who you bat after. The order is:

Kevin Morgan (2nd base)

Scott Michaels (SS)

Johnny Mars (CF)

Buddy Hoffman (RF)

Andy Peters (LF)

Mario Bruno (C)

Ken Ferry (1st)

Donny Demoss (3rd)

Jimmy Williams (P)

If you are not listed in the order, you are a substitute. Don't worry, I'll make sure all of you get to play."

As soon as those words came out of his mouth, Jimmy saw Joe Gurney's dad's truck and Joe Gurnsey jumping out of the back of it. He was wearing his blue Cubs hat and jeans with holes in the knees. He dashed to the bench with the biggest smile Jimmy had ever seen on his face.

"I made it just in time!!" he shouted out.

Coach Schmidt just glared at him, and Joe sat on the bench, oblivious to it. Jimmy shook his head, and he could see people in the bleachers, who had witnessed the late arrival, laughing. Jimmy also noticed the number of people in the bleachers had increased, and most them were wearing red.

"Boys, I want you to know that we are facing what is supposed to the best team in the league. They have the best pitcher, a kid named Paul Hart. But I have faith in you boys. I am sure you will do just fine." And thus ended the first pep talk of Jimmy's organized sports life. Some of the boys seemed genuinely inspired and cheered.

The Cardinals, on the other side of the diamond, were standing in a circle, their coach in the middle. He said some words Jimmy couldn't hear, but the tone rose to a crescendo, after which all the boys said in unison, "Let's win, Cardinals !!" which was followed by whistles and hoots and claps from the stands. The boys in red, when they trotted out to their positions, had the kind of stretch pants Jimmy had seen on players on television, and some of them had shoes with spikes. They threw the ball around with precision, as if they had a practiced routine. No way, Jimmy thought, could the Cardinals being doing this after only two practices like the Cubs had. In fact, Jimmy didn't think the Cubs could do it after ten practices.

And that was before he saw Paul Hart throw a baseball. After the first pitch Jimmy knew he may never, even when he was as old as Slugger, throw a baseball as hard as he saw Paul Hart throw it. Paul threw it so hard competing against him as a pitcher wasn't what was on Jimmy's mind what-so-ever, it was fully occupied with thoughts of being hit by a ball thrown by Paul Hart. More precisely it was focused on how to avoid being hit by a ball thrown by Paul Hart. And he could tell by watching his team mates watch Paul Hart throw they were thinking the same thing. But not only that, the kid was accurate. He repeated the same motion every time, and put the ball where he aimed it. Maybe he would strike out in three pitches and not get hit, Jimmy thought. He would consider that a positive outcome.

CHAPTER
Twenty-Two

I n a small town like Canton, youth league baseball was a very important form of summer entertainment. It was free, for starters, and the park was beautiful, and if you had a family the younger ones could play in the park playground while the older ones watched the game or played in it. It was more than probable everyone attending would have at least one friend or friend's child on one of the teams to root for, or have an enemy to root against, and for those few who didn't have either it was even more probable there was nothing else going on in town more exciting to do during these lazy afternoons.

The reputations of the boys of Canton as athletes started in Minor League baseball and culminated for those anointed few in their making one or more of the high school varsity teams in the years ahead. Not only would the baseball coach be there scouting, but also the high school football coach would come to most Minor League games to see who showed the potential to be his quarterback in ten years, and who would anchor his line. All the most important men in town would be there, urging their sons on to greatness, and making sure those same coaches knew who should be starting in a decade, and who would be signing their paychecks. The working-class families who made up the bulk of the town and the bulk of the teams ranged from those sitting as close to their superiors as they could in the bleachers, to soak up as much stray greatness as they could; to those who preferred to stay as far away as possible from the peculiar smell of the well-off and their lackeys. But everyone knew baseball and loved it, and once the game started, it became the most important thing.

Jimmy's father stayed as far away as he could from the rich and powerful, because despite Jim Crow laws not being in effect in states like Illinois, small towns like Canton had their ways of making sure black men knew their place. Choosing his seat was made easier by the fact the Cardinals were made up of the better off folks from the north end of town and he did not want their eyes on the back of his head, so he sat at the far end of the bleachers, as close to the Cubs bench and the other of the few Cubs fans as he could. Even though Jimmy knew where he was, it was like he was invisible as he sat so quietly. All the commotion around him had made Jimmy forget about Slugger as well, but when he thought to look for him, wondering if maybe he had slipped back into the trees, he found him where he would have least likely expected, sitting in the same row as his father, slightly more than an arm's length away. When Slugger had approached this spot, chosen so he could keep his eye on Jimmy as he warmed up, his father had given him no sign he would lash out if he came closer, but it was better to be prudent than rash and so he stayed far enough away to leap out of danger if he had to. Jimmy could tell they were not speaking, but at least sitting side by side with no one in-between, as the game began.

After watching Paul Hart mesmerize the crowd with his warm ups, Bill the Umpire strolled from behind the backstop, where he had been casually leaning against the chain link wall, and as he had hoped, all the boys stopped running and tossing balls around and stared back at him. Once he reached home plate he took the brush from his pocket, and used it to roughly wipe off the dirt. Then he stood and walked behind the Cardinals catcher, and called out to Paul Hart, "Are you ready?"

Paul Hart smiled and shook his head affirmatively. His teammates tossed the other balls toward their dugout, causing a mini-panic as balls bounced off balls and caromed about at unexpected angles, but order was quickly restored as they stopped spinning and were placed in a bag, one-by-one.

Bill turned to Kevin Morgan, who was standing off to the side of the backstop, swinging a bat too heavy for him, and said, "Batter Up!!!"

And with that Kevin walked to home plate to start the game amongst the enthusiastic cheers emanating from the bleachers and both benches. He was so nervous he walked into the batter's box on the left side, even though he was right handed. The cheers turned into speckled laughter as the crowd became aware of his confusion about where he should be standing, and how he should be holding the bat.

Bill looked at him with amusement. "Are you left handed?" he asked, knowing the answer already.

"No," said Kevin, realizing his mistake and dropping his head. He stepped across the plate, being careful not to put a dirty shoeprint on it, and stood as far away from it in the batter's box as the freshly drawn chalk line allowed. He raised the bat above his head in his batting stance, and Paul bent over to stare at the catcher's glove before starting his windup.

A sudden cacophony of sound assaulted the atmosphere as Paul started his motion, in the form of the Cardinals players yelling, whooping, and sarcastically singing out, "Hey batter, hey batter, batter, hey batter !!!" from the field and the bench. Little kids in the bleachers picked up on it too and the decibel level rose even higher as Paul twisted and turned, lifted his leg, and convincingly strode forward and threw. The mob of voices increased to a roar, singing, "Hey batter, batter, hey batter, batter, SWING!!"

Kevin's bat did not move.

"Strike one," said Bill the Umpire matter-of-factly as the ball snapped neatly into the catcher's glove.

183

Kevin's eyes, which even under normal circumstances were rather large, were now immense. What shocked him most was the fact that despite the huge size of his pupils, as the ball flew toward them it had not been seen by them. That might have been because he had closed them, but that fact was not apparent to Kevin Morgan at that moment. All he knew was he had heard the ball hit the glove before he had seen it.

The next pitch wasn't much better, except this time he kept his eyes open long enough to move the bat. By the time he had reached mid-swing the ball was already dribbling out of the catcher's mitt. It had impacted the glove and bounced out before the catcher could stop its escape.

"Ouch!!" he said, as he stood up and pulled off the mitt and shook his left-hand fingers. Once erect, the Cubs could see the Cardinals catcher was the biggest kid they had ever seen their age, taller and bigger.

"Come on, Hulk!!" called out one of the Cardinals in the infield, chuckling.

"Strike two," drawled out Bill, rather obviously.

Bill picked up the ball and threw it back to the pitcher.

Kevin Morgan did not know what to do next. He was still thinking about it when Bill, after watching the third pitch hit its target perfectly, leaned over and said, softly and firmly, "Yer' out, son."

As Kevin walked dejectedly to the bench and sat down, not a single Cub said a word of encouragement to him except the coach. No one laughed either, because they had no illusions of doing better.

Scott Michaels was up next. He decided he would be more aggressive. He used exorbitant amounts of energy to miss three straight pitches without ever threatening to hit anything other than the catcher's mitt, which he did after his last, most elaborate swing, on the back side as he let the bat go. Hulk was not amused, even though it did not seem to hurt him as much as catching the ball did. Scott glanced at the big kid he had just struck, picked up the bat as quickly as he could, and ran to the Cubs bench. This caused a slight delay, as the bat he was carrying was the bat Johnny Mars wanted to use. He had to trot over to pull it out of Scott's hands, who was sitting on the end of the bench farthest away from Hulk and was gripping it tightly, in case he needed it if Hulk came running after him.

Not that Johnny had any success with it either. He went to the plate with a ton of false bravado, and delayed the inevitable by stepping out of the box after each of the first two strikes, taking a few practice swings, and digging in the dirt with his toe. Unless he considered bothering Paul Hart enough with his tactics to get him to throw his first pitch outside of the strike zone, inside and high, making Johnny dive away and land on his backside, a success. At least Johnny had gotten one ball to go along with his three strikes, as the next pitch was right down the middle, and after the first two boys, it was an improvement.

CHAPTER
Twenty-Three

As the rest of the Cubs ran out to take their positions, Jimmy lingered in his seat, like the last drop of rain clinging to the car window before the wind inevitably rips it away. That slight hesitation only made his trot out to the pitcher's mound more noticeable. To see such a frail boy, his arms sticking out of his shirt like long brown pencils, brought a murmuring chuckle from the adults in the audience. The distinctions between Paul Hart and Jimmy Williams could not be greater and to the crowd were quite symbolic: Strong vs. Weak, Brave vs. Scared, Polished vs. Raw, Discipline vs. Chaos, White vs. Black. This game would be no contest.

Jimmy heard it as he picked up the ball Paul Hart had left next to the pitching rubber. He was used to it. Whenever he walked into a room of adults he could hear the whispers and looks of pity on their faces, as they gave their condolences to his mother. He had become accustomed to the self-assured look, that this boy would hold no threat to theirs, as weak as he obviously was. He had even developed a response, waiting and listening to the adult conversations which followed until he could answer some question or fill in some blank even the adults couldn't and do it with such nonchalance they knew it was a common place event, then watch out of the corner of his eye to see the look of surprise on their faces (and the look of pride on his mother's) when they realized his talent.

But those were mental victories, like spelling a word, or adding up numbers in his head, or singing a song, or reciting a Bible verse. When it turned to games of running and jumping and wrestling, Jimmy was the one laughed at and pitied, and he had never had to perform in a situation like this before, in front of so many people. He couldn't even begin to count them. More than twenty for sure, maybe more than one hundred, he couldn't tell. He stood with the ball in his hand and looked at all the faces.

"Hey Jimmy!!" called out Bruno, impatiently waiting behind home plate for Jimmy to throw him a few warm up pitches.

Jimmy turned and sheepishly realized he was supposed to be pitching. He went into his windup and sailed the first over Bruno's head. The ball hit the backstop and would have hit Bill the Umpire in the head if he hadn't bent over to pick up his water bottle. The crowd roared as he jumped at the sound of the ball hitting the chain link, and he quickly remembered turning his back on eight-year-old pitchers could lead to a large knot on the back of his head. Paul Hart was the exception, not the rule.

"I see I'm gonna hafta watch you, son," called out Bill to Jimmy.

The crowd got a larger chuckle out of that line. Jimmy didn't think it was funny, as he knew the ball should have been more accurate. He tried another, and it was also too high. Jimmy couldn't understand it. He was winding up correctly, but the ball was not going where he wanted it to. He forgot the crowd, the boys playing catch around him, and furrowed his brow, trying to decipher why the ball wasn't going where it should. Then he realized the pitcher's mound was truly a mound, and was above the level of home plate. This was a new experience for Jimmy, as he had only pitched from a flat surface before. But he figured out immediately what he needed to do to compensate, which was bend his knee further on his release, so with his arm at a lower level, the ball should be lower too. And he was right. The next few pitches were exactly where they should have been. He was happy, content, and he noticed the crowd had quieted and were busy occupying themselves with their popcorn, snow cones, and cigarettes.

But then Bill called out, "Batter Up!!", and Jimmy was no longer content. The first Cardinal batter stepped to the plate, and he was the shortest boy on either team. The strategy was obvious to the adults, but not to Jimmy. Most pitchers at this level, and most definitely in their first game, tended to be wild. If they started the game by walking the first batter it would set the trend and they usually ended up walking at least ten other guys before either the game ended or they had to be pulled for the next wild child. Then they brought up their Big Guns, three boys who were all taller, stronger, and meaner than anyone on the Cubs. The third of the three, called the 'clean-up hitter', was of course Chuck "Hulk" Hanson, the catcher, the biggest boy in the Minor League. If one of them walked as well, plus another got a hit, the Cardinals would be up two or three runs before the first inning was over, and the rout would be on.

Jimmy stood in his stance, and just before he wound up for the first time to a live batter in a real game, the rest of the Cubs started to chatter like the Cardinals had. Jimmy did not want chatter. Jimmy did not understand why anyone would do that to their pitcher. Jimmy needed peace and quiet to focus on his windup, not a bunch of chatter. Shrieks and whoops at inopportune times in his leg kick would be disastrous. How could he pitch with such nauseating noise?

But he of course had to. Everyone in the bleachers, everyone standing behind him making their monkeys-in-the-jungle racket, everyone leaning against their cars along the third base line, expected him to make a pitch, and soon. So, he did. But when he saw the boy lean toward the plate he did not try to throw the ball into the catcher's mitt, as he knew he should, but instead threw it as to make sure he did not hit the boy batting. Bruno reached out with his left hand and stopped the ball, which fell to the ground.

"Ball one!" called out Bill.

Bruno picked the ball up and returned it. Jimmy was conflicted. More than anything, more than his fear of his brother, more than his dread of being laughed at by the crowd, more than the shame of losing the game, and Jimmy hated losing any game, Jimmy did not want to hit the boy batting. He knew his greatest fear was being hit by the ball. Or was it being run over by a big boy like Hulk? He couldn't decide. He didn't want to decide, because he didn't want either of those things to happen to him. He would pick None of the Above, as he did on some of his tests at school, if he could have his way.

The next pitch was also outside. A little closer, but not nearly close enough. Jimmy took a deep breath. If he really, really, focused, he could throw it right on the edge of the plate, as far away from the boy as he could without taking the chance of hitting him. He went into his windup, and bent his knee, and followed through, not trying to throw it as hard as the first two times.

"Strike one!" called out Bill. The crowd cheered, but to Jimmy it was in a mocking way. The crowd was no doubt tilted toward the red side.

Jimmy then lost his focus on the next pitch, so happy to have thrown a strike, and the ball bounced before it reached home plate. Bill did bother to raise his voice much when he said "Three and one."

Jimmy again bore down, did his motion fluidly, but still slightly missed the edge he was aiming for.

"Strike 2!" said Bill. Jimmy was not expecting that call. He wondered if Bill's eyesight was bad. He also had realized by this time the batter had been instructed to not swing, and he didn't think that was fair to the boy either. If he had to take the risk of getting hit by the ball, he should at least get a chance to hit it back.

Jimmy was not as focused on the next pitch, as he was distracted by the thought of why people made other people do things those people did not want to do, but the pitch ended up in the same exact spot as the last pitch, at least to Jimmy's eyes. That was why he was even more confused when Bill called out to the batter in a calm tone, "Ball 4. Take yer' base, son."

Bruno held the ball in his hand, not knowing what to do next. The batter also stood, confused by Bruno's confusion, with the bat still on his shoulder. Bill looked down on them both with amusement. "You," he said to the batter, "drop your bat and go to first base. You walked." Then he turned to Bruno and said, "You might as well throw it back to him now," pointing to Jimmy standing on the pitcher's mound with a confused look on his face as well.

And so, he did. The crowd cheered as the boy trotted to first base to take his place next to Ken Ferris, who was standing on the base with his arm out, as if he expected Jimmy to throw the ball to him at any second. Jimmy looked over and declined, knowing the odds of Ken catching it were slim, and what would be the point anyway?

The next batter was another right hander. He was slightly taller than Jimmy, and much thicker, which does not mean he was fat, but normal sized for an athletic kid. Jimmy could tell by the way he walked to the plate, so unhurried but purposeful, he was in no way afraid of Jimmy. He was the kind of boy who pushed boys like Jimmy out of line at school. He was the kind who could sense fear in smaller boys and knew how to intimidate them. When he stood in the batter's box he glared at Jimmy to let him know he knew what Jimmy knew.

When Jimmy threw his first pitch to him, it was low and outside and Bruno had to scoop it up off the ground. He stopped it, but could not catch it. The boy at first base had started running as soon as the ball passed the plate and was standing on second when Bruno stood up with the ball in his hand. Jimmy saw Bruno was staring at him with a look of pity, the look he had seen in other boys' eyes when bullies stepped in front of him in the lunch line; like they knew it was unfair, but they couldn't help him.

"Come on, Jimmy!!!" he cried as he threw back the ball. Everyone in the bleachers, in the field, and on the benches, saw this thing getting out of hand rather quickly.

Jimmy threw again, once again outside, and Umpire Bill called out "Ball two!!"

Slugger was sitting in the bleachers, closer to his father now, as his view was blocked where he first sat by a supporting pole of the backstop. He knew Jimmy could do better than this, but he also knew Jimmy might decide he didn't want to and not try. If Jimmy did that, all he had hoped for would be lost. But knowing Jimmy like he did, he knew he had to be as reassuring as possible, he had to coax Jimmy. He had to choose his words carefully.

"Come on, Jimmy. Throw strikes!!" he called out, in unison with Coach Schmidt. The coach was on the edge of the bench, wondering if it would be better to go out and talk to Jimmy or not.

The batter heard the plea from the bench and the stands, and turned to his friends on the Cardinals bench and commented, "He's afraid to throw strikes!!"

When Jimmy heard the boy's snickering comment, and he knew the boy spoke the truth, he was instantly enraged. At that moment, Jimmy realized he did not like being laughed at more than any of the things he thought he was more afraid of before. When he turned to look at the catcher before his next pitch, he saw the batter leaning over the plate, taunting him to throw it at him, believing this skinny kid didn't have the guts to do it.

Jimmy threw the next pitch without thinking, as hard as he could. He didn't worry about aiming it, or hitting the boy, or anything, really. He just let out his rage in one coiled spring, as much rage as an eight-year-old can muster. And the ball, when it left his hand, felt like magic. It was not nearly as fast as Paul Hart's slowest offering, but it seemed to dance through the air and never straighten out until it popped into Bruno's glove.

Everyone in the stands went silent.

"Strike one!" called out Bill.

Bruno smiled as he stepped up and threw the ball back. "Nice pitch, Jimmy."

Jimmy thought so too. That was the same kind of pitch Donny Gomes couldn't hit when he tried. This kid batting, in fact, was not nearly as scary as Donny Gomes. His eyes had gotten big when he saw that pitch coming too. Jimmy suddenly was convinced this kid couldn't hit his pitching any more than Donny Gomes could.

The crowd came out of their brief trance, and started shouting out encouragement to the batter. He stepped back in for the next pitch, but did not lean over this time. If this kid threw another right down the middle like the first, he thought, he'd smack it. But when Jimmy threw it, a little harder than before, and this time aimed at the glove, he didn't. He closed his eyes, torqued his body, swung his arms, and the bat didn't even come close.

So now Jimmy was smiling. He had solved the riddle of the pitcher's mound, and now he had gained enough confidence in his control to not be afraid of hitting someone. The next thing he had to master was consistency, which proved to be a tougher trick. He was so happy after two strikes he could not focus hard enough for a third, and once again the ball bounced before it reached the plate. The runner on second scampered to third and things were now more serious than ever. If he threw another ball, the two strikes he had just thrown would be for nothing. If he threw another in the dirt, the guy on third would score, another guy would be on first, and there would still be no outs.

Jimmy had no other option he could think of other than throwing a strike, so he determined that was what he would do. He wound up, dropped his leg, and his foot landed awkwardly, sending the ball higher and farther outside than any of the pitches he had thrown before. To his shock, the batter swung anyway as hard as he could, and when Bruno jumped to catch the ball, Umpire Bill said, "Strike three, yer' out!!"

Wow, thought Jimmy. You could strike someone out on a bad pitch. That hadn't occurred to him before. He could throw the ball where the guy couldn't hit it, and if he swung, it would still be a strike. That seemed like a better way to do it than to throw it where they could hit it.

Jimmy liked to experiment. In fact, once he thought of one, he couldn't help but try it. It didn't matter if he was in the middle of the first inning of the first baseball game of his life, that there was a runner on third base with one out. He had to try it.

The next batter was a tall, slender, well-built boy with broad shoulders. He was the Cardinals best player and was expected to be the best hitter in the league, and had the calm, confident manner of the great athlete those around him were sure he'd become. His name was Carl David.

Jimmy could tell by his stride this boy could hold his own batting against Paul Hart and he needed to be very careful not to let him get a hit. He noticed Carl stood farther away from the plate than the first two boys, and seemed to be trying to get a better view of the ball, so Jimmy started his experiment by throwing the ball inside of the plate, in the space Carl had left open, but since Jimmy did not want to hit Carl he threw it softer than the ones he had thrown before.

As Carl watched the ball coming it ballooned into the size of a grapefruit and he swung at it with all his might, trying to make it explode into fragments and juice. The sound the bat made when it hit the ball was beautiful, even to Jimmy, and it was clear the ball had been hit as solidly as a ball can be hit. All eyes turned and watched it fly up into the air. It soared over the cars along the third base line and bounced off the farthest one's roof. The crowd cheered wildly, except one guy in the bleachers who called out

"Hey, kid, that's my car!! If you dented it, your dad's gotta pay for the repair!!" From his tone the crowd knew it was not his car and laughed, and the real owner of the car jumped off the bleachers and trotted over to conduct a quick inspection.

"Strike one!!" called out Bill, as the ball was clearly foul.

Jimmy was mortified when the ball was first hit, but quickly realized his experiment was working. The ball bouncing off the roof of the car might have looked and sounded impressive, but it was a strike like any other. However, Jimmy wasn't crazy. He wasn't going to try that again. On his next pitch, he reared back and threw it hard as he could, trying to get it low and outside. He missed his target but hit the glove anyway, as the ball danced from outside to right down the middle as it neared the plate. Carl's bat never moved, as he could not figure out where the ball was going either.

"Strike two!!" called out Bill. Carl David was not amused, but it was clearly a strike.

Jimmy's confidence soared. This kid wasn't getting a hit either. He assumed Carl would swing at the next pitch if it was anywhere close, so he threw it outside again. Carl David had enough discipline, remarkably to Jimmy at least, and did not.

"Ball one!!" said Bill.

Jimmy now was ready to throw a strike. Maybe Carl wouldn't swing again. He lifted his leg as high as he could and brought his foot down. The crowd gasped, as it looked like Jimmy would fall over. The ball screamed in, harder than any Jimmy had thrown so far. Carl swung hard, and Jimmy swore his eyes stayed open, but he missed anyway. Jimmy was surprised, but the ball was too far outside to hit.

"Strike three!!" said Bill "Two outs!!"

Jimmy now took a deep, deep breath. The next batter was the kid they called Hulk. Hulk was bigger than any kid his age. As the football coach watched him walk to the plate, he had a vision of the nose tackle for the class of 1977 staring at him through his cotton candy. This Cardinal team, he envisioned, had his nose tackle, and his best linebacker, and maybe even his quarterback, a decade from now.

Hulk was a typical big kid. He was self-conscious about being bigger than his friends, and had a gentle spirit. But if he was pushed and prodded, as he often was by those same friends, he could act out in anger. He liked being thought of as being the strongest, he liked that it was a fact, but he did not like it on those occasions he had to prove it. He came from a big family with several older brothers, so he knew about sports and his expected place in them, but he was awkward, and would not outgrow this awkwardness in time to help him in Minor League baseball.

Jimmy wanted to banish the chance of a kid this big hitting the ball back at him as quickly as possible, so he did not experiment with Hulk at all. In his universe, all the big kids he had ever seen on the playground were slow. If he didn't stand still long enough for them to grab him, they were less of a threat than the smaller kids who could run. Jimmy threw three straight, hard strikes and Hulk couldn't catch up to any of them. He swung at the first two, the last he stood immobile until Bill said, "Strike 3, yer' out, son."

Hulk swore he saw Jimmy snicker at him as he walked off the mound toward the bench. The kid had not only made him look bad, but laughed about it afterwards. Or so his team mate, Grant Roper, told him as he walked to the bench to put on his catching gear.

Jimmy was smiling from ear-to-ear as he trotted off the field. The people in the stands responded with some polite applause. His team mates ran from their positions on the field slapping him on the back laughing about how well he had done. Even Buddy Hoffman gave him credit, in a back handed way, when he said as he punched Jimmy not so playfully in the shoulder of his pitching arm, "Nice going. You had me worried at first, though."

CHAPTER
Twenty-Four

Paul Hart trotted out to the mound with an air of invincibility. The Minor League Cubs were just as pitiful as the Chicago Cubs. As the first batter, Buddy Hoffman, walked to the plate, Paul thought to himself, why waste any time with these guys? Why not strike every one of them out on three pitches and get this game over with as quickly as possible? He looked out over his shoulder into right field and beyond. He could see another game was being played on the next field, and knew his greatest rival, or so he had been told, anyway, Pat Hampton, was pitching for the Yankees in that game, against the Senators. With the sound of yelling and clapping, and the sight of boys running around the bases, that game seemed more interesting than the one he was playing in.

With an air of boredom, he threw the first pitch, right down the middle, past Buddy before he could blink. The crowd chuckled, not so much at the fact the pitch was so unhittable, but more from the look on Buddy's face when he couldn't hide the fact he didn't think he could hit it either. Despair would be the best word to describe it.

Like General Custer, Buddy was determined to at least go down fighting, and to swing as hard as he could at the next pitch. It did not matter to him if his eyes were open or not, whether the ball was a strike or not, he just wanted to swing the bat as hard as he could. He stared at the pitcher and gritted his teeth. The look on his face startled Paul, and when he threw his next pitch, it bounced before it reached the plate because he had not stepped as far forward as normal on his follow through. He had the thought in the back of his mind Buddy might swing so hard he couldn't hold onto the bat and it would slip through his hands and fly out to the pitching mound, so he didn't step as far forward on purpose to avoid getting hit with it. As it turned out, it was not an idle thought. When Buddy swung at the bouncing ball he didn't lose his grip as much from the might of the swing as from the contact the bat made with the ground when he swung down at it. The bat careened away, end over end, toward the Cubs' bench, making the boys scatter in both directions.

The crowd's chuckles turned to outright laughter. Coach Schmidt, standing next to first base, trotted over and scooped up the bat, which stopped a few feet in front of the bench, and walked slowly toward home plate. He leaned over Buddy while handing him the bat and said, "Make him throw strikes, Buddy."

But Buddy didn't listen. He was going to swing at the next pitch no matter what. Paul Hart, having been chastened by the result of his last pitch, threw the next high and hard, about level with Buddy's eyes, right down the middle. It would have been a ball, but Buddy, who kept his eyes open and could see this one, swung as hard as he could. He was still swinging when the ball bounced out of Hulk's hand.

"Strike three!!" said Umpire Bill. Hulk took off his glove and flexed his hand before sending the ball back to Paul. Catching, he was deciding as this torture went on, was not in his future.

Buddy returned to the bench dejected, but not totally dejected, because no one on the Cubs was totally dejected having survived batting against Paul Hart. If they were walking back to the bench and hadn't been hit by the ball, there was something positive to take from the experience.

AP was next, and he was the first batter for the Cubs who had an actual plan. He was going to keep his eyes open, and not swing unless he thought he could hit the ball. Not much of a plan, but better than the 'survive first' plan the rest of the boys had taken up to that point. Paul's first pitch, even though it was a strike, was in the second category. The ball was past AP before he could start his swinging motion. AP was the best athlete on the team, and had the instincts of an athlete even at this early age. He believed, rightly or wrongly, he could get on base, and each pitch was an opportunity. When the second pitch came, he was ready, having made an adjustment for the time it took for the ball to reach the plate. He swung hard, but with the purpose to hit the ball, not to swing as hard as he could.

The crowd, also becoming more interested in the excitement they were hearing from the next field, was brought back into focus by the sound of the bat hitting the ball, and then the ball hitting the backstop, as AP had managed to foul off the pitch up and over the catcher's and umpire's heads, having barely contacted the bottom tip of the ball as it sped past him.

But that was enough to alter Paul Hart's mood. He went from knowing he was invincible to having to prove it to the kid in the batter's box who had been lucky enough to touch one of his pitches. He stepped into his next pitch with complete conviction and threw the ball harder than any other pitch so far, but he overstepped, making his release point too high and the ball sailed over Hulk's head. Hulk did not make much effort to catch it and it slammed into the backstop.

"Ball one!!" called out Bill. AP had seen the pitch going high and had not moved the bat from his shoulder. He decided to step out of the batter's box and make Paul Hart wait to make the next pitch, just to see if it made him mad. It did and Paul Hart tried to throw the next pitch even harder. It wasn't as high, but still too high, and AP again watched it go by with his bat on his shoulder.

Hulk tried to catch it, got his glove on it even, but the ball had so much energy leaking from it that it snatched the glove off his hand and both fell together, the ball snugly tucked inside, about halfway between where he was standing and the backstop.

Bill looked over his shoulder at the glove and said "Ball two!!" and turning to Hulk he said, "Nice catch, son."

AP seemed to know the next pitch would be a strike, and he was prepared to swing before the pitch left Paul Hart's hand. Again, he made contact. This time the ball dribbled from home plate where he struck it and bounced a couple of times over the first base line and toward the Cubs bench. No one needed to scatter this time, as the ball stopped rolling long before it could reach the bench. Coach Schmidt picked up the ball and tossed it back to Paul. He clapped at AP.

This reminded the Cardinal players and fans they should be chattering. As they had become more drawn in by the drama they had grown more and more silent, but the clapping broke the trance and their noise grew louder than ever. Paul Hart went into his next windup thinking this kid had a chance hit his next pitch and he threw it outside to avoid this happening. AP, despite the crowd, many of them adults, telling him he must SWING, did not. It fit into his second criteria. It was too far away to hit.

"Ball three!!" said Bill.

Paul Hart was at a crossroads. He had expected to pitch a perfect game, strike out eighteen batters in a row, and go home a hero. Now he realized if he didn't throw a strike and get this kid to miss it, his day of perfection would be gone. He wound up, threw, and watched as the ball traveled through the air, higher than he had hoped but still hard to resist swinging at, and saw to his horror AP did not swing. AP couldn't tell if it was a ball or a strike, but he was certain he couldn't hit it, so he took his chances with Bill.

"Take yer' base, son," Bill said, rewarding his discretion.

The Cubs on the bench cheered as if AP was rounding the bases after hitting a grand slam. The crowd, not happy with the call, let Bill know about it immediately. The same guy who was wisecracking about his car getting hit stood up and held out his glasses. "Hey, you need these?" he asked mockingly, letting the crowd giggle for a moment, and then said, "No, really, you NEED these!!" And the crowd roared.

Paul Hart wasn't sure if the last pitch was a ball or a strike, but he chose to believe the crowd and not Bill. He was still pitching a perfect game, he just had an imperfect umpire. The kid would never have gotten a hit off him and he was only on base because the umpire was blind. Paul, also an instinctual athlete, had the trait all athletes must have to be winners, and that was to not allow the last failure to lower his confidence about the next attempt. In fact, the last result being unfavorable ensures the next to be favorable, not the other way around.

The next batter, Mario Bruno, felt the wrath of that trait in Paul Hart. Paul tightened his focus, gritted his teeth and threw two straight strikes poor Mario did not stand a chance of catching up to. But having Mario strike out in three pitches without swinging the bat was not enough for Paul, he wanted the batter to swing and miss. His ego demanded the batter fail to hit it, not fail to attempt to hit it. He threw his next pitch low, out of the strike zone, and not nearly as hard as the first two, and Mario obliged him by swinging with all his might.

The ball being so low, and the bat wildly swinging a few inches away from his head, was too much to Hulk, and he made a stab at it and missed. Bill, not the most agile of umpires, could not get out of the way and the ball grazed his ankle, right on the bone that sticks out and he jumped up on one foot and danced around in a circle, howling and grabbing at his ankle, already feeling it swell.

AP, seeing the ball bouncing away, took off running to second base at Coach Schmidt's urging. Hulk slipped as he turned to run after the ball, and fell again as he caught up to it.

People in the crowd, knowing the rules of baseball as they did, yelled at Mario to run to first base. This was the correct thing to do, as the player is awarded first base if the third strike is dropped by the catcher and the batter runs to first without being tagged or thrown out, but this rule was too esoteric for Mario, and since he knew the crowd was backing the Cardinals, he did not do what they told him. Even as the crowd screamed louder at him to run, he walked slowly back to the bench.

AP, now at second base, did not know what to do next either. Should he go on to third, or stay on second? He could have easily made it to third, but since he was not sure of what to do, he stayed put. By the time Hulk had retrieved the ball Bill had stopped hopping and looked around to see where everyone was. Coach Schmidt, who now realized Mario should have run to first base, yelled at him "Run to first, Mario!!" By this point Mario had walked halfway to the bench, but started running for first as his coach instructed. Hulk turned to throw the ball to first, but the first baseman was not there, as he had run to the pitcher's mound to congratulate Paul Hart on the strike out. Hulk could only stand next to home plate with the ball as Mario stopped at first base.

Bill, now standing on two legs, raised his arms above his head and said "Time Out!"

He then slowly limped toward the pitcher's mound, pointed to Mario at first base and said "Yer' out, son!!"

"What??" called out Coach Schmidt in Bill's general direction, then turning to Mario instructed, "You stay right there," as he ran toward the umpire.

"What do you mean, he's out?" shouted Coach Schmidt as he reached him. The crowd, for the most part, had the same question as the coach. They couldn't figure out why he was out either.

"He ran out of the base line," said Bill, matter-of-factly. Coach Schmidt didn't like the answer, but he did not argue further. The crowd groaned their way into appeasement of it as well. Despite the call going the way of their team it was distasteful to agree with an umpire on general principles. AP, still standing on second base, was not satisfied with the answer, but had a more pressing question. He called out, "Hey Mr. Umpire, could I have run to third?"

"No, you couldn't!" yelled out Grant Roper, the Cardinals first baseman.

"I didn't ask you!" shouted back AP.

"Yes, you could have," answered Bill. He shook his head as he walked behind the plate still slightly gimpy. "That's two outs," he said after re-taking his position.

The next boy up was Ken Ferris. Ken considered himself to be excellent at everything he did, because his mother had told him he was. It did not occur to him he would not get on base and he would not score a run every time, and he would not do well in every situation. He was so self-assured even when it should have been obvious to him he wasn't doing well he still believed he was, so he never had contradictory results in his past he could dwell on in positions like the one he was in now. What followed was an example of how being clueless was sometimes an advantage in the short term, but long term was usually not.

Paul Hart was no doubt distracted by all that had happened since he had thrown his last pitch. Ken Ferry, with his ridiculous slip on shoes, did not present the kind of challenge Paul needed to re-focus and he was lazy with his first 2 pitches and both were called balls. Ken Ferry wasn't going to swing at anything after that head start and Paul Hart went into a pattern of strike-ball-strike-ball which resulted in Ken Ferry triumphantly running to first base as hard as he could after Bill called out "Ball 4!!" Ken rounded the base as if he was going to keep running to second, and Coach Schmidt, who was again standing next to first base, reached out and grabbed Ken as he tried. "Stay here and don't run until I tell you," commanded the coach impatiently.

Now it was Donny Demoss's turn. Donny did not have much of a plan before he saw Ken walk, but that became his plan after he did. There were runners on first base and second, and the Cubs could score a run and take the lead if he could walk and then Jimmy could walk. Paul Hart had this figured out too, and he was none too happy about it, and put all his focus on the problem at hand. The first pitch to Donny was hard and accurate. Hulk did not have to move his glove to catch it, even though he would have liked to. Just because he was big didn't mean he didn't have soft hands, and catching balls thrown by Paul Hart was proof. When the second pitch came slightly outside but still close enough to evoke a "strike two!" from Bill, Hulk did not try to catch it cleanly, but rather knocked it down so he could pick it up off the ground in front of him. He bent over slowly to do so.

As soon as Ken Ferris saw the ball drop to the ground, he started running to second. There was no need to wait to for the coach to tell him to run, he knew he was supposed to run after watching the other boys run in this same situation. Halfway to second he could tell Hulk was in no way going to be able to throw him out, and he started smiling broadly. AP, who was still standing on second base, watched Ken running toward him in horror. He had also seen the ball drop from Hulk's glove, but he could also see it dropped right in front of him and all he had to do was pick it up. No one had told him to run to third, and since he wasn't sure he could make it, he didn't run.

"Go back, go back!!!" AP yelled at Ken, waving his arms up and down in the universal sign of shooing someone away. Ken stopped smiling, but kept running. He had forgotten completely about AP being on second, but he was still sure he had done the right thing, and kept going.

AP's yells brought to everyone's attention who hadn't already noticed Ken was running to second and soon two Cubs would be occupying second base. Hulk now had the ball and tossed it back to Paul, who then turned to see Ken Ferris and AP both standing on second base. Ken said to AP, "You should have run."

AP, looking confused and angry, said, "No, you should go back to first," and shoved Ken off the base they both had their foot on. Ken fell to the ground but quickly stood up and put his foot back on the base.

The crowd was hysterical. Paul Hart, still holding the ball, realized he should throw it to the second baseman, who was standing next to the two boys, laughing. He didn't see the throw, since there were tears in his eyes, and the ball thudded off his stomach. Paul then ran to where the ball dropped and picked it up and touched each Cub with it. He then turned to Bill, who had also trotted out to the scene at second base.

Bill looked at all the boys and said, "One of you boys is out, and it doesn't matter which. That's three outs."

CHAPTER
Twenty-Five

Jimmy watched this unfold from what was called the "on-deck" circle, which was just a patch of dirt between the bench and the backstop where the next batter would swing a bat or two bats if he was trying to impress everyone with how strong he was. Jimmy swung the lightest bat he could find. When he saw the action at second base, and heard the crowd laughing at his team, a wave of determination came over him. Jimmy did not like to be laughed at. His older brother and sisters laughed at him every chance they got, because they knew how much it bothered him, and he always strove to minimize the times they could do it. By this time in his expansion he was becoming more and more adept at avoiding it, and he was also getting better at hiding how upset he was when he couldn't.

But this was something different. He felt the same as when he heard the people in his school or in the store laugh at Black people. Even though they weren't laughing directly at him, they were laughing at people who looked like him. Whenever a Black man was laughed at for using poor grammar or not understanding something in a public place, Jimmy felt the need to say something intelligent, or do something intelligent, to make up for the man, even if the laughter was only in their eyes. This felt the same, Jimmy realized, as he dropped his bat and walked to the bench where his glove was. He had to do something about this laughter too.

He couldn't find his glove when he got to the bench and went into a mini-panic. He heard laughter from behind, Joe Gurnsey's laughter. "I was just keeping it warm for you," he said, handing him his glove.

Jimmy smiled as he turned. He took the glove and trotted out for his warm ups. The fear had left him. He had to stop the people from laughing at the boys in the purple shirts, which was the same shirt he was wearing. Every warm up had a purpose, and that purpose was to stop the laughter.

The first batter was nervous. Jimmy could see it in his eyes. Ignoring the chatter behind him, all around him, he gritted his teeth, wound up, and threw. The ball seemed to dance around in an ever-tightening circle until it landed in Mario's glove.

"Strike 1!" called out Bill.

The next pitch Jimmy threw with even more confidence. "Strike 2!!" called out Bill.

The boy standing with the bat in his hand looked dejected. He had never been in a real game before, and the kid was throwing the ball left handed, and he couldn't figure out when to swing or where the ball was going. Jimmy saw the dejection and gritted his teeth harder. The next pitch would stop them, he thought. It was the hardest of all, high but straight, and the kid took a heart-rendingly pathetic swing at it, eyes wide shut, and missed without scaring the ball at all.

"Yer' out, son!!" said Bill.

Jimmy looked at the crowd, and listened, and when he heard no more laughter it warmed his heart more than the scattered cheers which supported him. The next kid would fare no better, except he didn't swing at the high pitch. In fact, he did not swing at all. After ball one came three straight strikes. "Two outs," called out Bill.

The next guy was Paul Hart, and Jimmy looked very closely at his stance. He wanted to make sure he knew where Paul was standing, because he didn't want to hit him, even by accident. He didn't want to hit him even more than he didn't want to hit Hulk. With that in mind Jimmy threw the first pitch outside, but not by much, and Paul did not swing. "Ball 1," called out Umpire Bill.

This seemed appropriate to Jimmy. Maybe Paul Hart would do the same for him. The next pitch hit the same spot. "Strike 1!!" said Bill.

Jimmy realized this umpire was not reliable, or he did need the glasses the guy in the stands had offered him, and he better make sure he left no margin for misinterpretation on the next one. He threw the next pitch far enough outside Bill had no choice but to call out, "Ball 2!!" and so he did.

The next pitch was between the last two, and a little low as well to Jimmy's eyes, so he was as surprised as Paul, Paul's dad, and Paul's uncle when Bill called out "Strike 2!!"

Jimmy could see Paul was not pleased. It seemed to Jimmy Paul was mad at him, not Bill, for throwing a pitch Bill saw as a strike but was not. Paul looked at Jimmy like he was a cheater, and cheaters always pay. The next pitch from Jimmy left no doubt. He bounced it in. "Ball 3, full count!" called out Bill.

Jimmy did not know what to do next. If he took the risk of hitting Paul, he would probably strike him out. He had never pitched this well in his life or had better control than he had for the last two batters. The risk of hitting Paul was low, but if he did hit him, it would be a disaster. Jimmy looked at the next kid, waiting to bat, and thought, with two outs he'd rather not risk it. He can get the next kid out, no problem. The next pitch bounced in as well, and Mario had to take it off his chest protector to stop it. Jimmy felt sorry as he watched Mario squeeze his stomach in pain, but not nearly as sorry as he would have been if he'd hit Paul.

Paul trotted to first base before Bill could tell him to go, looking over at Jimmy with distain. Since he was a pitcher himself, he knew another pitcher when he saw one, and he knew Jimmy had walked him on purpose and he also knew why, because Jimmy was afraid of him. Despite Jimmy's talent he knew he could prey on what he saw as his lack of guts. Just wait until Jimmy had to face him. He'd have him afraid to pitch to anyone.

With the threat of Paul Hart now safely at first base, Jimmy buckled down to the task at hand, which was getting the next guy out. As he stepped to the plate, Jimmy could see the boy was scared. Jimmy figured he could throw it softer than he had before, to make sure he threw a strike even Bill could not miss. He wound up, went through his mechanics correctly, but did not push off as hard as normal or kick his leg up very high. The ball flew straight, over the plate, a perfect pitch to hit. The boy with the bat knew it, the crowd knew it, and Jimmy knew it. When the boy uncoiled his bat with an unexpected fury, Jimmy flinched. He heard the sound, and when he could not locate the ball, he assumed it was coming straight at him and he ducked even further. The laughter from the crowd, and the fact the boy was not running, made him realize the ball had been hit foul, bouncing past the Cardinals bench.

Jimmy stared at the crowd and took the ball when it was returned with a new-found resolve. No more soft pitches. The next pitch was done with full commitment: high leg kick, big step, big bend of the knee and then his back, and the follow through to fielding position, picture perfect. And the ball, seeming to have a mind of its own, but knowing to come home to the glove once it had finished its darting and dancing, was not in any danger of being hit again. "Strike 2!!" called out Bill.

That pitch made Jimmy a little tired. Up until then, Jimmy had more pep than he needed, in fact when he started the inning before he had so much pep it was hard to control. The thought of getting tired had not even occurred to him. But now, he looked over to the bench and had the urge to sit down. All it would take was one more strike and he could do it. He took a deep breath, and then a second, and went into his wind up. The ball was hard, low, and inside. The boy hopped back with his hands above his head.

"Ball 1!!" said Bill.

The batter looked at Jimmy angrily. "You tryin' to hit me, boy?" he asked. Someone in the crowd laughed at the thought of the little white boy calling Jimmy a boy in that tone, the tone reserved for black men.

From the first pitch of the game until that moment, Jimmy had forgotten Slugger was there watching. When he heard the word 'boy', he instantly thought of him and looked for him in the stands. Surely he wouldn't start a fight, but Jimmy could never be sure with Slugger. This kid had to be struck out and right now.

As he wound up, Jimmy felt the extra juice flow from his hip up to his arm from the thought of Slugger diving into the crowd after whoever it was who had laughed. Jimmy, as the ball left his hand, thought of his Gramma. He wondered how many times she had told Slugger what she told him, and why she had wasted her breath. Grammas never feel like they are wasting their breath, concluded Jimmy.

"Strike three!!" called out Bill. Jimmy didn't know if the boy had swung or not. He had turned his head to start walking for the bench before the ball even reached the catcher. He had done everything right, so he was not concerned about the boy hitting it. To everyone else who watched, it seemed like arrogance, but the truth was Jimmy was trying to get off the field as soon as he could so he could rest. When the other boys coming off the field crowded around him as he walked to the bench and cheered and patted him on the back, he spotted Slugger in the stands, now a little closer to his father, smiling.

"You should get a hotdog," said Harry Williams to his son, when they made eye contact as Jimmy walked off the field. He handed him a dollar bill. "Get me one too, with mustard," he continued. "And get some chips and something to drink, if there's enough money left over."

Slugger started to decline, but a hotdog sounded like a steak to him at this point. He hadn't been starving in the last week, as he had called in a few favors from his friends and acquaintances, but a hotdog would fill the bill quite nicely. He took the dollar without saying a word and trotted off to the Concession Stand.

Harry Williams watched as Slugger walked away, and he was quite amazed at his rebellious charge. He had to give him credit. He knew what he wanted, and was stubborn enough to someday get it. But what amazed him even more was the job he had done preparing Jimmy for this day. Harry had no dreams about his young son being a star athlete. He never played sports himself, and was fully aware that he had passed on his lack of an athletic body to his frail son. With Jimmy's string of illnesses and surgeries, just keeping him healthy enough to make it to adulthood was all he could ask for. He had assumed before seeing what was unfolding Jimmy being picked as pitcher was more of an indicator of Slugger's influence than Jimmy's talent and had come to the park dreading the worst. The best scenario he had imagined was there would be at least a few other boys playing who were worse than his son, and he wouldn't get hurt. Watching his son trot off the field to the cheers of not only his team mates, but from the crowd around him as well, was more than he could accept as reality. He must be dreaming.

"Hey, is that kid pitching your son?" a man sitting in the row below him turned and asked.

Harry Williams came out of his trance and realized he had been awake. "Yup, that's my youngest son," he said, unsure of quite how to say it.

"Well, he's a pretty darn good pitcher," said the man.

Harry Williams just shrugged, but it was a proud shrug.

CHAPTER
Twenty - Six

J immy was next to bat when the last inning ended, so he went
to the bat rack and grabbed the bat he had been swinging before, and put on the batting helmet. The team had two helmets
total, a smaller size and a larger size. Jimmy and most of the boys
used the smaller helmet. As he fidgeted with the strap under his
chin which tightened the helmet to his head, he tried not to look
at Paul Hart warming up. It was the top of the third inning, and
the score was tied zero to zero, and Jimmy was going to bat for
the very first time in a real game. It took all the courage he could
muster to step into the batter's box and as he looked out at Paul
Hart staring at the catcher's glove, he prayed for something to
happen, a sudden downpour or earthquake or something, so he
could avoid having to stand a few inches from the bullet which
was about to be hurled at him.

As if he was an answer from God, Bill stood from behind
Hulk. "Time Out!!" he cried. Bill motioned for Coach Schmidt.
"Hey Coach, this kid wasn't batting last inning when the third out
was made. You better get the right guy up here, or you'll be batting
out of order."

Jimmy swiveled to look at Bill, confused. That was the first
time he noticed Hulk, standing a few inches away, between Jimmy
and the umpire. In fact, Jimmy couldn't see much of Bill because
all he could see was Hulk. Hulk was staring down at him with an
angry look.

"What?" asked Coach Schmidt. He was also confused.

Bill took a few steps toward the Cubs bench, looking weary, but in truth he was happy he could now show everyone his expert grasp of the rule book. "The batter who was up when the last out was made at second base should still be up."

"Oh," said Coach Schmidt.

Donny Demoss did not wait for his coach to figure out who had been up, he knew it was him. He ran to where Jimmy was standing, a few steps out of the left batter's box, and said, "Give me the helmet."

Jimmy handed Donny the bat, but left the helmet on.

"That's not a helmet, Jimmy," said Donny with amusement.

Jimmy pulled the helmet off and handed it to Donny, then retrieved the bat and went to the on-deck circle while Donny put the helmet on and strode to the plate. Donny stepped into the right batter's box and then stepped out with a confused look on his face. He looked up at Bill and asked, "Do I start where I left off, with one ball and one strike, or do I start over?"

Bill looked down at the boy and started to answer his question, but then thought about what the boy had said and replied, "The count was two strikes and no balls, but we start over."

Children sometimes have moments of comic inspiration which adults just can't match. Donny said with perfect timing, "What, you called that last pitch a strike? Didn't the catcher drop it?"

Everyone within earshot laughed except Bill. Bill just stared, open mouthed, as he could not believe this kid was arguing a call which was wiped out anyway. Then he remembered he was a baseball umpire, and anyone will argue anything with a baseball umpire. "Just get in there and bat, son," said Bill.

Donny stepped into the batter's box and was greeted by a high, hard, and inside pitch from Paul Hart. Paul didn't think Donny was funny either. To him, Donny was just delaying the inevitable, which was he was about to get struck out. "Ball 1!!" called out Bill.

"Are you sure ??" called out someone from the crowd, assuming Donny would be too busy picking himself off the ground to continue razzing Bill and needed the help. This time Bill knew not to answer.

Paul Hart decided he needed to take something off the next pitch, to make sure it was a strike. This kid wasn't going to hit it anyway, so why not put it right down the middle? He wound up, and threw it right where he wanted to.

Donny, who had seen enough of Paul Hart after the first pitch, swung with a fury. If his eyes weren't closed, he was at best squinting. The Crack that followed startled everyone. No one, not the crowd, not the Cubs, not the Cardinals and surely not Bill, had expected Donny Demoss to hit the ball, and therefore no one moved. The ball bounced once, then twice, before Paul Hart realized it was coming right for him and Donny Demoss realized he should be running and the moment of silence that occurred after the Crack ended and everyone was furiously moving and shouting. Donny ran. The Cubs on the bench jumped up and shouted "Run, run, run!!" The Cardinal infield sprinted to the proper positions as they had been trained to, and Paul Hart reached down to catch the ball.

Paul declined to bend low enough and the ball declined to bounce high enough to get into his glove cleanly, and it squirted between Paul's legs and spun around on itself a few feet behind him. Donny kept running. The rest of the Cubs kept cheering. The crowd yelled at Paul, "Turn around, it's right behind you!!" and so he did. When he saw the ball, he lunged, and with one swift move picked it up, spun, and threw to first base, where Grant Roper stood waiting. Paul threw it hard, the only way he knew how, but the spin left him off-balance and the ball sped toward Grant in such a way he had to step toward home plate to catch it. When he did so, he saw Donny Demoss charging at him, only two steps away. Not wanting to get run over, he stepped off the base and stretched out in front of the base line, stabbing at the ball as Donny ran past. Grant managed, quite miraculously, to almost catch the ball, even though Donny was going to be safe at first anyway, but he did not quite catch it. The ball dribbled out of his glove and rolled away toward the Cubs bench.

"Go, go, go, go!!!" shouted the Cubs to Donny, seeing the opportunity for him to make it to second base. Donny dashed off, never looking back to see if Grant had picked up the ball before he reached the base. To his surprise, the ball sailed past his left ear as he neared the bag, and the Cardinals shortstop, Carl David, reached up to catch it. Luckily, Donny was standing on the bag before the tag came.

Paul Hart was also standing next to second base by this time, and the look of disgust on his face was palpable. His perfect game was ruined and now his no-hit game was ruined. Other pitchers may have considered what had happened to be an error, not a hit, but not Paul Hart. If it was an error, it would be Paul Hart's error, and Paul Hart did not make errors. Any kid could get a lucky hit, when he didn't throw it as hard as he could, but the idea Paul had made an error was not acceptable to him. Then Paul arrived at an even better solution. It was not a hit, and he had not made an error. Grant Roper had made the error. He should have caught the ball and tagged the runner out. Paul Hart, in his universe, still had a no hitter, and his error sheet was also still clean.

Plus, the Cubs still hadn't scored even if it was a hit. He could still pitch a shutout. But to do so, Paul knew getting the next batter out was crucial and he had to strike him out. And who was the next batter? The skinny pitcher who was scared to death of him, that's who. Just to make sure he knew who was boss, Paul Hart threw the first pitch at Jimmy's head. Well, it should be clarified Jimmy thought Paul Hart threw it at his head. The pitch was high, hard, and much too far inside for Jimmy's comfort. He didn't fall, but he skipped back two steps to get out of the way.

The next pitch, right down the middle, was called strike 1 by Bill to Jimmy's relief. Maybe Paul Hart wasn't going to hit him after all. Jimmy was not very sure of this, however, and backed away from strike 2. On the third strike, which came next, Jimmy was at least able to stand still, almost, as the ball sped by and into Hulk's glove. The bat never left his shoulder.

"Nice try," snickered Hulk as Jimmy turned to walk back to the bench.

Kevin Morgan had renewed hope when he came up next. Donny Demoss had hit the ball. Why couldn't he? When the first pitch was thrown, he took a mighty swing and managed to foul off the ball to the backstop. The next pitch was low, the following high, and Kevin was feeling good about himself. That ended on the next pitch, as Paul threw the ball too far inside, and it bounced off Kevin's leg.

"Oww!! Oww!!" he screamed and did a hopping dance in a circle around the batter's box.

"Take yer' base, son," instructed Bill.

"Are you OK?" asked Coach Schmidt, running to check on the boy.

"Uh-huh," replied Kevin, fighting back tears. He limped and skipped toward first base as the crowd clapped.

Paul Hart watched the drama from the pitcher's mound, and shook his head. These Cubs were peskier than he thought. He had to bear down. Now there were two on.

Scott Michaels was next, and Coach Schmidt was thinking he had done the right thing with his lineup. He had his best two hitters up with one out and two on. What could be better? Scott strode to the plate with all the confidence he could muster. Paul Hart was human. He could be hit.

But not on the next pitch, or the second, both of which scooted by Scott without a care. He swung at one of them, but only symbolically. The next pitch was low and outside, and Scott literally threw his bat at it. By some miracle he contacted the ball in this fashion, even though it was fouled off toward the Cardinals bench. Both the bat and the ball came within a few feet of it. The boys on the bench did not scatter, but lifted their feet to let them pass underneath and Scott ran over to retrieve his bat sheepishly. When he returned, Paul was ready. Just in case Scott had ideas of leaning over for the next pitch, Paul made it easy to dissuade him by throwing it inside. Scott jumped back, chastened even further. He watched as strike three came next, and left the rally up to Johnny Mars.

In his first at bat Johnny hit a foul ball that at the time looked like the best the Cubs would do all day. This time he proved that foul was no fluke, as he managed to foul off not one, but both of Paul Hart's first two efforts. He was proud of this, and thought he was doing well, until he realized now he had two strikes and no balls, and he would have to swing at anything close or he'd be out. The third pitch did not qualify, as it was outside by a large margin, so he let it pass.

"Strike 3!!" called out Bill.

Johnny Mars looked up at Bill in disbelief. He must not have heard him correctly. But all the Cardinals were running off the field, so he had to believe it.

"Where'd they find that guy?" Johnny Mars called out to the cosmos as he walked away in disgust.

CHAPTER
Twenty - Seven

Now came Jimmy's turn again. It was the bottom of the third inning and the score remained zero-zero. This classified the game as a pitcher's duel, and as one of the pitchers, he had to keep up his end of the bargain. As Jimmy warmed up, he couldn't help but notice it was more difficult to throw the ball as hard now than it was in the first inning. His arm felt slightly sore and a dull ache was starting to throb through it. But when the first batter walked up to the plate, the kid named Grant Roper, he forgot about that and focused on what to do next. Grant was a tall kid with a sneer on his face that let the whole world know he was above it all. Jimmy decided he would conserve his energy by not throwing as hard as he had before, to make sure he threw only strikes.

The first pitch he threw made him rethink that strategy, as the ball came right down the middle of the plate, waist high, and Grant took a mighty swing at it. Just when Jimmy thought he would miss it, he heard the crack of the bat connecting with the ball. It bounced past Jimmy on two hops to his left and went on toward Kevin Morgan, who was crouching between first and second base as a second baseman should, waiting for the ball to reach him. Grant was steaming up the line with more effort than speed, and the crowd was shouting and cheering him on. The ball took a bigger hop the third time than the first two, which did not seem possible to Jimmy as he watched it, but it certainly was helpful to Kevin. It bounced so high that not only could it not go between his legs, the expected outcome, but instead so high he had to catch it or it would have hit him in the face, forcing him to catch it.

The next step for Kevin was to turn and throw the ball to the waiting Ken Ferry at first base. Ken was holding his glove out in classic first baseman fashion, while feeling around with his foot for the bag. As Kevin threw the ball Ken looked down, because he couldn't locate the base with his foot. When he stepped on the base and raised his eyes the ball was on him and he couldn't move the glove the required nine inches to catch it. The ball slipped out of his grasp, or more precisely was never in his grasp, as he barely touched it with the glove. It rolled away behind Ken toward the Cubs bench.

As Ken ran after it Grant reached first base, and his coach was swinging his arm vertically in a circle and yelling "Go, go, go!!!!", and Grant turned and headed for second. When Ken reached the ball, which had stopped rolling in front of the Cubs' bench, Grant was two steps from second. Ken turned to throw it to second base, and when Coach Schmidt saw that, he shouted, "Don't throw it, Ken!!"

But Ken thought he knew better, and threw it anyway. Accuracy was also not one of Ken's strong points, and the ball flew past Scott Michaels, the shortstop who was standing on second waiting for the throw, and Kevin, who was not, and on into the outfield between the centerfielder, Johnny Mars, and AP, the left fielder. As they ran together, trying to catch it, Grant Roper started out for third base. Johnny arrived first, and turned and threw the ball into the infield without looking for someone or somewhere more specific to throw it. Jimmy was standing to the right of the pitcher's mound spectating, not covering a base as he should have been, so he was in the perfect place to catch it. When he did he looked over to third to see Grant standing on the bag with a self-satisfied look on his face, a sneer of sneers.

Jimmy did not throw it, as that seemed useless, and walked to the pitcher's mound with the ball to face the next batter. He would not make the same mistake twice with this kid, thought Jimmy. To make it a bit more difficult the next batter was the short kid who Jimmy faced to start the game. "Just what I needed," mumbled Jimmy to himself as he went into his windup, raised his leg as high as he could, and threw the ball with all his might. Mario jumped up, Bill ducked, and the ball sailed over both of their heads and clanged against the backstop. Jimmy and Grant both took off running for home. Jimmy won the race, as he had much less distance to travel to get there, but they both arrived before Mario could pick up the ball and throw it. The crowd went wild as Grant stepped on home plate. Mario threw the ball to Jimmy as the cheering swelled.

"Safe!!" cried out Bill.

Bill didn't bother to say 'ball 1', but Jimmy assumed it was as he walked to the pitcher's mound in utter dejection. The score was now Cardinals one, Cubs zero. Jimmy didn't know what to do next. Good thing Slugger was there. He called out, "Don't worry about it Jimmy, just get the batter out!"

That made perfect sense to Jimmy, and that was what he set out to do. He wound up and threw the next pitch as softly as the one he threw to Grant. The batter did not move. He wasn't thinking about swinging after the last pitch he had witnessed.

"Strike 1!!" called out Bill "The count is one and one."

Jimmy took a deep breath. He knew that last pitch could have been hit too, if only the batter had swung and from the look on the batter's face he could tell he knew it too. Jimmy's first thought was to bear down and throw the next pitch harder, but the look on the kid's face reminded him of his experiment. The next pitch he threw just as softly as the last, but he threw it outside, not across the middle. As Jimmy expected, the kid swung at this bad pitch because he was upset about not swinging at the last good one, and he could not connect.

"Strike 2!!" called out Bill.

Now Jimmy went for the kill. He did his best Juan Marichal and brought his leg down with a purpose. The ball went right down the middle and crossed the plate before the batter could decide whether to swing or not.

"Yer' out, son," said Bill softly, almost apologetically.

OK, thought Jimmy, walking around the pitcher's mound to gather his thoughts, now I need to get this next guy. The next guy after him was Carl David, and the next kid after him was Hulk.

Jimmy went after the next batter with a fury, throwing two strikes and two balls, none of which was hit. On his next pitch Jimmy had no choice but to throw it softly, as his footwork was wrong and he couldn't get much on it. The boy at the plate took a mighty swing, but the ball dipped slightly before reaching the plate and he only tipped it, and it bounced before reaching Mario's mitt.

"Still 2 and 2," called out Bill.

Jimmy looked at Carl David and knew he didn't want to have to pitch to him, so he had to give it all he had on the next pitch. He was extra careful this time, put his feet in the proper positions, and threw another perfect pitch into Mario's glove.

"Strike 3!!" called out Bill "Two outs!!"

Next up was Carl, and Jimmy's plan didn't change. He was not going to give him anything to hit. First he threw low, then high, then outside. Carl let all three pass as he had the discipline to not swing at bad pitches, but his eagerness to swing the bat overwhelmed him on the fourth pitch. Carl stepped forward to swing before he realized where the ball was going and when he realized it was inside he had no choice but to hack at it in self-defense. He smacked it sharply and loudly toward his own bench.

"Three and one," called out Bill.

Wow, thought Jimmy, this kid could hit bad pitches and good pitches! On the next pitch, Jimmy didn't take any chances and he bounced it in for ball 4. Carl trotted down to first, mildly upset he didn't get a pitch to hit, but at least he was on base this time. As Hulk was up next, Jimmy forgot about Carl and went about the business of getting the big kid out again.

He wound up, lifted his leg high, and threw. It was outside, but Hulk swung at it anyway. The torque and energy expended were impressive, but the bat did not come close. Mario took a stab at it and managed to knock it down, but could not catch it. Carl took off to second and Mario, who had seen bad things happen from throws already this inning, did not make one.

"Strike 1!!" called out Bill.

Hulk was not happy. He couldn't touch this kid's pitching, and he knew it. As he stomped and snorted in the batter's box, he couldn't help imagining picking Jimmy up and throwing him down the hill next to the field, then he thought of how much easier and more satisfying it would be to break Jimmy's back over his knee. While he rummaged through his mind trying to think some other, more sinister way to hurt Jimmy, the next pitch came, high and hard, and he almost forgot to swing at it. As it was high and out of the strike zone that would have been the proper course, but he made a late swing at it anyway.

"Strike 2!!" advised Bill.

OK, thought Jimmy, one more pitch and I can go sit down and rest. He used the lack of effort which goes along with that line of thinking and as soon as it left his hand he knew it would not make it to home plate without bouncing. Jimmy started running toward home, assuming Mario would not be able to catch it. Mario did catch it, or rather trap it between the ground and his glove, but that did not stop Carl from running to third. Hulk was leaning over the plate watching Mario grab at the ball, so Mario had no choice but to use the same logic as before and not throw it to third either. He couldn't see past Hulk to throw it if he had wanted to.

Now Hulk had a purpose. If he could get Jimmy to throw it wild, Carl would score and he wouldn't need to get a hit to get an RBI. He leaned over the plate as far as he could, and dared Jimmy to throw a strike. Jimmy saw this, and reared back and threw it outside, or so he thought. The ball had a mind of its own and despite starting out outside as Jimmy intended it to, it slid across the plate, missing Hulk by a couple of inches.

"Strike 3!!" called out Bill. "That's three outs!"

Hulk was in shock. The ball had almost hit him, and it was a strike? If he was a cartoon, steam would have been coming out of his ears. He balled both fists, including the one with the bat in it, and stomped off to the bench, kicking the dirt into a cloud on his way.

CHAPTER
Twenty-Eight

Everyone on the Cardinals team loved seeing Hulk get mad, assuming he wasn't mad at them personally. It was one of their favorite forms of entertainment, making him mad at someone else. Paul Hart was still chuckling as he walked to the pitcher's mound to start the fourth inning. He now had the lead, one to nothing, and as far as he was concerned, that one run was enough. The Cubs would not be scoring on him this day, he was sure.

As Buddy Hoffman came to the plate, watching Paul warm up, he did his best to convince himself the ball wasn't coming as hard as it was the last time he batted. Maybe if he waited for a perfect pitch, one right down the middle, he could make contact this time. He stepped into the batter's box with a surge of confidence. Paul went into his windup and the ball, coming as hard as it had on his last at-bat, was too far inside for Buddy to do anything other than step back out of the way.

"Ball 1," called out Bill.

The next pitch was low, almost bouncing before it made it to the plate, but Buddy took a hack at it anyway.

"Strike 1!!" said Bill.

Buddy knew he shouldn't have swung, and repeated his mantra in his head again, "Don't swing unless it is perfect." The next pitch wasn't and he didn't.

"Ball 2," called out Bill.

Paul Hart looked at Bill incredulously. Someone in the crowd, sensing what Paul was thinking, shouted out "Where was it?"

Bill, despite not having to answer to the crowd, couldn't help himself. "That pitch was high," he announced.

Several hoots from the bleachers let him know his was the minority opinion, which made him feel more powerful, as he knew his was the only opinion that mattered.

Paul Hart, feeling the need to show Bill what a high pitch truly was, threw his next offering over Hulk's outstretched arm and over the ducking umpire, and it bounced noisily off the backstop.

"Ball 3!!" said Bill, and he looked around to see if anyone would argue that one. No one did.

Now Buddy knew if he could restrain himself from swinging again, he would have a good chance of walking. Paul, as if knowing Buddy's weakness, threw another pitch as low as the last one Buddy swung at, and was quite surprised when Buddy didn't swing. It was not like Buddy wouldn't have swung, but just before Paul released the ball a bright orange butterfly had flitted its way into Buddy's field of vision, and Buddy was fascinated by butterflies. He could not help himself and turned his head to watch it as the ball flew past him. The pop of the ball into the glove brought him back into the present, but at that point it was too late to swing.

"Ball 4," cried out Bill. "Take yer' base, son."

Paul took the ball back from Hulk, and paced around the pitcher's mound while Buddy trotted to first base, smiling at the sliver of orange now floating away toward the trees. The next guy, Paul promised himself, would pay for this injustice. The next guy was AP, the first guy to get on base off him. It was an undeserved walk, Paul remembered, and that made him even more furious. He reared back and threw the first pitch as hard as he could.

AP closed his eyes and swung. He didn't open them until he felt the sting of the ball as it connected with the bat. The pitch had been inside, and it hit the bat just below the label, almost smacking against AP's hands instead of the wood. AP started running before looking at where the ball went. He was halfway down the first base line, completely focused on making it to first base, with his head down, when he heard the crowd laughing. He looked up and saw Buddy Hoffman still standing on first base, looking back at him, and when he looked over his shoulder, slowing down but not stopping, he saw Bill standing to throw another ball to Paul Hart. He then stopped in his tracks and looked toward his coach, confused.

"That was a foul ball, AP, go back," Coach Schmidt explained. The ball had travelled between the backstop and the Cubs bench, and rolled across the road and into the trees. It had been struck solidly enough to be launched through the air about twenty feet. AP, despite the laughter, was rather proud of himself when he realized how far he had hit it, even though what it amounted to was strike one.

"Wow", AP said softly to himself as he trotted back to the batter's box, "I can get a hit off this kid."

Paul Hart, now so mad he was foaming at the mouth, also thought the same thing. How dare this kid run to first base? He decided to turn the tables and instead of AP getting a hit, AP was going to get hit. He didn't throw it as hard as he could, just to make sure he hit him, and that allowed AP time to lean out of the way. The ball whizzed past, barely swiping the sleeve of AP's tee shirt.

"Take yer' base, son," called out Bill.

AP looked at the umpire with some confusion. That was only ball one, as far as he was concerned. It was also only ball one as far as the Cardinals coach was concerned as well. He jumped from his seat on the bench and ran over to Bill.

"What was that?" asked the coach.

"He was hit by the pitch," informed Bill.

The crowd hooted, Hulk turned around and looked at Bill in disgust, and AP, now understanding the call, dropped his bat and began his trot to first base. As he was passing as close to Paul as the base line allowed, Paul called out to him, "Next time, I'm going to really nail you!!"

He had tried to say it too softly for his coach to hear him, but he failed. Instead of saying what he was thinking of saying to the umpire, the coach now knew his most important priority was to settle down his pitcher. He turned his back on Bill and slowly walked to the mound, where Paul Hart was standing, his chest heaving.

As he made his walk, Joe Gurnsey started the boys on the Cubs bench singing out; "Pitcher's blowin' uu-up, pitcher's blowin' uu-up!" All the boys joined in except Jimmy, who was not so sure Paul was blowing up yet. By the time the coach arrived on the mound, he knew what to say to get Paul re-focused.

"You hear that, Paul?" he asked. "Well don't let it get to you," he said softly. "You have to get control of your emotions, Paul. If you control your emotions, you can control your pitches and throw strikes. If you can't throw strikes, or if you hit someone again, I'm going to bring in another pitcher."

The coach knew that would do it. He could tell from Paul's eyes he in no way wanted to be replaced as pitcher. The fear of that outcome would outweigh Paul's anger, he was sure.

"OK," said Paul. "I'll do it. I promise."

The first to test this promise was Mario Bruno. Mario had been watching in anticipation, and realized he could be the hero if he could just get a hit. He went into a purposeful crouch, and since he was short in the first place, made it very difficult for Paul to throw the ball low enough to get it into his strike zone. It didn't matter however. When Paul's first offering came in high, Mario swung anyway. He didn't come close.

"Strike 1!!" called out Bill needlessly.

"Make him pitch to you, Mario," implored Coach Schmidt.

Mario listened and let the next pitch, thrown perfectly down the middle, waist high, pass.

"Strike 2!!" called out Bill.

Mario thought to himself listening to the coach wasn't helping him become the hero he imagined himself being, so the next pitch was going to be hit, no matter what. Paul, getting back into his groove, fired the next pitch with more enthusiasm than the first two, and it split the plate in two again. Mario swung, and heard two sounds. The first was the ball barely grazing the bat, and the second was the ball hitting Hulk's glove. By some miracle it did not fall out.

"Strike 3!!" called out Bill.

"What?" called out Mario. "That was a foul ball!"

"Yeah, but I caught it," answered Hulk menacingly.

Mario looked at Hulk, then at Bill, hoping for a different answer. Bill shrugged and said, "Yer' out, son."

Next was Ken Ferry, standing in the on-deck circle, swinging two bats instead of one. He had seen guys do it on television, so why shouldn't he do it, especially after his success the first time he was up? Paul watched him as he dropped one of the bats and walked to the plate and the slip-on shoes made him shake his head in disgust. Only a Cub would play a baseball game in slip-on shoes. The other Cubs, with their mismatched jerseys and tennis shoes, were bad enough, but this kid was well beyond his ability to respect.

Ken decided he would walk again, as that had worked so well the last time. Paul Hart, after throwing his first pitch for a strike and seeing Ken not even contemplating swinging, made short work of him. He struck Ken out on a count of 1 ball, 2 strikes, with a three-quarter speed lollipop he wouldn't have thrown to anyone if he thought they would swing at it. When Ken didn't and Bill leaned over to tell Ken his time was up, Paul breathed deeply, relieved the kid had not surprised him by taking a hack.

"Two outs!!" called out Bill.

Donny Demoss was next. Paul remembered this was the kid who hit the ball between his legs and bore down extra hard on his first pitch. The result was the pitch was low and it bounced in front of Hulk. Hulk made a valiant effort to stop it and was mostly successful, except the ball caromed off his glove and up to his backside, then landed directly behind him.

Buddy remembered what had happened the last inning, and took off for third before AP could join him at second. AP, once he saw Buddy go, sprinted off first base himself. Hulk was spinning around, looking for the ball which was right at his feet, as the crowd laughed and the other Cardinals frantically called out to him, "Look down!! It's right there!!" By the time he found it and picked it up, both boys had advanced successfully, and were standing on second and third.

Hulk shook his head in disgust. As he did, he noticed Jimmy standing in the on-deck circle to bat next, and he had an idea. He trotted out to Paul to hand him the ball instead of throwing it. He put his glove over his face, so no one could read his lips, and said to Paul, "You should just walk this kid. Look who's up next." And he tilted his head toward Jimmy.

Paul did not like the thought of walking anyone on purpose, but the thought of striking Jimmy out with the bases loaded was too good to pass up. He looked at Hulk with surprise, as Hulk was the last person on the team he would expect to come up with such a sound strategy. He nodded to Hulk in agreement and Hulk walked to his position behind the plate. Paul then gave Donny a free pass, throwing the next pitch inside and the last two outside. Donny trotted to the vacant first base triumphantly.

As Jimmy stood swinging his bat in the on-deck circle watching the scenario unfold, he could see the other game on the next field was ending. People were drifting toward their cars, and boys were walking off the field. Minor League games were governed by the Mercy Rule, which meant if one team was ahead by ten runs or more by the end of the third inning or later, the game was ended. It was deemed better for a team's psyche to lose 10 -0 rather than 30 - 0, even though losing by the Mercy Rule was no psychological picnic either. The game between the Senators and Yankees had ended that way, and just like in the real world, the umpire had shown mercy on the Senators and put them out of their misery after falling behind 13 to 0 in three innings.

Fans of that game were drawn to the Cubs v Cardinals contest, first because they wanted to stop at the Concession Stand and reward their heroes, and second because they saw what looked like a much more interesting game to watch than the one they had just witnessed. By the time Jimmy came up to the plate, the stands were almost filled.

To Jimmy, the game situation, the bases loaded in a one run game, was not as daunting as having to stand in the batter's box and face Paul Hunt again. He felt a chill in the warm June air, despite the sun beaming down and the temperature not being conducive to chilliness. Goose bumps rose on his pencil thin arms. His teeth chattered. Dogs for miles around could smell the fear oozing out of him.

Paul could see it too, and he decided to have a little fun with Jimmy before striking him out. He threw his first pitch as hard as he dared, and made sure it was high and inside. Not a wild pitch, for sure, but a message pitch. Jimmy ducked and jumped at the same time, and almost inadvertently got himself hit in the head by the ball in his awkward attempt to avoid it.

As Jimmy collected himself outside the batter's box, he could hear Slugger and his coach, and a few guys on the bench say, "Don't be scared in there." "Just swing the bat." or just plain, "Come on, Jimmy!" He knew all of them were correct, but his fear drove him to another conclusion. He had to end this as soon as he could. The quickest way he could get out of his current situation was to hit the ball, and on the next pitch. He decided the best way to ensure this was to not try to hit it, but to just stick his bat out and let the ball connect with it, the way he had done in practice. That way the screaming in his head would be over as soon as possible.

Paul looked over at his coach, and could tell by the look on his face if he walked Jimmy he would get pulled off the mound. It was standard practice in baseball if a pitcher walked in a run, his time was over and someone had to be sent in to relieve him. Paul could not let that happen. His next pitch had to be a strike. Since in his mind Jimmy was even less likely to swing than the kid with the slip-ons, he threw the same, three quarter speed piece of candy to Jimmy he had used to strike out Ken.

Following his plan, Jimmy stuck his bat out in what could best be described as a three-quarter swing, just enough to extend the bat across the plate to where he thought the ball was going. Jimmy was too afraid to close his eyes, so he didn't, and he watched as the ball took a direct course toward his bat. Just before contact was made, Jimmy eyes ballooned. There seemed to be no doubt he was going to hit it! The ball flew off the bat, more from the momentum of the throw than the swing, and shot through the air close to the shortstop, but it was not hit hard enough to get there without falling to the ground and bouncing. The shortstop, Carl David, reached over and down to his right, but the ball scooted underneath his glove and bounced a couple of times beyond him before it stopped on the outfield grass.

All the Cubs were running, including Jimmy. Buddy Hoffman sailed across home plate with ease. AP ran to third and stopped, looking for where the ball landed. DD stood on second and Jimmy was still running to first when Carl reached the ball, as it stopped closer to him than the outfielders. Coach Schmidt's mouth dropped open, in shock over what had just happened, and he did not recover in time to stop AP, who was being commanded by the now swollen crowd to "Keep going, Keep going !!" until he could no longer resist the urge to score. Carl, thinking he may still have time to throw out the slow-moving Jimmy, wound up to throw to first. When he saw Jimmy two steps from the bag, and then saw AP take two steps from third heading for home, he changed his mind and instead pivoted to throw to the waiting Hulk. The ball arrived a step before AP did, and Hulk did not so much tag AP out as he did push him down when he reached out his leg to touch the plate.

Bill, who had moved from behind the plate at the sight of the ball leaving Jimmy's bat, was standing in the perfect position to see the play and make the call. "Haaaah- oow!!" he cried, while pointing his thumb up in his outstretched right hand, the OUT signal.

The crowd went wild. AP picked himself up off the ground and dusted himself off. The boys in the outfield trotted in. Donny and Jimmy clung to their bases, not leaving without further in-structions. They soon received them from Bill. "That's three outs, boys," he informed. Then he turned to the crowd and said, "Score tied, one to one, bottom of the fourth!"

CHAPTER
Twenty-Nine

As Jimmy trotted in from first base, he suddenly realized how tired he was. He had been throwing for longer than he ever had in his life, but it was the sprint to first base that wore him out. His legs felt heavy, which for Jimmy's bird legs was quite an accomplishment. He had never felt heavy in his life, unless his sister was sitting on him. As he scoured the bench, looking for his glove, he wondered how it could be no one had brought it to him, to allow him to save a few steps. It was almost right where he left it on the end of the bench, but in the excitement of the last inning, it had been knocked off into the dirt. By the time he retrieved it, the rest of the boys were already in position, waiting for him. He took a couple of warm-ups, which were more like wear-downs, before signaling to Bill he was ready as he was ever going to be.

The fact the Cubs had tied the game re-energized his teammates, however. They had slowly decreased the volume of their chatter as the first three innings went by, but now they were back at full throat. To Jimmy they sounded twice as loud, and his head began to ache. He gazed into the stands to find his brother and father, who were forced to sit shoulder to shoulder as the bleachers were now completely full. Not only were there Cubs and Cardinals fans, there were now Senators and Yankees and their fans, eating snow cones and popcorn; the Yankees in victorious splendor, the Senators in dejected silence, but all quite dedicated to filling their stomachs.

The first batter was standing in the batter's box, with Paul Hart on deck. Jimmy was not intimidated like the first time he saw Paul waiting to come to bat, he was too winded. His first wind up was labored, and he did not bend at the waist as he should, and the ball sailed high. The batter did not budge. "Ball 1!" called out Bill. Jimmy took the ball from Mario, and slowly walked to the pitching rubber. After a deep breath, he wound up again, but this time concentrated on bending at his release point as he knew he had to if he wanted to keep the ball down. It came straight across the plate, shoulder high. "Ball 2!" called out Bill as the batter let it pass again.

Jimmy couldn't believe the call, but he did not have any energy to waste getting upset about it. The Cardinal's manager saw Jimmy's condition, and called time out. He trotted out to the batter, and whispered in his ear, "This kid is tired. Don't swing at anything. He'll walk you for sure." When he went back to the bench, he told the next batter and the next to do the same thing.

He was right, of course. Jimmy threw the next pitch in the dirt, and the next outside, and the Cardinals had a man on first without the bat leaving his shoulder. The crowd noise increased, as they all could sense this was the beginning of the unraveling, and the Cubs sensed it too. Their response was to chatter even louder, thinking Jimmy would pull through with their added support.

Paul Hart, obedient to a fault, stepped to the plate and waited to get walked like his predecessor. Jimmy, ever observant, recognized Paul was told not to swing, and focused on throwing strikes without worrying Paul was going to try to hit it. He remembered his form, and his brother's words of encouragement. He wound up and threw it where it was intended, even though there was not much velocity behind it. "Strike 1!' said Bill.

Jimmy took three deep breaths before the next pitch. His windup was stilted, his arm angle off, and he threw the next one outside. Paul, after letting the first pitch go by, couldn't let this one. He swung and missed by a foot, which was about how far outside the pitch was.

"Strike 2!" called out Bill.

The Cardinals coach was livid. After getting Paul's attention, he threw up his arms in the universal symbol of "What are you doing?", and the glare on his face let the world know he had better not take a swing at the next one.

It seemed to Jimmy like his brain was swelling. The noise and his mounting exhaustion were destroying his will to focus. But he only needed one more strike and he would be one step closer to sitting down and resting again. After a rest, maybe he could come back stronger the next inning, but he doubted it. He wound up and threw. The ball, which he did not think stood much of a chance of making it to the plate before it bounced, somehow did not. "Strike 3!" called out Bill, much to Jimmy's surprise.

Jimmy had felt pain in so many places of his body at different times in his life, but never in his shoulder before now. It was not the type of pain he felt when he was stuck with a needle; it was more like the ache he felt in his stomach when he ate something that he could not digest well. He was too tired to even sweat.

The next batter, the kid who had called him a boy last time, was more obedient than Paul.

Jimmy did not want this kid to see anything but strikes, but his first pitch denied him that wish.

"Ball 1!" called out Bill as the ball slid outside.

Jimmy used even less effort on the next pitch.

"Ball 2!" called out Bill, with an air of caution in his voice. He could tell the boy on the mound was not trying as hard as he thought he should, and he hated to see what he was about to see.

Jimmy tried harder on the next pitch, but his ability to control his body throughout his throwing motion was fading. It bounced before it reached the plate, and Mario stuck his glove down and stopped it before the kid on first could think to run to second. Jimmy rationalized he could save energy by walking the batter, and focus on the next kid. Deep down he knew that was not the right thing to do, but it was a lot easier on the surface. The next pitch was not even close to the strike zone.

"Take yer' base, son," said Bill.

Now there were 2 on, and only 1 out. The crowd cheered, as they saw the end was near. Harry Williams saw the sag in his son's shoulders, and he knew the boy was tired. He looked over at Slugger, who was now focused solely on his brother since he had finished his hotdog, but didn't say anything to him. He didn't know what he should say. Slugger, so much stronger and more able to handle this situation than his little brother, did not know what to say either. They watched in solemn silence as the next batter stepped to the plate.

The next boy, who Jimmy had struck out with ease the last time, was in no mood to let Jimmy walk him. The first pitch, low and away, he swung at with all his might and managed by some miracle to foul off. That got him a short discussion with his manager, who let him know he would not see another at bat if he swung again. Despite Jimmy knowing this, his body betrayed him on the next three pitches, and now he was facing a count of 3 and 1.

"Just throw strikes, Jimmy," implored Coach Schmidt, who was now on the verge of taking Jimmy out. He hesitated, and let Jimmy throw again. It was low, the boy did not swing, and off he went to first base.

Now the bases were loaded and only one out. Jimmy felt that his arm was dangling more than hanging off his shoulder. He did not know which hurt more: his shoulder, his arm, or his pride. At that moment, he knew what his brother meant by 'rag arm', because that was exactly what he felt was hanging from his shoulder, a rag, not an arm anymore.

Up came Grant Roper. He stepped into the batter's box and waved his bat in Jimmy's direction. This was the bat that got the hit that led to the run that started Jimmy's downfall. He smiled at Jimmy to let him know he was in no way afraid of him and Jimmy was too tired to care whether Grant was afraid of him, he just wanted all the noise around him to stop, but he could not block it out as he wound up and threw.

He threw as hard as he could, but his motion was not complete when he let the ball go. From its trajectory, everyone including Mario saw it was sailing over his head. He jumped and the ball ricocheted off his glove and up into the air. All the Cardinals on all the bases sprinted ahead. Jimmy ran, but could not beat the boy coming from third, and Mario could not throw it to Jimmy in time anyway. The crowd was standing now, yelling at everyone and no one in particular, as the second run crossed the plate.

Roper, standing off to the side watching the action, could not help but to call out to Jimmy, staring at the ball in his hand next to home plate, "Nice pitch. Keep 'em coming."

Jimmy walked back to the mound with what seemed like the last bit of energy he could muster. Grant Roper's words were ringing in his ears. Keep 'em coming, he had said. Jimmy decided he would do just that. It wasn't like Grant's words had given him renewed energy; it was more like an emotional charge. His next windup was done with more vigor than the last, and he managed to put some heat on it. Grant was leaning over the plate. The ball came inside, but not too far inside for Bill. "Strike 1!" he called out.

Grant took a step back and gave Bill a hard glance. The main heckler in the crowd shouted out, "I guess it didn't hit him, so that makes it a strike!!"

Now Grant was ready to swing. When he blasted another hit, he would be the no-doubt hero of the game! He waved the bat with a fury as he waited out Jimmy's next delivery. It was high, up about Grant's eye level, and he swung. "Strike 2!!" called out Bill.

One of the new arrivals, who had come from watching the other game, decided he would heckle the heckler, "I guess he swung, so THAT makes it a strike!!" The crowd laughed. The two men in the crowd eyed each other, already deep into mutual dislike. Heckler 2 would do his best to cancel out Heckler 1 from then on.

A few more deep breaths, a few more grinds of his teeth, and Jimmy was ready again. Juan Marichal, he thought, Juan Marichal. He twisted and turned and lifted his leg. The ball screamed, or maybe it was Jimmy's arm that screamed, as it left his hand. Grant was distracted by all the effort Jimmy put into it more than the velocity of the pitch itself and did not have time to lift the bat off his shoulder. "Strike 3!!" called out Bill, and he couldn't help himself but to turn and look for a response from his friend in the third row. It didn't come. "Two outs!" he proclaimed.

Coach Schmidt relaxed a bit. He wanted Jimmy to finish the inning and bring on another pitcher for the next one, and with two outs, it looked like Jimmy would make it. One more walk and that would be it, however. Even he knew if a pitcher walked 4 guys in the same inning, he had to be pulled.

Jimmy was thinking the same thing as his coach. One more out and the torture would be over. Just three more strikes. His heart sank when he saw the short kid coming up to bat again. Somehow, to Jimmy, he looked even shorter than he did the first time he was up. How could he fit the ball into such a small window? He knew that was what he had to do, because the kid would not be swinging if he didn't. That much was clear. After the first pitch, which despite all his efforts Jimmy couldn't keep low enough, he was defeated. The second and third pitches were thrown high as well, and with much less conviction. As he took the ball back from Mario, he could tell from the chatter his own teammates did not have much hope for him either. But he was determined he wouldn't miss high again, and he didn't. In what to Jimmy was an impossibility he threw the ball above the ground, and it didn't bounce before Mario caught it, but Bill still had the nerve to call out, "Ball 4, take yer' base, son."

That was enough for Coach Schmidt. He started the slow walk from the bench to the pitcher's mound. He looked out to centerfield, where he knew Johnny Mars was waiting impatiently for his chance, and over to shortstop, where Scott Michaels stood. As he walked he weighed his choice. The Cardinal players, as they saw the Cubs coach amble off the bench, started the chant, as the Cubs had done, "Pitcher's blowing uu-up, pitcher's blowing uu-up!!"

Grant Roper was enraged by the fact he had struck out, and had to watch as the other boys stood on first, second, and third. He should be out there, not sitting on the bench. He just could not accept he had let that scrawny kid strike him out. As the other boys chanted, he silently gritted his teeth. Then he had a moment of inspiration. As the boys started the next round of the chant "Piii...he broke in and sang in a loud voice, "Nigger's blowing uu-up, Nigger's blowing uu-up!!" A few in the crowd snickered at Grant's display of humor, others gasped, and most of the Cardinals bench, after they stopped giggling, joined in. If anyone had not heard what Grant had said, it was clear and loud by the time Coach Schmidt reached Jimmy. "NIGGER'S BLOWIN UU-UP, NIGGER'S BLOWIN UU-UP."

Jimmy, as he saw Coach Schmidt coming out to save him from his dilemma, was at first relieved. He knew he was failing, and the Cubs were losing, and his eyes started to well up with tears. Then he heard the boys singing, and the first tear escaped his long, feminine, eyelashes. By this point the coach reached him.

Coach Schmidt was a good Christian man, and more than that a father; and his heart broke as he heard the chanting. This was an eight-year-old kid, for God's sake. It was bad enough that he was taking him out of the game, and these people could not help but call him names, that name? He had forbidden his own children to speak it, and he did not understand how those he worked with, went to church with every Sunday, lived on his block, and he knew loved their own children, were so comfortable with it. As he reached Jimmy, he changed his mind about what he was about to do.

"Jimmy," he said, clasping the boy by his shoulders and bending over to look at Jimmy eye to eye, "I came out here to take you out." He paused to compose himself. He had to be strong enough for them both. "But now I'm not."

Jimmy looked up at him, at that point no longer caring about baseball, the Cubs, or anything other than escaping the noise he heard around him. He was tired and felt all alone. He thought of his father and brother, having to sit there and listen, and wanted them to escape too. The tear fell, followed by another.

"Stop crying, Jimmy," the coach said softly and firmly. "Wipe off your face."

Jimmy dutifully swiped his face with his gloved arm. Wet streaks ran down it. He looked at Coach Schmidt, and saw the tenderness in his eyes. The coach continued.

"You can get this next kid out," he said, somehow believing it himself, despite all the conflicting evidence. "Just bear down and throw strikes," he said, seeing he had the boy's attention. "Don't let us down."

Jimmy looked at his coach. Don't let them down? He hadn't been thinking of them up to that point. Then he noticed Scott Michaels and Mario, who had trotted over when the coach came out, and realized, he was not quite alone. Scott looked at him with the kind of pitied look on his face Jimmy abhorred. "OK," he said to his coach.

Coach Schmidt let go of Jimmy and stood tall, turning to look at the crowd in disgust as the chant continued. Once they realized he wasn't taking Jimmy out, as they had all been willing to bet their house on just seconds before, they went silent. Even the ones who weren't chanting were surprised. But the spell was broken.

"Come on, Jimmy, you can do it," said Scott, who up to that point was sure he would be pitching to the next guy. He wanted to pitch, and badly, but now he wanted even more for Jimmy to overcome.

Coach Schmidt then retreated to the bench, wondering why he had just done what he had done. Jimmy was exhausted, and he knew it, and by any rational analysis he should have taken him out. But the feeling in his chest was too much for logic. His brain said "mistake," but his heart had overruled.

This was not something the crowd had expected. As they watched Jimmy, now standing again alone on the pitching mound, a slight tickle of remorse came over them. After all, this was an eight-year-old kid, and a skinny one at that. They could see him wiping the last of the un-escaped tears out of his eyes before they fell, and for just a second they had to root for him just a little bit.

Jimmy was wondering if he could wind up again, let alone throw the ball where he needed to. He thought of his Gramma. Sticks and stones, she had said, sticks and stones. He looked around and saw the runners waiting impatiently at each base, waiting for their chance to circle the bases and claim their piece of glory. They had no confidence in Jimmy, that was for sure. He looked at Johnny Mars in the outfield, at Ken Ferry at first base, at Joe Gurnsey sitting on the bench. They didn't seem to have much confidence in him either.

Bill, standing behind the plate, had had enough drama and wanted to get home before it got dark. "Play ball!!" he commanded.

The next kid was ready to make history. He wanted to hit the first grand slam of the Minor League season. All he had to do was get a hit off this rag armed coward on the pitching mound, and that was assured. None of the Cubs could catch it. All the Cardinals would greet him at the plate as he triumphantly came home. As he wallowed in his imagination, Jimmy threw the first pitch.

The ball wasn't thrown straight, but it was thrown true. It sailed over the plate like a ship bobbing in the waves. It was high, low, and right down the middle, all seemingly at the same time. The swing, while commendable, was not effective.

"Strike 1!!" called out Bill.

The Cardinals coach, even though he had given strict orders to his players to not swing, didn't react. The bases were loaded, the pitcher was tired, and his kids were here to play baseball, not take a stroll. After what he had just seen and heard, the kid deserved an honest at bat.

Jimmy now had hope, even if he did not have control. Maybe he could get out of this after all. The batter, however, lost a little hope. That last pitch was all over the place. He decided a walk wouldn't be so bad. Jimmy threw again, and this time did not induce a swing. Mario reached out and caught it despite it being outside.

"Ball 1!" called out Bill.

"Booooo!!" responded Heckler #2. The crowd laughed.

Jimmy did not think it was funny. Each throw made him grimace, and wasting throws was disheartening. At this point he felt drained of not only energy, but also emotion. The only thing he had left was technique. The next pitch was strictly that, a technical toss without any verve. It was high. "Ball 2!!" called out Bill.

Coach Schmidt's brain began to chastise his heart. His stomach turned. What should he do now?

Jimmy didn't give him time to think about it. He went into his windup. This time, he thought about the window in his garage, his brother patiently waiting beneath it, daring him to throw it too high. Bend at the waist, Jimmy, and bend your knee on the release, was the mantra in his head. The ball, without much velocity, went right where it was supposed to.

"Strike 2!" called out Bill, encouraged. He wanted Jimmy to escape, too.

Now the crowd forgot their compassion, and went into a frenzy of partisanship. "Come on," Heckler #1 cried, "Just hit the ball, will you?!" he implored the batter.

The crowd broke Jimmy's concentration. He would have preferred to pitch to the sounds of a symphony orchestra, and for the crowd to be as quiet as the symphony audience had to be or be removed from the auditorium. All this noise was not helping. He forgot technique and just threw it. At the last second the batter, who had decided he was not going to strike out looking, saw it was out of the strike zone and checked his swing. Well, at least the Cardinal fans and players thought he had checked it. The Cubs and their growing legion of fans thought otherwise. Ken Ferry started trotting to the bench.

"Ball 3!!" shouted Bill. His, of course, was the only opinion that mattered.

Now it was all on the line. Ball 3, strike 2, two outs, and the bases loaded. Jimmy knew this was his last pitch, no matter the outcome. Why not go all out? He went into his windup, lifted his leg as high as he could, which wasn't nearly as high as it was the inning before, and let it go. It was high, and he knew it the moment he let it go.

But to the batter, it was perfect. What luck, he thought, this was a home run pitch if he ever saw one. He swung, in the upward arc most batters use as their home run swing, and the ball, as if it could see the bat and wanted a good spanking, dropped just enough for the bat to make contact. It sounded sweet, even to

Jimmy, especially when he saw the ball climb up and over Mario and Bill and clang off the backstop.

"Foul ball," called out Bill, rather anti-climatically.

So, it wasn't his last pitch. Jimmy was happy and not happy at the same time. He had to do it one more time. It wasn't over yet. Bill threw him a different ball, as he had determined the last one was dented by the metal cross beam of the backstop. For some reason this calmed Jimmy down, to know he didn't have to throw the same ball which had allowed itself to be hit like the last one. This new ball felt more cooperative in his hand. He licked his lips, tasting the salty remnants of his tears and sweat. Jimmy hardly ever sweated. He lived his life too dehydrated to waste much moisture on sweat. He needed to keep a store of tears ready, and sweat was a luxury his body could not afford. It felt strange to him to feel it creeping down his forehead now.

That was what he was thinking about as he wound up again. Not the game situation, not the chanting of the Cardinals, not how his arm felt or even his technique, but the wonder of a drop of sweat falling down his forehead and how rare that was for him. When he let go the ball, it felt so good he wanted it back, to have that feeling of sweet release stay for more than just the flash of an instant it had lasted. A pitch would never feel so good again in his life. The ball wandered over the plate. There was no better way to describe it. It did not zip, it did not float, and it did not swerve. It wandered. This time the swing was in vain.

"Strike 3!!" called out Bill, happy the swing allowed him to avoid having to make what to at least half the crowd would be an unpopular decision. "That's three outs. Top of the fifth, two to one, Cardinals."

The cheers of the crowd and the pats on the back carried Jimmy all the way back to the bench.

CHAPTER
Thirty

The fifth inning felt like the start of the game to the Cubs, which was not good. Having the lead again rejuvenated Paul Hart as he took his warm up pitches. He wasn't tiring as Jimmy was, and all he had to do now was conquer six more bums and the game was his. When he looked at Kevin Morgan, the first batter of the game and the first batter of the inning, he had no doubt this would be a piece of cake.

As Kevin took his place in the batter's box, Coach Schmidt realized he needed to start getting the kids who had not started into the game. Each boy had to bat or play the field for at least an inning or the Cubs would forfeit. Before the coach could stop the action and make a substitution, Paul threw, or better yet over-threw, his first pitch.

"Ball 1!" called out Bill.

Coach Schmidt looked down his bench and saw the three boys who still needed to get in. His first thought went to his nephew, Derek. He had been asked by his brother to put Derek on the team and this would be the first and last attempt the brothers would make to pull Derek out of the world he preferred, the land of dolls and dresses, and into the world of macho men, and he had to be the one who did it, to make sure the boy did not have to play on a team without the protection of an adult with the proper sensibilities. Coach Schmidt was indeed sympathetic, and loved his girlish nephew, but he wasn't naïve enough to think Derek would blossom into anything different than what he had shown from early on in his life, and Derek himself was not conflicted by his preference to play with dolls, or that he cared more about the way his uniform looked than how he played in it.

Then there was Joe Gurnsey and Steven Albright. Joe, he couldn't be sure what to make of, since he had not shown up for either practice. Steven, on the other hand, had shown some potential. As he rummaged around in his head for the right combination of moves, Paul Hart wound up again, and this time fired a bullet right down the middle. Kevin flinched at the velocity and did not swing.

"Strike 1!" called out Bill.

Coach Schmidt continued his planning. If he replaced Kevin Morgan with Derek, he probably wouldn't get to bat, and that was a good thing. No way could he put Derek at second base, though. He couldn't catch, couldn't throw, wouldn't try, and wouldn't care. He could hide him in right field, where no one would probably hit it. But that would mean he had to either take Buddy Hoffman out or move him to a different position and take someone else out. This was getting complicated.

Kevin had even more complicated things to think about than the coach. Paul Hart was throwing some serious smoke. The next pitch, thrown harder than hard, came inside, and when Kevin saw it coming he swung at it to avoid the ball hitting him, because it was thrown so hard he could not have gotten out of the way if he had tried. To his surprise, the ball did not hit him. Not to his surprise, he didn't hit the ball either.

"Strike 2!!" called out Bill.

Now what to do with the other two boys, thought the coach. No way was he going to let Jimmy pitch the next inning. He had given all he had to give, and then some. He wondered, should it be Scott or Johnny Mars on the mound next? Either boy would have to warm up first, and it was best they did so off to the side, while the Cubs were still batting. He was still mulling it over when Paul Hart threw his next pitch.

The ball was not threatening to hit Kevin this time, and his only response was to breathe a sigh of relief. He did not even think of swinging.

"Strike 3, yer' out, son," said Bill with conviction.

Up came Scott Michaels. Coach Schmidt looked at his batting order. Johnny Mars, then Buddy Hoffman came next. Paul threw the first pitch to Scott. It sailed over the strike zone, and Scott managed to let it go by without swinging.

"Ball 1!!" called out Bill.

Coach Schmidt could not decide what to do. He delayed his decision by telling himself the best strategy in this situation was to wait and see. Maybe it would be obvious what he should do if he just waited. He did not have to wait long. On the next pitch Paul took a little off, so he could keep the ball down in the strike zone. His adrenaline was countering his attempt at control, and while the pitch was indeed lower it was still too high.

Scott didn't care. Boys his age love to swing at what they can see best, and what they can see best is a pitch thrown at eye level. It was too high to hit cleanly, but too enticing to let go by, so he swung a hearty swing and the ball connected with the bat with a load crack and flew high into the air, and Scott was off and running. The ball arced up, and up, and up, and all the boys on both benches and the crowd in the stands gasped as the ball seemed to go into orbit. It didn't reach quite that far. In fact, it didn't even make it out of the infield. Carl David had the best view in the house. All he had to do was lift his glove and let the ball fall into it. As he did, the crowd came out of their trance and cheered.

"Two outs!!" called out Bill.

Coach Schmidt now had a plan. He first went to Buddy Hoffman, now the next batter after Johnny Mars. "Buddy, I'm taking you out." He reached out his hand to take the bat from him, and Buddy reluctantly complied.

"Steven Albright, you're up after Johnny," he continued, turning to his bench and holding out the bat to Steven. The coach had concluded that Scott Michaels would pitch next, and Steven would replace him at shortstop. That way he could put Derek in right field. So far, so good.

"Joe, you're going to play second base next inning," continued the coach, which allowed him to put Derek in Kevin's spot in the batting order, and made it unlikely he would get a chance to bat. Again, sound strategy. Second basemen were usually not asked to do much, so Joe would hopefully not have to prove he could catch either. That meant Kevin Morgan was out too.

He thought he was done, but now he had ten guys playing nine positions. The obvious thing to do was take Jimmy out, and all would be clear. But, the coach thought, wasn't Jimmy the only guy who had a hit so far? He deserved one last chance at the plate, plus where was Joe going to bat? As he looked at the boys sitting in a row, waiting for his next instruction, he saw some slip-on shoes jutting out, and decided that was where Joe would bat.

"Jimmy, you are going to first base," he decided. "That means you're out, Ken, and Joe will take your spot in the order."

All this activity distracted Paul Hart from the task at hand. He started Johnny off with a pitch in the dirt, and followed it with another slightly higher Johnny swung at and missed, to make the count 1 and 1. Johnny, having seen his buddy, Buddy, taken out of the game, decided he better not swing at one of those again or he'd be next. He let the next one go by without challenging it even though it looked good to him and most everyone else who was watching.

"Ball 2," said Bill, who had not quite been watching. He had been distracted by a pretty woman in the bleachers who had bent over to catch her young daughter, teetering on the end of the stands attempting to see where her snow cone had fallen. Her mother had seen this before, and knew her daughter would retrieve it and eat it, dirt and all, unless stopped. Snow cones covered in dirt still tasted delicious to a four-year-old. Heckler #1 had also been distracted, and therefore could not let Bill know he had missed the call.

"What's the count?" asked Hulk, whose mother it happened to be.

"Uuh, two and one," said Bill.

Paul threw the next pitch high, and Johnny took it. "That's three and one," said Bill before anyone could ask. He had to concentrate.

As Paul wound up for his next pitch, Joe Gurnsey jumped off the bench, in a delayed reaction to the realization he might get to bat this inning. As there were several batters ahead of him, this was unlikely, but he had hope enough to not be able to sit still. Paul caught the movement out of the corner of his eye and was startled, and the ball slipped out his hand when he threw. It was at least a foot outside.

"Take yer' base, son," called out Bill to Johnny, who had also been distracted and did not swing.

Coach Schmidt turned to his older son, who was serving as his assistant, and said, "Go warm up Scott. He's pitching next inning."

Scott, still consoling himself at the end of the bench after popping out, was instantly revived when he heard those words. He was finally getting to pitch! Off he skipped with the coach's son and a ball and a dream. As the coach marched off several paces, Scott could barely contain his excitement.

Jimmy watched him as he threw. His wind up could not be described as anything but funky. He bent his knees funky, his elbows funky, and he did not follow through like the encyclopedia recommended, but he could throw the ball harder than Jimmy ever could, and the relief he didn't have to face the crowd again, at least on the pitcher's mound, more than overcame any resentment Jimmy may have been feeling.

The longer Steven Albright had been watching the game from the bench, the more he came to believe he could hit this kid Hart's pitching. He felt he should have been starting anyway, and when he stepped into the batter's box it was to prove just that. After the first pitch, however, he lost a little of that confidence, as it was thrown inside and came at him a lot faster than it looked from the bench. He thought about swinging at it, but by the time he had decided to it was too late.

"Ball 1!" called out Bill.

Paul looked over at the Cubs bench, to see if anyone was about to jump up and distract him before he threw again. No one did, but the pitch was outside anyway.

"Ball 2!" called out Bill.

Now Paul was mad. He was mad at himself, no doubt, but still mad. He went into his windup, did everything perfect, threw it straight down the middle, and watched in horror as Steven Albright swung and connected. The ball was hit hard, right at the first baseman, Grant Roper. Halfway down the baseline the ball hit a pebble and ricocheted slightly toward the Cubs bench, causing it to bounce outside of the base line. Steven was running and the crowd saw a collision in the making and so did the first baseman, so he only took a halfhearted stab at it, more concerned with not getting run over, and it bounced off his glove. As the ball bounded away from Grant he jumped out of the way of Steven before they collided and Steven rounded the base on his way to second.

"Foul ball!!" called out Bill, causing Steven to end his journey abruptly halfway between the bases.

Heckler #2 did not agree. "That was fair all the way!!" he cried.

Bill, turning to walk back to his place behind the catcher, decided to respond.

"You're right. It was fair. Until it went foul, that is," he said with certainty.

As Steven trotted back to the batter's box, passing a few feet away from Paul as he went by, he said, "You got lucky."

Paul Hart, while in silent agreement, said publicly, "Get back in there and bat, and we'll see who gets lucky."

"The count is 2 and 1," said Bill.

"Are you sure?" asked Heckler #1. His rival had been getting the best lines in lately, and even though Bill had made the call he preferred, he had to say something.

Bill just rolled his eyes. Steven decided to taunt Paul even further. Before Paul went into his windup Steven stretched his bat over the plate and called out, "Put it right here, tough guy."

Paul decided he didn't want to bother Steven with the need to swing at his offering. He threw the ball at the bat as it sat on Steven's shoulder. Steven had to step forward to keep from getting hit. Hulk dove, if a kid his size could be said to dive, and stopped the ball with his glove. Johnny Mars, back at first after running to third on the foul ball, sprinted off to second. Hulk picked up the ball and threw it blindly. It was aimed directly at Paul Hart's head, and he caught it in self-defense.

"What are you trying to do, take your own guy out of the game?" called out Heckler #1. The crowd laughed, not only at the words, but at the sight of Hulk and his lack of agility.

Hulk hung his head and crouched into his stance for the next pitch.

Hulk's mother was a pretty blond. She had managed to keep an admirable figure, for someone who had borne five children. All four of her sons were big like Charles, but he was by far the most sensitive. It was difficult being the biggest kid. No one knew how the names he was called hurt him, except her. She had dried so many of his tears and knew his temper came from that place. Someone had to make him mad, to pester him until he was forced to lash out, or he was as gentle as a lamb. A big lamb, no doubt, but still he was her sensitive lamb. He was the only one who had his father's heart; the kind, warm, gentle spot he kept hidden from the world she had seen in his eyes when they met; and though her family was unified in the opinion she could have done much better, allowed her to see past his intimidating size and the rough exterior to his soul. It had taken her four tries to find a son who had that same light and until now she had managed to protect him from his coarser older brothers, but now was the time she knew she could not. His journey to find his place in the world had begun.

And then she had kept going, so at least one girl would come out. The old saying, be careful what you ask for, applied to her youngest. Precocious was not an apt enough description but it might be the best word she knew. Being a girl around the bigger, older boys in the house had in no way made her shy or reclusive. This girl seemed to know what she wanted from birth and was not only never afraid to say it, but also never afraid to do it without saying it. Her brothers knew from an early age not to cross her, or they would regret it. She ran the house, in her own mind at least, from the time she could walk.

"Three and one!" called out Bill.

"Pitch to him, Paul," called out the Cardinal's coach.

Paul tried to comply with his next pitch, and made a valiant effort at throwing a strike, but he missed outside.

"Ball 4," said Bill, "Take your base, son."

251

Now there were two on and two out and the Cardinals were clinging to a one run lead. This game was not supposed to be this close. The Cardinals had also cleared their bench of all the reserves, but the plan was for Paul Hart to pitch a complete game, as befitted the start of what was expected to be his glorious career as one of Canton's best pitchers of all time. He was being groomed to not only lead the varsity to the state baseball title in high school, but maybe even to have a professional career as well, such was his perceived talent. The coach was hesitant to pull him, as that would not sit well with the city fathers who were already plotting his legendary future, but if he walked another Cub he would risk doing it anyway.

It was up to AP to decide. He walked to the plate ready for action. One hit, and the Cubs were back in business. Paul Hart had to pitch to him, not just throw it, or there could be a miracle in the Cubs' future, so Paul pitched to him. No nonsense, no distractions, no emotion, just his raw ability showing through. The count was no balls, two strikes, before AP could get the bat off his shoulder. It wasn't even fair. The third pitch, low but hittable, wasn't. Everyone admired AP's handsome but futile swing, however. It was honest, and true, and was attempted with the utmost of resolve. He didn't come close.

"Strike 3! Three outs. Bottom of the fifth inning," said Bill.

Anyone who has ever rooted for the Cubs knows this outcome all too well.

CHAPTER
Thiry-One

As Jimmy trotted out to first base he was thinking of Willie McCovey. Nothing about Jimmy would remind anyone of McCovey, a large and tall man, quite imposing if you were standing next to him. Jimmy had never been considered physically imposing a single day of his life. He could only think of one thing they had in common, long legs.

In the prior innings while Jimmy took his warm up pitches, the rest of the infielders warmed up by rolling the ball between each other, and scooping it up and throwing it to the first baseman. Once the first baseman caught it, or retrieved it if he missed, he would roll it to the next guy, who would scoop it and throw it back. With Ken at first base it was a fifty-fifty proposition he would catch it if they threw it well, and the chance of him catching it if he had to move was about nil. Most of the warm up time was spent with Ken chasing the ball after it flew past him. Jimmy decided if he used those long legs of his, he could stretch out for the ball and improve those odds, just like he had seen McCovey do on TV. The boys threw high, low, left and right, and Jimmy caught almost every one, assuming the crowd would be watching his every move. When one bounced in front of him and he missed it, he was surprised when no one said a word, except his coach.

"Let it go, Jimmy," he said. "That's enough of a warm up."

The crowd was more focused on Scott Michaels warming up, trying to decipher his wind up. It was as confusing to them as it was to Jimmy. They came up with a different chant for Scott. The boys on the Cardinals bench pulled out the old classic, "We want a pitcher, not a belly itcher. We want a pitcher, not a belly itcher!!" No matter how many times the people at the game had heard that one, it was still funny.

Carl David was the first batter to face Scott. After having to face a left-handed pitcher for the first time, Scott throwing from the right side was like a gift from God. The ball came from the angle it was supposed to. He could see it and tell where it was going. The first pitch, he could tell immediately, was zooming straight at his head. He ducked under it, and looked out at Scott in surprise.

"Watch out," called out Heckler #1, "This kid is a wild man!" The crowd laughed in agreement.

Scott took the ball from Mario, and turned his back to the catcher to re-assess his plan to throw it as hard as he could.

"Come on, quit belly itching and pitch!" said Heckler #1, not too originally. Heckler #2 looked over at him and shook his head slowly, side to side, in response to his lack of creativity.

Scott composed himself and wound up again, with less emphasis on velocity and more on accuracy. This pitch was lower and slightly outside, and Carl took a hack and connected. The top half of the bat connected with the lower half of the ball, and the ball flew up, up and up, and all heads turned skyward to watch its flight.

Jimmy saw it was hit in his general direction, but to his left, and he watched it in flight for a fraction of a second before running after it. After a few steps, he realized the ball was hanging in the air for so long if he ran as fast as he could, at least as fast as he could with his head tilted to track it, he might be able to catch it. As it began its descent, he heard voices in the crowd, sucking in their breath loudly, gasping, and Jimmy wondered why. After his next step, he heard a woman let out a piercing scream. The ball was shooting downward now, and Jimmy knew all he had to do was take a couple more steps and he could grab it. That was when he saw, just at the bottom of his field of vision, Buddy and Kevin Morgan diving away from him in either direction. With his next step, he saw the bench on which they had been sitting until the moment they realized Jimmy was not going to stop before he ran into it.

Heckler #2 jumped up and shouted "Look out!!" but it was too late. Jimmy saw the ball, the bench just a step away, and knew it was too late as well. He was no doubt going to run into the bench, he realized, so he might as well catch it. He reached out his glove as he took his next and last stride, and just before he felt what he was sure was going to be a painful impact with the stiff wooden bench, Coach Schmidt, who had dived toward Jimmy as the others dove away, caught him in mid-air, inches from the wooden planks which would have most certainly gotten the best of the coming collision. His arm encircled Jimmy's skinny waist, and Jimmy stretched his arm out as far as he could, still trying to bring the ball into his glove. It bounced away, just beyond his grasp, on the far side of the bench.

The crowd breathed a collective sigh of relief. They did not want to see what they were sure they were about to see. A cheer went up. Only two boys were disappointed, wanting to see Jimmy crash, Grant and Hulk. "What an idiot," said Grant loudly.

"Nice catch, Coach!!" called out Heckler #2. With that he looked over at his adversary. He had won their battle for sure, now. The crowd's nervousness turned to laughter. Yes, he thought, he had won for sure.

"Strike 1!" called out Bill as the coach released Jimmy from his grip, and let the boy trot back to his position. He spanked Jimmy on the butt as he went, in the universal athlete show of approval and Jimmy flushed with embarrassment. He had completely forgotten the bench was there until it was too late, so he didn't feel so brave. He agreed with Grant it may have been the stupidest thing he had ever done in his life.

No one watching was more impressed by what he had just seen than Carl David. He hadn't even bothered to run once he had hit it, since it was obviously going foul. As he watched the kid run after it anyway, he thought of what his dad had told him many times: great champions would run through a wall, if that was what it took to win, and he had, for the first time in his life, seen someone willing to do it. Well, not a wall, but a bench, but that was close enough. The thought Jimmy hadn't seen the bench until it was too late did not occur to Carl. To him, guts were guts, and this little black kid had 'em.

"The count is 1 and 1," continued Bill. He had things to do later that day, and this game was dragging on longer than he had expected. Carl needed to stand back in the batter's box so they could get on with it.

The next pitch he let pass, but it was close enough for Bill, if not Carl. "Strike 2!" called out Bill. The crowd did not agree, but since they had not yet recovered from the near disaster they had so recently almost witnessed, they did not object.

Scott wound up for his next pitch, and threw what could only be described as an accidental screw ball, a pitch no kid his age could throw on purpose but more than a few could on accident, and Carl went down swinging. The ball was not supposed to move like that.

"One out!!" called out Bill.

Up next came Hulk. After not being able to touch any of Jimmy's pitches, he had renewed vigor when he faced Scott Michaels. Now was the time for him to show his teammates he could do what they expected of him, and that was hit the ball harder and farther than anyone else his age.

When Scott saw the look of rage and determination on Hulk's face, he decided he didn't want to risk hitting Hulk, so he threw the ball purposely outside for ball 1. That seemed like a good plan, so he tried it again on the second pitch. Again, he threw his accidental screw ball, and it drifted over the plate instead of staying outside as he planned, and Hulk took a mighty swing. The ball shot off his bat, on a down sloping line between second and third base, and bounced hard in front of the feet of Steven Albright, who could not get out of the way, which would have been his reaction if he had the time to react. All he had time to do was place the glove in the way of the ball before it bounced up into his stomach.

Hulk dropped his bat and started chugging up the first base line, like a train leaving the station. The ball was too strong to be stopped by Steven's glove and popped up into the air, above his head, and by some miracle did not fly over him. All he had to do was to wait for it to fall and he could catch it. Hulk was watching the ball instead of running at full speed and saw it was not going to make it into the outfield, so he increased his pace as best he could, knowing he had to beat the throw, if there was a throw. The ball came down to Steven, and he bobbled it but did not drop it. He knew if he did not throw it as hard as he could, even a kid as slow as Hulk would beat it to the bag, so he spun and heaved the ball with all his might.

Jimmy was standing on first base by this point, watching Hulk charging toward him out of one eye, and watching the flight of the ball with the other. He quickly prayed for the ball to be thrown straight at him, but as he watched it, he knew it wasn't. In fact, it wasn't even going to make it to him in the air, it was going to bounce first, and having been thrown while Steven was still turning caused it to sail far to Jimmy's left. Jimmy saw it was not so far off he needed to step off the bag and he should be able to stretch just far enough, with his left foot still on the base, to scoop up the ball if it hopped up high enough, just like he had seen McCovey do.

Hulk was only a few steps away when he saw Jimmy stretching out. He was standing in the base path, and if the skinny kid did not get out of his way he was going to run him over. That thought was so delightful he smiled through his gritted teeth. He could have his revenge and get on base for the first time of his life. What could be better than that?

The ball bounced, just as Jimmy dreaded it would, and as he saw it rising from the ground he could hear Hulk's footsteps, his labored breath, and what he thought was a low growl. The ball was coming, and Jimmy knew he could catch it. But if he caught it, there was no way for him to get out of Hulk's way in time. Hulk's shadow loomed so large Jimmy was plunged into the dark, and Jimmy did not know what to do, but by now he had waited too long to decide and no longer had any other choice but to catch it as the ball was already reaching him. He squeezed it in his glove.

Hulk eyes opened wide when he saw Jimmy catching it in the baseline and he charged ahead as hard as he could, but surely, he thought, this scrawny kid would jump out of the way before he ran him over, catch or no catch. Then he took another step and realized Jimmy couldn't jump out of the way in time, and his thoughts turned more sinister. He lowered his shoulder and did his best impersonation of Dick Butkus, plowing into Jimmy with all the momentum he could muster.

Jimmy did not feel the impact at first. He was too busy looking at the puffy clouds in the sky. There was a jet trail. Two birds were dancing with each other in the air as they raced between the trees. He wondered, how could he have been looking at the ball entering his glove in one instant, and the next into the heavens? Were the stars out in the daytime, or were the sparkles he saw inside his eyeballs?

Then he felt the impact. It was not the impact he expected, that of Hulk's body smashing into his, but the impact of his back hitting the dirt. He had been flying above the ground like a trapeze artist and had missed the net. Every drop of the precious air in his lungs escaped, all at once. Then he felt the second impact, and that was Hulk, landing on top of him at the tail end of what to the crowd was an instant in time, but to Jimmy was an eternity in a heartbeat. Hulk had managed to trip over Jimmy's foot as he bulldozed him, and he became airborne following Jimmy, and landed with a splat on the helpless Cub. What had been for Jimmy a moment of the sweet bliss of pure weightlessness was now a moment of the crushing weight of suffocation. The air that had escaped had no place to return.

Hulk's body covered almost every inch of Jimmy, lying immobile underneath him. Only Jimmy's right arm and gloved hand stuck out from the wreckage. The ball had rolled out of the glove and was lying as helpless as Jimmy was on the chalk of the base line. Hulk stood up and looked down at Jimmy, saw the ball had been dropped, and stepped on first base, triumphantly.

Jimmy did not feel any relief from the weight being off him, he couldn't breathe. He knew what had happened, as it had happened before, his brother had made sure of that in many past episodes. Jimmy had the wind knocked out of him. He went into a fetal position to die. The Cubs were running, the coach was running, and Bill was running to first base to see if the kid still had a pulse. Jimmy felt himself losing consciousness, and wondered if this was the end of his short life. When he had lost all hope of survival, his lungs expanded and let in some air and he could breathe again. He sat up, still semi-fetal, and wrapped his arms around his knees.

Bill, looking down with some relief, asked the obvious question, "Are you OK, kid?"

"Yeah, I'm OK," answered Jimmy, not meaning it, but knowing what was expected.

Bill then turned to Hulk, and said not so obviously, "Yer' out, son."

"What!!??" screamed Hulk, the self-satisfied smile which had been on his face gone in a flash. "He dropped the ball!!!"

Bill shrugged and said, "He held it long enough. Yer' out!" He said it with enough emphasis Hulk knew not to argue, and he put his head down so he didn't have to see the look on Jimmy's face as he trotted across the infield toward the Cardinals bench in shock and anger. As Jimmy stood up gingerly the crowd started to clap. They had been so fearful he may not rise again they were in no mood to argue the call. It was justice being served, if not a correct call, so what could they do other than clap?

Jimmy dusted himself off and went back to his position, and everyone else did as well. He was breathing again and was amazed, after checking each part of his body twice, he felt no pain. As Hulk arrived at the Cardinal bench, still fuming and gritting his teeth, he saw Grant Roper, laughing hysterically, doubled over.

"What's so funny?" asked Hulk, with gathering menace.

As this was one of the funniest things Grant had ever seen, he did not stop laughing immediately. "You almost killed that little Nigger," he said in what to him was stating the obvious.

"What??!!" shouted Hulk, incredulously.

Now Grant stopped laughing, sensing danger. He decided he needed a further explanation. "I mean, if he had any brains, he woulda gotten outta your way."

Hulk turned his head slightly, as if to let it sink in. Then he leaned over, face to face with his teammate.

"So, is that what you would have done?" he asked, his tone demanding the correct answer or else.

"Well, yeah," said Grant sheepishly, not sure if that was the answer Hulk wanted to hear, but at least it was the truth.

Hulk was more furious than ever, and grabbed Grant by both shoulders and squeezed as hard as he could. "So, what you're saying is, is that kid has more guts in his little finger than you have in your whole body!!"

Then Hulk let Grant go, and sat down on the bench with a thud, feeling absolutely defeated and spent. Grant swallowed hard, and did not say another word the rest of the game. He still thought it was funny, but he knew to keep it to himself.

At this point Bill signaled for the game to continue. Every game he umpired had drama, but this was beyond his experience. He knew it needed to start again, to conclude. To break the spell, he called out, "Play ball!" and so they did.

Scott Michaels had no trouble with the next batter. A couple of balls, a trio of strikes, and he had completed his first inning as a pitcher without allowing a walk, hit, or a run. His only regret was no one would remember it.

CHAPTER
Thirty-Two

Derek Schmidt loved his father, and his father loved him back just as dearly. Because of this, they both tried to do what they could to make the other's life as happy as possible. To Derek's father, that meant introducing Derek to as many of the manly arts as he could think of, starting with baseball. If he could get Derek to do what the other boys his age did, maybe he would grow out of his feminine nature and become a happy man. To Derek, that meant eagerly agreeing with his father's wishes. Derek was drawn to sports anyway. He loved watching athletes run and jump, and saw the beauty of physical exertion. Seeing the light in his father's eyes when he came home from work and Derek was wearing his Cubs jersey made it all worthwhile.

The possibility of playing, instead of merely watching the other boys and cheering, never occurred to him. He had assumed his uncle would just let him sit. It's not as if Derek had any desire to excel in sports. He was pudgy and soft, and liked his body to feel that way. What if he fell, and bruised his nearly flawless skin? What if, heaven forbid, he started to sweat and smell bad? The time he spent standing in right field, looking away from what was going on in the infield, was filled with terror. He reasoned if he didn't watch the action, the ball would never come his way, and he wouldn't have to take a chance on hurting himself or getting dirty. No one was happier for Scott Michaels than Derek was as the boys streamed off the field after the third Cardinal out of the fifth inning. He joyously skipped to Scott and put his arm around his shoulders.

"Good job, Scott," he gushed as they trotted along.

Scott thought the hug lasted a little longer than he felt comfortable with, and shrugged Derek off. He felt a slight queasiness at Derek's touch, but had no clue why he felt that way. The other boys did very similar things, slapping him on the backside with their gloves, rubbing him on the head, faking a kiss on the cheek, but those felt different somehow. When Derek followed, and sat next to him on the bench, Scott suddenly felt thirsty and not so casually bounded over to the water fountain for a drink. His plan was to sit as far away from Derek as he could when he returned.

Mario Bruno was the first batter in the top of the sixth. It took him some time to prepare, as he had to take off the shin guards and chest protector he was wearing behind the plate. As with all catchers his age, his eagerness to bat made getting the gear off even more time consuming. It took him more time to prepare to bat than it did for him to perform the act of batting, as Paul Hart was in no mood to mess around.

Paul saw he was three outs away from the game being his, and he wasn't going to let little Mario do any damage, or even have any hope of doing any damage. His first two pitches were right down the middle, and despite Mario's best efforts, he could not catch up to either one. On the third pitch Mario started swinging at the same time the ball left Paul's hand, and he managed to foul it off. It bounced off the water fountain as Scott took his last gulp. Scott, already wide eyed from his recent encounter with Derek, literally jumped out of one of his shoes. He had untied it when he first sat on the bench, and jumped up so quickly to go to the water fountain he hadn't bothered tying it again.

The crowd appreciated the added entertainment value and laughed and clapped, and the hecklers couldn't think of anything more to add. Even they were getting spent by this point in the game. As Scott sat in the grass, tying his laces, Paul put Mario out of his misery with his next pitch. It came in so hard no one could see it. If it had of been three inches left or right of his glove, Hulk could not have caught it. However, since it wasn't, he did, and Bill had no choice but say, "Strike 3, yer' out, son," to Mario.

Joe Gurnsey was next. After having to sit and watch for so long, Joe wasn't going to let his time in the batter's box go by as quickly as Mario had. This kid Paul Hart did not scare him at all. Not to say Joe had an actual plan, other than not swinging at the first pitch. When Paul threw it, it whizzed past him, high and inside.

"Ball 1!" called out Umpire Bill.

A sheepish grin spread over Joe's face and he called out to Paul, "Nice pitch!" He now formulated a plan, maybe Paul would hit him and he could get on base that way. He leaned farther toward the plate to bait him.

It worked, as Paul once again threw inside. For some reason, self-preservation most probably, Joe stepped back to avoid it, defeating his own purpose.

"Ball 2!!" called out Bill with more enthusiasm.

Now Joe's temper came to the fore. He changed his plan again, and went back to no plan at all, other than anger. The Cardinals coach stood from his bench and called out to Paul impatiently, "Throw strikes, Paul!!" To make sure he knew he meant it, he motioned to two kids sitting next to him to start warming up by playing catch behind the bench.

When Paul saw this, he indeed did get the message, and returned to the business of putting the Cubs out of their misery. His next pitch was thrown for a strike, but was not thrown with the intensity of his last few pitches. As if to make up for the years of oppression and broken treaties his people had suffered, Joe put the bat on the ball and it shot off it, over Paul's head and into right center field. From the sound of the crowd, it was as if the game was being held in Wrigley Field. Joe made the turn at first base and chugged toward second as the faithful cheered him on.

The ball landed near the feet of the centerfielder, who let it bounce next to him without much of an effort to catch it in the air. Carl David ran to second base to take the throw, if the outfielder would ever pick it up and toss it. When he did, Joe was securely on second base. Carl caught the rather errant throw by jumping up and snagging it before it could get past him, a rather unlikely outcome as far as Joe was concerned. He took two steps toward third before he realized, yes, Carl had indeed managed to bring it down. Despite his best efforts to retrace his steps to second, Carl touched him with his glove, the ball inside, before Joe could put his toe back on the bag.

Bill was running from his place behind Hulk and shouted "Yer ooooouuuuu..." as he tripped over the pitching rubber, and he fell in the exaggerated style of the comically clumsy face first in the dirt while raising his hand to make the call. To more than a few people watching from the bleachers, this was the best high-light of a game filled with highlights. Most of the other things that happened in this game happened in other Minor League games, but seeing the umpire eat a mouthful of dirt was a once in a year event, if that often, as most umpires weren't in good enough shape to run that far in the first place. His thick chest protector saved him from serious damage to his body, but nothing saved him from the serious hit to his pride.

It's funny how when bad things happen to someone else it can bring people together. Hecklers 1 and 2 shook hands, convinced they should be taking mutual credit for Bill's literal downfall. After all, if they hadn't been on him so much, he wouldn't have felt the need to get such a close look at the play. Maybe they should be working together next game.

As Bill pulled himself up to a sitting position, Hulk's little sister called out "Are you OK, mister?" He smiled at her as she stuck her face against the chain link fence. Her mother had given up trying to keep her still in the bleachers and allowed her to run along the sidewalk behind the backstop. Anything to wear her down was good, as far as her mother was concerned. No one else had bothered to ask about his condition, they were too busy crying and coughing, as laughter was not enough of a reaction for what they had just witnessed. Bill waved to her, and rose to his feet, the spell broken. Joe trotted to the bench with his head down, in agreement with Bill what had just happened was not funny.

So now the Cubs were down to their last out. Since games for boys this age lasted only six innings, if the Cubs did not tie it now, the game was over and there would be no need for the Cardinals to take their last at bat. It was all up to Donny Demoss to keep the game going. Jimmy would be next if he did, and then Derek Schmidt.

Coach Schmidt was not ready to give up. He gave Donny strict instructions to let the first two pitches go by. Paul would have to throw three strikes to end the game, not win by getting Donny out on a bad pitch. As he had hoped, Paul was a little rattled by what had just happened. Joe Gurnsey had smacked his last pitch out of the infield in the air, although it was not thrown with maximum effort. He decided he couldn't take that chance on another pitch and threw the next as hard as he could. The ball sailed high.

"Ball 1!" called out Bill.

The pitch was no doubt high, but Paul was not pleased at Bill for whatever reason. He threw the next pitch just as hard, and just as high.

"Ball 2!" called out Bill.

The next pitch he overthrew and underthrew at the same time. It was low and away. The bat did not leave Donny's shoulders.

"Ball 3!" called out Bill.

Now Paul began to feel the first tickle of fatigue himself. He wanted to conserve energy, but still did not want to give Donny a good pitch to hit. The next one he aimed more than threw, and it was even lower than the last.

"Take yer' base, son," murmured Bill.

Jimmy came up next. Now he could be the hero. The look he saw in Paul's eyes was familiar to him. Paul was tired, he could tell. Maybe he could hit it much harder this time, even harder than Joe. Coach Schmidt could not give Jimmy the same instructions he had given Donny, as what he had thought was a brilliant line-up change was now looking rather dull. If Jimmy did not get the game tying hit, winning or losing would be up to his nephew, so he couldn't tell Jimmy to try to walk.

Jimmy took the first pitch anyway, as it looked outside to him. He was not in agreement with the call from the umpire, which was clearly stated as "Strike 1!"

The next pitch, clearly inside to Jimmy's mind, but not Paul's, was labeled "Ball 1," by Bill, who of course had the only opinion that mattered.

The third pitch came out of Paul's hand with a purpose, and Jimmy swung with even more purpose. He closed his eyes, torqued his body quite impressively, and connected with the clean fresh air.

"Strike 2!" called out Bill.

Jimmy stepped back into the batter's box, which he had fallen out of with his last swing. "Just make contact, Jimmy," he heard from both inside and outside his head.

Paul had also been impressed with Jimmy' last swing, and decided he would rather have Jimmy swing at a bad pitch than a good one, so he threw the next one outside. Jimmy thought about swinging, which means he didn't have time to accomplish it.

"Ball 2!" called out Bill. No argument from Paul this time, as he had thrown it where he wanted to, outside the strike zone. He decided to try again, just a little closer. Jimmy couldn't let this one pass, it was too close to tell whether it was good or bad, but not close enough to warrant his best swing. He stuck his bat out to impede the ball's progress more than swung at it. The ball bounced harmlessly over to the Cardinals bench.

"Foul ball," called out Bill for those who could not figure it out without his help. "The count is 2 and 2."

Paul was trying to paint a pretty picture instead of pitching at this point, and he tried to split the difference between his last two throws. He missed by an even wider margin than he had before. Jimmy had no choice but to let it pass.

"Full count," informed Bill.

Now was the time for heroes. Full count, two outs, the tying run on base, and the lead run at the plate, namely Jimmy. Wouldn't this be the greatest day in Jimmy's life if he could pull the ball over the right fielder's head, down the hillside to the next ball diamond, and trot around the bases like Willie McCovey had on TV?

Paul Hart was thinking the same thing, except it would be the worst day of his life if it happened. He reared back and threw the next pitch as hard as he could. Jimmy would have to earn his hero status. He wouldn't have it given to him by Paul. The throw was not made with much of an attempt at accuracy, only velocity. As usually happens under such circumstances, it was not even close to being a strike, but heroes don't need a perfect pitch to get a home run, and Jimmy was swinging. The ball bounced before reaching the plate and neither Jimmy nor Hulk could touch it with their bat or glove before it bounded past them.

The crowd, not sure if Jimmy knew what to do next, screamed at him, "Run, Jimmy, Run!!!" and Jimmy, after a fraction of a second of dejection thinking he had struck out to end the game, realized if he could make it to first base before Hulk could retrieve the ball, he would be given a reprieve. Off he went, and Donny went off to second. Hulk spun around, lost his balance and tried to stay on his feet as he started after the ball. Before he reached the backstop where the ball had landed, he fell. As Jimmy reached first base, sure the ball would hit him in the back as he ran, he could see Coach Schmidt swinging his arm in a circle, the sign Jimmy should continue to second base. Hulk had managed to catch up with the spinning ball in time to see Donny headed to third base. He threw it as hard as he could toward the third baseman, but it was too high for him to catch. As Donny rounded third, he saw out of the corner of his eye the third baseman was in no way going to be able to bring it down and his heart leaped ahead of his legs toward home. Jimmy was halfway to second when he heard Coach Schmidt call out, "Stop, Donny!! Don't run!!"

Carl David always seemed to know what to do when it came to sports. He automatically assumed Hulk would throw it to third, not second, and he would probably throw it over the third baseman's head. He therefore ran behind him and was standing in the exact spot he needed to be to catch the ball before it sailed into left field. Donny, remarkably, heard his coach's command and turned far enough to see Carl as well, and stopped in time to scramble back to third base before Carl could tag him out. Jimmy was standing on second base as the play ended.

So now the crowd was hyper, the Cubs bench was hyper, the Cardinals in the field were hyper, in fact everyone in the park was hyper except one person. That person was Derek Schmidt. He held a bat in his hand and was waiting with outward nonchalance as he saw the other boys running and yelling. If anyone in the crowd assumed he was thinking about becoming a hero, they were mistaken. If anyone thought he was nervous, they were mistaken. What Derek was thinking, more than anything, was if he could get this over with as soon as possible he could go home and change clothes.

And wouldn't you know Paul Hart knew Derek Schmidt? They went to the same church. The other boys in Sunday school knew all about him, that he was queer, as they called it. They weren't sure what being queer meant, they had learned the word from their older siblings, but they knew he couldn't throw like they did, or run like they did, didn't like to play with them, and didn't care. That was what they all thought was the strangest thing about him, downright scary, in fact, the fact he did not care. They didn't even bother to tease him after a while. When he wanted to play with the girls instead of them, they let him be.

Paul had no doubt he could make short work of Derek and end the game. In fact, the look he saw in Derek's eyes as he came to the plate told him the same thing. All he had to do was not throw the ball wildly, and it was over. You can imagine his surprise when the first pitch, thrown with three quarter's speed right down the middle, was swung at. Maybe waved at was a better way to describe it, but it was more aggressive than Paul had expected.

"Strike 1," said Bill, snickering at the boy's batting stance and style.

Derek looked at Bill, realizing from the tone he had heard many times before Bill's apparent lack of respect for his form. But then again, Derek did not care for Bill's style either, so they were even in his mind.

The next pitch Paul threw with a little more intent, but not so much as to test Hulk's agility. When Derek swung at this one, his eyes were not closed, but not looking at the ball either. They were looking up at the sky. It was such a beautiful day.

"Strike 2!" said Bill.

Derek looked down at his pudgy arms and legs, and realized if he exerted himself much longer he would start to sweat. Nothing in this world would be worse than that. He had to get out of the sun, and soon.

Paul's next pitch was low, and it bounced right on the plate. It did not matter to Derek. He had made up his mind he would swing at the next pitch no matter what, and not because he wanted to hit it. He swung and Hulk dropped the ball and Donny and Jimmy, who knew the drill, started yelling at Derek to run, hoping Hulk would lose the ball under his body and make a wild throw so they could run home. Hulk sort of did lose sight of it, but Derek did not move, and Hulk reached down and picked up the ball and touched Derek with it, still standing in the batter's box.

"OK," said Bill, with a shrug. "That's it. Game over. Cardinals win, 2 to 1."

The crowd cheered wildly, having gone back to Busch Stadium after the short excursion to Wrigley Field. Once again all was right with the world. The team which was destined to win won, Paul Hart had the first of the many, many wins to come in his pitching career, and the Cubs fans would have to wait until next year, as always.

CHAPTER
Thirty-Three

As soon as the game was over, when the last pitch was thrown and missed, little Becky Hanson grabbed her mother by the hand and dragged her with all her might toward the Concession Stand. She wanted to be the first in line, and her mother was taking way too long. Becky was on a mission. "Come on, Mom," she commanded. "You have to buy me a snow cone!"

"Now Becky," her mother admonished. "You've already had a snow cone, and some cotton candy. That's enough for you."

"But it's not for me, Mommy," she answered as sweetly as she could.

Her mother looked down at her daughter with surprise and admiration. Becky wanted to give her brother a reward for winning the game. She allowed herself to be pulled along by her daughter, and they did indeed make it to the front of the line before the rush.

Before the boys were released, they were told to form lines, and run past each other shaking hands. Most of the Cubs, of course, did not feel like doing it, and some of the Cardinals did not think it was necessary either. For Jimmy this was the scariest part of all. What would Hulk do when he had a chance, crush his hand? Put him in a head lock? Punch him? But he forgot that series of outcomes when he saw Grant Roper spit on his hand before reaching out to grab his. Jimmy had seen this trick before, and pulled his hand back before getting it wet.

Carl David was halfway through the line. He stopped for an extra second to shake Jimmy's hand an extra shake. "Good game, kid," said Carl, "You're really something." Jimmy looked at Carl with his eyes wide, and Carl smiled and moved on.

Then came Hulk, and his handshake was softer than Jimmy expected. He grumbled "Good game," as required, almost inaudibly. When Jimmy made it through to the end, he couldn't keep the smile he had been holding back from rushing forth.

As the boys went through the handshake line, the people in the bleachers started to filter out. Some went directly to their cars, others formed a line behind Becky and Mrs. Hanson at the Concession Stand, and others stood around chatting, waiting for their sons to pack up their gear and join them. Jimmy trotted toward the end the bench where his glove was, and saw his father and brother standing between the bench and the backstop, side by side, waiting for him. "What are you smiling about?" asked Slugger, wondering if his brother got it. He had lost the game, hadn't he? He wasn't supposed to be happy about it. He didn't realize Jimmy had been more worried about surviving the game intact than winning or losing. Living to tell the tale was enough for him. Jimmy did not answer but instead continued to the far end of the bench, where his glove and Joe were sitting.

"Good game, Jimmy," said Joe, properly sad about not only losing, but the fact his brother and father hadn't stayed to watch the game. He looked around and didn't see anyone from his family and realized he would have to walk home.

"Thanks, Joe," Jimmy responded. "You got the best hit of the game!" He did not mention the ultimate outcome of that hit, knowing Joe felt bad enough about it already.

Jimmy then walked back to his heroes, still standing side by side, and realized his work for the day was not over. He had something to do for his mother. As he thought about what to say next, he saw the little blond girl running across the grass with not one, but 2 snow cones. As it turned out, the Concession Stand was going to close after the game, and they had started selling snow cones for half price.

Becky ran over to Umpire Bill, who was standing by the backstop, gathering his gear and his dignity by wiping the dirt off his clothes and equipment. Becky looked up at him and said with the utmost sincerity, "Sorry you fell down, Mister Umpire. I hope you feel better." With that she handed him one of the dripping cones in her hands.

"Well, thank you, Missy," he said with more than a little surprise.

Her mother smiled. She knew this had not been the reason her daughter had asked for the snow cone, but it was a wonderful gesture on her part to think of the umpire with her extra prize. She was standing next to Hulk now, with her arm over his shoulder. Becky turned and smiled at them both, but instead of going to join them, she ran to the opposite team's bench instead. Jimmy was still thinking of what to say to his father and brother when she stopped in front of him.

"This is for you," she said to Jimmy, handing him her remaining snow cone. She wanted to say more, but the words froze in her mouth. Instead, she reached up with her now empty hands and grabbed Jimmy's arm and pulled it down. With Jimmy's head now low enough to reach, she kissed him on the cheek, and then ran smiling as fast as her legs would carry her to where her mother was standing, whose mouth was wide open in shock and amusement. Becky grabbed her mother's leg and hid behind her, peeking around it at Jimmy to see his reaction.

Jimmy did not know any other way to react so he simply stood there holding the cone, wondering what kind of crazy creature Becky was. In his universe, girls could never be counted on to do anything that made sense. But what he did know was he didn't want the snow cone. After wiping Becky's real or imagined slobber from his cheek, what he should do next became apparent. He handed it to Slugger.

"Here Slug," he said. "You can have it. The last time I ate one of these it made me sick at the stomach," which was true. About half of everything Jimmy ate, especially sweet stuff, did make him sick.

As Slugger reached down to take the snow cone, Jimmy did something he could never remember doing before, and never, ever did again. He reached up and took Slugger's free hand in his. As he held Slugger's hand as firmly as he could, he looked up into his eyes and said in the firmest tone he could, "You are coming home with us." It was not a request, it was a command, the first one he had ever given to his older sibling, and with that the trio started walking toward the car.

As they walked away, Joe called out from behind them, "See you later, Jimmy."

Jimmy turned and saw Joe standing there alone. "You need a ride?" asked Jimmy. Jimmy looked over to his dad, wondering if he had over stepped his bounds. The look on his dad's face told him he hadn't.

"Naw," said Joe.

"OK," said Jimmy, "You can have one anyway. Come on." Once again, this was an instruction, not a request. Joe followed his order and fell in behind the group headed to the car. Jimmy realized this would solve another problem. When they arrived at the car, Jimmy decided he would go for three. "You sit in front, Slugger. Me and Joe can sit in the back."

With that the four men climbed into the vehicle and drove off, through the park, under the gently swaying trees, and out into the fascinatingly unreliable world beyond. Jimmy and Joe did not waste the time talking. They kept their heads stuck out of the back windows so they could feel the rush of air on their faces as they went.

CHAPTER
Thirty-Four

The next day, after church, Jimmy sat at the dinner table with all his family back together. It was the happiest family dinner they had in a long time. His older sisters made a special effort to tease Jimmy even more than usual, just to make sure he did not think anything had changed because of yesterday's events. He was still their scrawny little brother, and they could make his life just as miserable as they had in the past. They could still sit on him and he wouldn't be able to get up before they decided to let him up. They could still trick him into getting in trouble. Nothing had changed, and they wanted to make sure he knew it.

But somehow, they knew, and he knew, something had changed, and that was why they needed to make a special effort. Even though they had not been there to witness it for themselves, they had seen and heard enough to know Jimmy was not going to be the little boy they tortured much longer. He was going to grow up much faster now. When dinner ended and the children were taking their places at the sink to do their assigned clean up tasks, the phone rang.

Jaqueline was closest and reached it before the other girls could react. After saying hello, she turned to Jimmy, his back turned with a towel and a wet glass in his hands.

"Jimmy, it's for you," she said, with as little enthusiasm as she could muster.

Jimmy turned to his mother, who was busy putting the leftovers into the refrigerator.

"Can I?" he asked. He knew from past experiences before he could play after Sunday dinner he had to finish drying the dishes. As receiving phone calls was still a novelty, he did not know whether they trumped that rule or not.

"Go ahead," she said.

Jimmy went to the phone and spoke into the receiver "Hello, this is Jimmy."

He heard a familiar laugh on the other end.

"I know who it is," said the familiar voice.

"Who is this?" asked Jimmy.

"It's Donny, Donny Gomes," said the voice.

Jimmy was speechless.

"Are you deaf as well as dumb?" asked Donny. With that question, Jimmy knew it was indeed Donny.

"How do you know my phone number?" asked Jimmy, dumbfounded.

"It's called a phone book," said Donny with considerable sarcasm.

"Oh," said Jimmy.

"I'm putting together a baseball game at Anderson Park," continued Donny. "You have to play."

Jimmy took the phone away from his head and looked at it, amazed at what had just come out of it.

"No, I don't," responded Jimmy firmly.

"OK, Jimmy, will you please come over to the park and play baseball?" asked Donny in the most demanding, threatening voice he could use while still being polite. "I need you to be my pitcher."

Jimmy said nothing.

"I heard about the game yesterday. I heard you did pretty good. And if you can strike ME out, I know you can strike out the other kids around here too," he continued. "Maybe you can win this time," he said with a chuckle, not able to stop himself from getting in a zinger.

Jimmy thought about it. Playing baseball in the park, without all the coaches and spectators, did sound like fun, even if it was Donny asking him. Not that he was going to give in that easy.

"Only if Joe can play too," he responded.

Donny paused. He hadn't thought of Joe, but the more players he could muster, the better.

"OK," he said, "You can bring the Injun with you too," and just to let him know he hadn't forgotten their last encounter he added, "You can tell him not to be scared. I won't pound him, this time."

"OK," said Jimmy, satisfied with the bargain he had made. If things got out of hand, Joe would fight Donny and he wouldn't have to. Then he remembered he had something else to do first. "I'll be there in a half hour, as soon as I finish drying the dishes."

"What??" laughed Donny. "You can't get your sisters to do that for you?"

Jimmy did not answer.

"OK, Jimmy," said Donny, trying to gain the upper hand again, but somehow realizing he never would, "Not a minute more."

And with that he dropped the receiver as hard as he could, to try to make Jimmy's eardrum burst. It didn't. Jimmy hung up the phone and picked up the towel and the next wet glass. He finished the last dish without his usual quality control standards, which weren't that high to begin with, as he was too filled with excitement to wipe with his normal tenacity, and ran for the back door as soon as the towel was on its place in the rack. As he opened the screen, he saw his brother was standing outside, talking to Jim Gurnsey.

Jimmy ran to Jim, ignoring his brother, and asked with much enthusiasm, "Is Joe home?"

"Should be," said Jim, chuckling at the energy spilling from the boy's mouth.

Jimmy ran past, headed for the patio where his glove was stored.

"What's the big hurry?" asked Slugger as his little brother breezed by.

"I'm goin' to the park, to play baseball," said Jimmy without slowing down. He had retrieved his glove from the toy box and almost reached the alley when he realized he had not told his mother where he was going. "Could you tell Mom?" he shouted to his brother.

"Sure, Jimmy, sure," replied Slugger, and as he watched Jimmy trotting and skipping away into his own unique destiny he thought to himself, after that, my job is done.

54123172R00173

Made in the USA
San Bernardino, CA
08 October 2017